fahrenheit

THE POWER OF THREE LOVE SERIES

Leigh Lennon

Editing by Editing 4 Indies
Proofreading services by Deaton Author Services
Formatting by Ink It Out Editing
Cover design by Najla Qamber
Beta Readers: Nancy George, Kymberly Dingman, Mary Moore, Megan Damrow, Melody Hillier, Megan Harris and Kelly Green

about fahrenheit

The Red Head

Growing up in foster care, I never had a family I could call my own. I'd finally found my place in this world. The only problem, it was in the arms of not one, but two men. Two distinctly different men I'd never be able to choose between.

The Doctor

Finally, I'd found the woman I wanted to spend the rest of my life with. We were deeply in love. There was only one catch. She loved another, too. A surprising compromise was thrown my way. We'd share her, in a committed relationship. But, sharing wasn't my style. Until, that was, I started to long for him just as much as I did her.

The Fireman

My redhead seductress had laid claim to my heart, along with the good doctor. He denied loving me but I would catch him watching me, with the same hunger in his eyes as he had for the woman we loved. They are both mine, he just didn't know it yet.

dedication

For those who love outside the realm of what is traditional in the eyes of the world.

To the one person who taught me if you were lucky to find love, it didn't matter who they were. I miss you every day.

playlist

Aerosmith, "Love in an Elevator"
Air, "Redhead Girl"
Alabama, "Angels Among Us"
Alicia Keys, "Girl on Fire"
Bon Jovi, "Bad Medicine"
Brooks and Dunn, "Boot Scootin' Boogie"
Charlie Puth, "One Call Away"
Coldplay, "A Sky Full of Stars"
Counting Crows, "Good Time"
David Crosby, "Triad"
Foo Fighters, "Everlong"
Frank Sinatra, "Fly Me to the Moon"
Gabrielle Aplin, "Light Up the Dark"
Maroon 5, "Animals"
Maroon 5, "What Lovers Do"
Nickelback, "If Today Was Your Last Day"
Panic! At the Disco, "High Hopes"
Pink Floyd, "The Dark Side of the Moon"
Slow Club, "Not Mine to Love"
Snake River Conspiracy, "You and Your friend"
Soundgarden, "Black Hole Sun"
Spin Doctors, "Two Princes"
The Beatles, "Here Comes the Sun"
The Veronicas, "Revenge Is Sweeter"
The White Stripes, "Fell in Love With a Girl"
Thompson Twins, "Doctor! Doctor!"
Zac Efron and Zendaya, "Rewrite the Stars"

prologue

levi
twelve years ago

I watched him intently. The signs were there. It was like this all day. The way his hand quickly touched my own. Or how our eyes met when one of us looked at the other for too long.

My date had stood me up. Of course, her brother was the one who answered the door when I came to pick her up. "Want to come in for a beer?" he'd asked. Sure, I wouldn't be getting what I wanted, so a beer sounded like the next best thing. We'd been acquaintances, friends of friends so it wasn't odd to hang out for a couple of hours. After all, I certainly wasn't scoring with his sister.

I finished my fifth beer when he stood. "Want another,

man?" I nodded, but my eyes followed him as he stood, his ass causing my cock to strain against my jeans. Fuck, that was uncomfortable, but surprisingly so, I was not uncomfortable with the hot and young lawyer who had been flirting with me all day.

"So tell me, Levi," he asked when he handed me a beer, "what do you do for a living? Stephanie told me, but I forgot." He sat next to me, the closest he'd been since I entered his house.

"Um, I'm a fireman." His hands moved up my arms. They stopped at my biceps when he squeezed them.

"You're sure strong." It was his only reply. But Dane was just as big as I was. Placing my hand on his bicep, the closest one, I did the same thing to him.

"Yeah, right back at you." After that, all bets were off. Dane wasn't gentle when he grabbed my face and pulled it to his. Before his mouth was on mine, his lips found my ears.

"Babe, I've wanted you since the second I opened the door. Fuck, my sister is a moron for standing you up. But you gotta tell me, do you want me as much as I want you?"

I leaned back to see the electricity racing in his eyes. "Fuck yeah, I do."

I tried to kiss him, but he stopped me. "Been with a man before?" Dane asked.

"Um, no. But that doesn't make me not want you any less." My voice was needy. I sounded like a pussy, but fuck, his dick inside me was all I could think about at the moment.

"Well, you're in for a treat, baby. I'm going to ride you so much, I may just turn you from pussy to cock."

And it was then, I realized I loved both. I never said goodbye to the touch of a woman, but fuck, did I enjoy the touch of a man just as much.

chapter 1

scarlet

His fingers caressed the inner folds of my thighs. I shouldn't want this—not this way. Not when I was equally in love with two men. How could I choose? I'd been asking myself that question as his hand worked farther up. It didn't take long for my pussy to start clenching around his fingers when he found my G-spot. My hips bucked, and small moans floated from my mouth. I couldn't form a coherent sentence.

His gaze locked on mine, and then he was over me, pulling his fingers from me and licking my juices from them. "Hmm, it's exactly as I'd expect. You taste like cantaloupe."

My eyes narrowed on him. My pussy had never been compared to a melon before, but it could be worse. At least he didn't associate it with chicken or salmon.

My inner dialogue along with his mesmerizing smile

had me giggling. One look at this man, I could see the sometime broody, very serious persona of him. The way the hazelnut hues of his dark chocolate eyes narrowed or how his lips curved down in an indifferent frown, was one sign of his heavy minded attitude at times.

"Don't overthink things, Red." His pet name for me had my pussy gearing up for round two, but I did have a lot on my mind. Mainly, was this fair to him? Was it fair to the other man? I'd been open with them from the beginning.

"Listen" — I grabbed his hand — "you know I'm not ready for a commitment like you are. I mean, if we do this, it's sex. I'm not ready to decide."

A frown covered his face. "I'm a man, Red. I get it. I want more than you're willing to give at this point. I'm the one who could be hurt, but I want you anyway." Even his words held hope. And I wished there was some way I didn't have to choose between the two men I had fallen in love with.

I wiped the bright red lipstick that rivaled the color of my hair from his cheek with a smirk. "You think if I sleep with you tonight, you'll wow me, and it'll be the deciding factor?"

His lopsided grin was panty melting. "Well, fuck, Red, if I answer you, it will make me sound like either an egomaniac or desperate. So, I plead the fifth for now." His lull, his pull, and everything I'd come to know from this man in the past couple of months made me wonder if I could say no to him. My desire to have him was palpable, but was it fair?

"Listen, Red, I'm ready. I know the risks, and I still want you. It's not like we just met. We've been doing this song and dance for what, three months? You've been brutally honest with me, so now let me be brutally honest with you."

We're still standing in front of the beautiful skyline of Chicago boasted by my thirty-seventh-floor apartment. Bringing me closer, I asked, "Um, okay, what is it?"

"If I can only have you for one night, let me worship your body like the temple it is. If you decide later that your choice is, well, you know — not me — no harm, no foul. Your body will be the one I compare all future women to, but I'll accept your decision and be happy for you."

Hell! How could I say no? I mean, his body was made to be worshipped in his own right. His olive complexion, the darkness that sparkled in the hazelnut of his chocolate eyes, and his speech, hell—I surrendered it all to him.

With a tilt of my head, his lips crashed to mine. I jumped into his arms, and he made his way to my room. He'd been here many times, so he knew his way around. He was going to get as familiar with my body as he was with my apartment.

Continuing to kiss me, he walked to my bed and tossed me on it gently. Staring at me from above, he had removed his button-up shirt, leaving me face-to-face with his tattoo. And his abs—I could have washed my clothes on. "Hell, your body doesn't stop," I said, watching where that V disappeared into his jeans. "Can I see more?" My breath was needy, and it was barely audible when he grinned.

"I think I need to hear you beg more, Red." His lopsided grin was back.

"Fuck!" I screamed, and he had me where he wanted me.

"Red, I'm waiting, sweetheart," he chimed in again.

"Fine," I huffed at his request, but I needed his cock inside me now. "Would you please, pretty please with sugar and a cherry on top, too, undress so I can see more of your body and your fabulous penis?"

"I'm sure you can do better than that, Red?" he teased with an obnoxious albeit sexy smirk still adorning his face.

"I'll give you a blow job." When my words escaped my mouth so quickly, I slapped my hands over my lips, almost embarrassed about what I had said.

"Um, not what I was expecting, Red, but hell, that works."

The second his pants and boxers were gone, I was smiling. He wasn't a man in front of me. He was a fucking sculpture, and someone had formed him perfectly. "Thanks for asking so nicely, Red. Now, about the blow job ..." He was standing in front of me while I laid on my bed. Sitting up, I grabbed his waist, bringing him over me so his body straddled mine.

"Hold your horses there." I pulled him close to me. Leaning over to his ear, I added, "And you are welcome, Jordan."

chapter 2

jordan

I had been straddling her, but her words and that promise had me flipping her over in one fluid motion. She was above me after we changed positions. She leaned over me. When her tongue touched the tip of my cock, the heavens opened and angels sang. Her mouth was made to wrap around me. She traced the tip of my cock over her lips as if it was a tube of lipstick, painting her lips. Her almost hazel brown eyes looked up, locking on my own eyes as her blow job was that of legends.

She popped her head up, smiling at me, with one hand on the base of my shaft and her other hand on my bare ass. My eyes rolled back in my head when her mouth enveloped my cock. With my fingers wrapped in her fire engine red hair, I was able to set the tempo for the best blow job—ever.

"Hell, Red," I could barely croak out. I'd imagined the touch of her tongue for months as I had waited for her to make a decision.

When I was close to creaming her mouth, I pulled my cock from her lips. "If I'm going to come, it's going to be from your tight little cunt for the first time." Sure, I'd promised her no pressure, but she was right. Once she had me, I hoped her need for me was like my need for her. If only he were not part of the equation.

When I'd asked her out on a date shortly after Elliot's accident, and her eyes had immediately dropped to the floor, I didn't think she was interested. Then she grabbed my hand, and the sweetest smile formed on her lips. "Um, I'd love to go out with you, but you gotta know I'm sort of seeing someone. We aren't exclusive, though, so if you're okay with it, I'd love to see where you and I could go."

Our chance encounter was three months ago, and in our time together, I'd fallen head over heels for her. Of course, I wasn't expecting the other guy to be the one man who made me question so many things about myself sexually. The pussy and the cunt were all I'd ever been interested in. Until ... fuck, I couldn't even say it.

I looked up, she was on her knees, and my heart overflowed for her. Sure, sex with her would be all I had ever dreamed of. But it was meant to physically express how great we could be when our bodies finally fused together.

The other man? I knew what she saw in him. I wasn't blind; he was good looking in his own right. What was I saying? I had never looked at a man as attractive, especially one I considered competition. Shit, why was this fogging my mind when the beauty of my redhead was before me. But his winks every time we were within arm's reach were distracting as hell.

I tipped her head down to me. "I need to be buried deep inside you, Red. Right. Fucking. Now," I commanded when I found the zipper to her loose skirt. At work, she wore these tight pencil skirts I loved, but in her personal time, her skirts were looser, allowing me access to her cunt without getting her naked. But right then, I pulled at her bright purple skirt. It came off easily, even if she was over me.

"I'm not stopping you, Doc." The name rendered me immobile. It wasn't until he started calling me this that Scarlet began using the same little term of endearment, too. And I loved it, but if truth be told, it got under my skin in a good way when he called me this. And what got me was he never acted as if I was his competition for Red. In his eyes, we weren't rivals for her affection. For me, he was my rival, but he treated me like his long-lost best friend.

"What are you so deep in thought about, Doc?"

With her skirt off, it was my turn to kneel. I flipped her around as easily as I had the first time, then pulled her lacy purple panties off her body with my teeth. I was face-to-face with her pussy, greeted by trimmed little red curls. My hooded eyes didn't stop me from touching her, eliciting a moan from her that caused my dick to harden more. Her fingers mussed up my hair. When I looked up, I saw she'd thrown her head back.

"You're perfect in every way." Pulling my finger from her clit, I sampled the goods and almost howled at her taste again. "Shit, I love your aroma and your taste. It's all Scarlet, all you." My speech was almost incoherent, but I was able to at least articulate what her flavor did to me.

"Are we going to talk or fuck?" Her smartass mouth was only one of the many reasons I was falling in love with her.

I stood, bringing her with me when my eyes popped wide. My movement was a little rushed, and I squeezed her tight to me. I'd never manhandle this woman, and understanding me, she laughed. "I'm almost as tall as you, Doc. I won't break. I love it a little rough."

Shit, could this girl seriously be any better? In my eyes, it was a fuck no!

I picked her up, mainly because I could. I wanted her fused with my body. When my need to enter her had become too intense, I threw her on the bed gently, and she laughed. "Fuck, Doc, as I said before, I won't fucking break. Show me who's in charge. Own me tonight. I'm yours to have your way with."

I was naked, and my dick was leading me to my sweet redhead. "You're going to unleash the beast," I warned.

With a loud laugh, she pointed at my cock. "I see the beast is unleashed already." I wedged myself between her knees.

"There are two beasts, Red. You're about to meet them both."

"Have me. Tonight, I'm yours."

Her words were all it took for me to push deep inside her and claim her. The only problem with tonight and her words ... I wanted her every day. I wanted her as mine. And I wanted and needed him out of our lives—for good.

chapter 3

levi

Scarlet was all I could think about when I woke. I had been seeing her for three months, and she'd been up front with me—both of us—from the beginning. I held nothing against the good doctor. Well, except for the fact he wasn't into guys like me. But really, how could I blame Jordan Peters? Scarlet was stunning¬—A redhead seductress who'd had sex with him last night. Again, the only sad part of the statement was that I was not asked to be a part of it.

That lucky bastard. Plus, the man was as stunning as she was. But what Scar and I shared was special, too. I had been as forward with her as she had been with me. I loved women. I loved men. She was certainly familiar with this setup because her bosses and best friends had this same relationship. Again, they were some fucking lucky bastards. Although I tried not to think too much about this aspect since the woman in their life was my twin sister. But I'd love to have what they had. Three people, equal partners. But what Arden, Daimen, and Ell had was rare.

As my mind floated to the good doctor and my redhead seductress, jealousy didn't fill me. Sure, I'd like to be there. Fuck, I wanted her in that way. And we would get there soon. But shit, I wanted to watch them.

When we spoke at lunch yesterday about her and the good doctor's relationship, I listened, curious about the change of subject from the Chicago Cubs, which she knew very little about.

"Um, Levi." Her voice had a twinge of nervousness. "I've been thinking. I care for you both. You know that, right?" I thought for sure this was a goodbye and the end of what we had built for the past couple of months. Sure, we'd kissed, and I'd fingered her here and there. The minx was certainly a sexual being. But she only continued, "I can't make a decision. And quite honestly, we never claimed to be exclusive."

I grabbed her hand. "Scar, beautiful, you know how I feel about the matter. You know how I feel about the good doctor, though he can't stand the sight of me. But yes, we aren't exclusive. So what is this about? Are we breaking up?" I'd always been matter of fact in my questions.

"No, but I'm going out with Jordan tonight. I think it's the night that I—"

Again, my forwardness was apparent. "Fuck him." I finished her sentence. I knew it was going this way, plus a boner sprouted from this image.

My mind was racing, and my cock hardened further at the good doctor taking our redhead seductress. My visual at the moment was him nailing her in the ass. I made a note to go home and take care of myself with this image.

"Wow, now that is a step. But what does that mean for us? I mean, don't get me wrong, the thought of you and the good doctor together is hot. But I won't deny I want you. I want my cock to stretch your sweet cunt." She reddened but not because she was embarrassed. I had gotten her all hot and bothered.

With a large smile forming on her face, she squeezed my hand tighter. "Yeah, Levi, that's exactly what I'm saying. I can't choose, and I don't want to, but you're next. The next time we're together, you can fulfill your deepest desires with me." And hell, right then, I was hot and bothered and ready to devour her.

Every vision of how the good doctor could be taking my redhead seductress was all my mind had room for. Were his fingers in her? Did his cock fill her all the way? Was he a kinky bastard, wanting to claim her ass? Would he taste her? And of course, the pièce de résistance was imagining her luscious lips wrapped around his glorious cock.

My dick thought someone was here to play with him because he was undoubtedly at attention. "Sorry, buddy, it's just you and me," I murmured, trying to pull my sorry butt out of bed. But I had so much ammunition to jerk off to. And the good doctor and my redhead seductress were all I needed to get off.

The brick structure in front of me gave me peace. Even if every time I put on the uniform, I wondered if today would be the day the flames I fought would finally claim me. But it was fleeting, and the beep of my phone drew me out of my morose thoughts.

A silly ass grin covered my face with a picture of Scar in bed, her red flames of hair fanned out over her pillow.

Redhead Seductress: *Good morning, my fireman! Wanted to send you this little selfie. And to let you know you're next.*

Well, fuck me sideways. Did she just send me what I think she did?

Me: *Scar, beautiful, is that your freshly fucked self?*

Again, my dick started to wake at the thought that Scarlet was near me. He was not the only one who wanted this. I waited for her response, watching the time—I wasn't needed for my turnover for a while. In my office now, I had the privacy I needed. Details were what I wanted. Of course, I might have to close the blinds and lock the door for some sort of release.

Redhead Seductress: *Yeah, I knew you'd get off on my picture. I can't believe you're okay with this.*

The truth was, I could see myself with Scar in my future. I was not a possessive man, and it could have been because I wanted the good doctor just as much as I wanted Scar. But that was not a consideration—not with the tight-ass doc. And boy, would I like to test the theory of him having a tight ass.

Me: *Yeah, fuck! I'm in my office, and my cock needs some attention.*

Her reply was so quick, I barely had a chance to console my own cock.

Redhead Seductress: *How about tomorrow night? I will give your buddy some attention. Oh, and you, too, of course.*

Um, was that even something I had to answer?

Me: *Beautiful, you better be ready for me. Because I'm all ready for you.*

Redhead Seductress: *Then it's a date. I'm looking forward to it, Lieutenant Hottie.*

Shit, I loved her nickname for me. And fuck, looking at my watch, I had thirty-six hours before I could fill my redhead seductress. It was going to be agony.

chapter 4

scarlet

Could one love two men equally? I often wondered that about Elliot when it came to Arden and Daimen. I didn't know if I needed an answer to the question itself because my situation was different. Those men I knew as my brothers were in a unique realm of circumstances than I was in. And shit, the idea of giving up either Jordan or Levi hurt.

After my texts with my fireman, I sat in a state of almost pity. And I hated pity. It was unnecessary. It would not change my past of being shuffled from home to home or sometimes having drunk foster dads become a little too handsy after they found their way in my bed late at night. I mean, it was par for the course in the system, right?

But why did it need to be? So many wanted children but they didn't want me. And I wondered if a man even wanted me. Jefferey and I were exclusive for years, though he'd always claimed marriage was not for him. I had him in my bed, and he'd always argued that should have been enough. But I wanted it all. I wanted the new last name. The last name of Reeves had never done anything for me, not after losing my parents. And as stupid as Jefferey made it seem at the time, I wanted that silly marriage license. I needed a firm commitment and to understand it would not be torn from me again. Not like it was that fateful night my parents had not come home from their date at the age of seven.

Yeah, to know love and then to be placed in the most loveless system in the world was a hard pill to swallow. I remembered my mom and dad. Katherine, my mother, was a baker. She made baking a ten-tier wedding cake look easy. My dad, Michael, was a disabled veteran. Having been in the Navy, he loved being a sailor. And though we didn't have much, we had a small boat we'd take out on Lake Michigan as much as possible. Being a sailor was part of his soul, part of his blood. My parents weren't rich, but we had each other.

I had my parents to thank for the fire color of my hair. They were both redheads, so I didn't stand a chance. We were three peas in a pod. But Dad got free tickets to the theater one night, and Mom loved a good play. On their way to the car, they'd been robbed for all they had. They got very little from my parents that night since we lived hand to mouth. But just like Bruce Wayne's parents in my favorite comic book, my own parents suffered the same doomed luck.

But I hadn't had a mansion to continue to live in or an Alfred to help raise me. The neighbor across the way loved me. She was the grandmotherly type and petitioned the court for custody. Funny and fucking ironically enough, they said I wouldn't be safe in her care. We might have had little, but Miss Maizie, as I called her, would have put me first in everything just as my parents had—certainly unlike every fucker who tried to hurt me within the system.

No, the law mandated I be placed with a more

appropriate couple. I was willing to bet Miss Maizie would never have crawled into bed with me to cop a feel or lock the pantry for three days as myself and the others in the home starved whenever our foster parents were on a binge.

I attempted to keep my mind away from the past. Wandering through the memories really only caused deep-rooted reminders that never could heal the pain I'd experienced at the hands of those who were supposed to care for me

But on the worst day of my life, my eighteenth birthday, when my foster mom threw me to the streets because her dead-beat husband groped me one too many times, I ended up cuddled in the corner of a laundromat near the heaters. It happened to be that two very hot men came in late at night when I was again being harassed by a shithead trying to cop a feel.

The men took me back to their apartment, a one-bedroom they shared with another man. Though I should have been scared shitless these men would rape me or hurt me, I was oddly at peace. Plus, I was out of options.

All three men gave me the only bedroom, telling me to lock it until I felt comfortable while they took residence in the living room, and I never moved out. They had become my family. To this day, they still were. At one time, Arden and Daimen's childhood friend was part of my life, too. I loved Spence as a brother until he'd changed into someone I didn't recognize anymore. He was killed tragically months ago, but I missed who he had been to me once. I mourned the man who I had considered a brother like Arden and Daimen.

I was deep in my thoughts of these men and the love I had for them when my phone rang. Smiling and pulling my dreaded memories of the past, I answered it with a huge grin covering my face.

"Hey." It was Levi. He surprised me since we'd just been texting back and forth.

"Hey, beautiful." His voice could cause an earthquake of quivers through my body without any effort on his part. Well, him and the man showering in my bathroom.

"Hey to you. Thought you were going into your morning turnover," I asked.

"Yeah, it was very short this morning. Anyway, I need more details. You know I'm not jealous of Jordan getting your rocking body first. If anything, I was jealous because I wasn't included in the mix."

My cheeks reddened, turning the same color as my hair. "Yeah, I get that, Levi. I don't think he does, though." I turned him on; it was as obvious as the nose on my face. It wasn't a large stretch to admit Jordan did something to Levi, too. And I was okay with it.

"Ah, at least you could indulge my desire with the good doctor a bit, my redhead seductress."

The little bit of his defeat was gone, and he was back to making me laugh again. The man, even when beat, showed a measure of hope. "You are so confident. I didn't think I had to stroke your ego."

"Hmmm," he began, "there's actually something else you can stroke, you know." And just like that, with this man on the phone and the other man I'd also fallen in love with in the bathroom, desire spread like wildfire through my body.

"You're so bad," I replied, but it wasn't my normal voice. No, it was my bedroom tone, and if anyone knew this, it was the man on the other end. Well, and the good doctor in the shower.

"You're turned on, Scar, aren't you?"

"Well, yeah, of course I am," I added.

"So he's taking a shower, I betcha, or he'd be pissed by this call. So tell me how glorious his cock was. I bet you it was long and not lean but not as thick as mine." Levi's words were fanning flames I wasn't sure even the fireman in him could put out. "But it's okay. He can have the length because I have the girth." A moan escaped my lips. "And I betcha his fingers are skilled, and he knows how to work the clit and G-spot at the same time, right?"

I was breathless at his words, though I couldn't answer him. "Well, I did my job, so I'll let you go. If you give him a blow job, I need more details." He ended the call promptly, and I was ready to orgasm at his words. Shit, I had no doubt I loved both these men.

chapter 5

jordan

Her phone was in her hands, and she was naked against her black satin sheets, looking like a goddess. A smile covered her face, smattered with her cute freckles. I stood at the door, watching every little move she made. It was as if her enjoyment came from lying naked on her bed, waiting for my return.

"Red?" I pulled her out of her world. "You look poised and ready for another round."

Tossing her phone over to her end table, she stood and walked toward me in her birthday suit, wearing a grin. The girl was born to live in a nudist colony. Her soft curves, the long legs I was born to be between, and her supple ass were just a few physical attributes that had Scarlet Reeves embedded deep in my heart.

She pulled me with her, crawling back onto the bed. As

I climbed between those legs made to wrap around my body, a text on her phone brought me out of my sex coma. It might have taken us a while to get to this point, but if last night was any indication, our physical connection was a lethal combination of lust, pleasure, and desire.

"Who've you been chatting with this early?" A pang of jealousy hit me, and I hoped I was wrong. She'd been up front with me about the fireman — the bane of my existence.

But with Scar, there was never any remorse or doubt in her own mind over her choices. Her arms wrapped around my neck, bringing me close to her lips. "Oh, it was Levi."

Fucking ball busters. I broke the connection of her fingers around my neck when I pulled away from her.

She propped herself up, sitting against the headboard, and grabbed a sheet to cover her beautiful nakedness. "Shit, Jordan. We covered this last night. I'm not ready to be exclusive, and you knew that. You accepted this."

My hands didn't remain at my sides. My animated gestures were sure to make matters worse, but I had several things on my mind, and I was just about to get started. "Yeah, that's true. But do you think you could have waited until I was out of your presence before you texted your other guy? I mean, what is this? Why would you tell him? I wouldn't think he'd want details." I was the one who wanted to gloat. I had her first — it had to mean something. The second this arrogant ass of a fireman was out of the picture was the day I could call Scarlet Reeves mine and mine alone.

"You know what, Jordan? You have your whole life to be an asshole, so why don't you take today off?" Her voice carried the resentment to my previous words and was now as far away from me as she could get. Her movements were just as animated as she grabbed my jeans and threw them at me. When the metal of the belt hit me in the head, she didn't flinch. "Shit, that was an accident, but I won't apologize. Maybe it was Karma for being a dick." Her voice was a little softer, and with the accidental injury, it seemed to have calmed her a bit. "And anyway, you don't know Levi. You refuse to befriend him. You don't know how he thinks. His view on life is in complete contrast to yours."

Rubbing the knot that was forming by the second on my forehead didn't stop me from asking the most obvious question. "Why the hell would I want to get to know Levi? It's going to be you and me or him and you. Why would I put myself through the torture of getting to know the asshole?"

A chuckle escaped her mouth, and one of her hands moved to her lips. "You know, I care for the man. I shouldn't have to stick up for him. You should have enough respect for me not to bad-mouth him in front of me."

Leaning down on the opposite end of the bed from where her eyes were boring in me, I tried not to laugh at her ridiculous remark. "Really? Like he doesn't hate me as much as I hate him. Just on pure principle. Though I'm not an arrogant prick like him."

I'd forgotten redheads had a temper on their own. And with Scarlet, it seemed to multiply by ten when she was pissed off. I'd forgotten the keys I'd put on her end of the bed last night just as they got slung at me. "Levi is a little cocky, sure, but he's not an asshole. Not like the man I just slept with."

I lifted my hands. "If I had a white flag, I'd wave it, Red. Can we start over?" I sat on the side of the bed, trying to figure this all out. "Red, honey, I'm sorry. But I find it hard to believe Levi is all innocent about me as you claim."

This time, she flashed her beautiful smile at me, sitting on the bed. When she pulled at my hand, she placed a kiss on it, and I grabbed her, bringing her close.

"Innocent? It certainly would never be a word I'd used to describe Levi when it comes to you. But not in the way you're thinking."

My eyes narrowed, questioning her silently.

"Believe me, Levi is not an asshole. He thinks quite highly of you. Sure, you both may be after the same girl, but he doesn't look at it as a competition. I'm not some prize to win.

And quite honestly, Jordan"—she paused for a second, her hand finding my erection that she had woken up—"I care for you both. Fuck, I think I may love the two of you."

Her loving another man should deflate my dick, but it didn't. She loved me. And I didn't want to share her. I didn't plan to. I'd make it my mission for her to love me more than that arrogant prick of a fireman.

After the revelation that Red loved me, I had a little pep in my step, but fuck, the idea of Levi with her was like an anchor weighing a ship down. But I settled for a small victory, and it was the fact we both loved each other.

The emergency room at the hospital was quiet, which told me we were waiting for all sorts of crazies soon. But I was not ready for the next patient, or for the crew who brought her in, as a woman very pregnant started to scream through evident contractions. "Somebody get this baby out of me!" I wasn't OB, and Dr. Phillips appeared out of nowhere. "I got this, Jordan." And they rushed her to labor and delivery. That was it for me, or so I thought.

"Hey, Doc." A deep voice wrestled me out of some papers that had held my attention. Turning to him, I knew it was him before I turned around. Arrogance followed this man.

"Lieutenant." I acknowledged him to his face and turned back around.

"Jordan." His voice was a bit more demanding when he asked, "Can we chat for a second?"

Tossing my pen on the desk, I turned back to him, and a smile covered his face. What did he have to be smiling about? I slept with Red last night, not him.

"Um, sure." When I turned to head down the hallway, I sensed his presence behind me. Entering a triage room, I shut the automatic glass doors and pulled a curtain across it to give us privacy. "What's up?" I remained casual, not giving him a care in the world that Red's love for him bothered me.

"Listen, Doc, I know about you and Scar. About last night."

I lifted my hand. "I'm not talking about my sex life with you when it comes to Red." I had begun, but he cut me off.

"I'm not bothered by it. I'm not threatened by it either. I just wanted to chat with you. Now is not the time or the place, but I'm off all day tomorrow. Scar and I have plans in the evening."

It was a low blow, and the punch fucking hurt. She loved us both, so of course he'd sleep with her when given the chance, and tomorrow was his chance. "I'm off tomorrow afternoon, too. Want to meet for lunch?" He raked his muscular hands through his curly locks.

"Um, actually, why don't I bring lunch your way, or you can meet me at my place?" Fuck, at least in public or at his place, I could leave if he pissed me off.

"Let's meet at your place," I offered, "and I can pick up lunch then. You're at Ell's old loft, right?" I asked. Fuck, I hated I knew this about him.

"Yeah and hey" — he handed me his phone — "put your phone number in here, just in case something happens." I hated to give him my number, but I did. Surprised he already had a name loaded in his contacts for me under The Good Doctor, I smiled for a second as I added it.

"Okay, cool. I'll text you in a second so you have my number, too." He left the triage room, and I felt a vibration on my phone.

Unknown number: *You are saved under The Good Doctor, so feel free to save me under The Sexy Fireman.*

Yeah, when pigs fly, I thought to myself. Pulling up the contacts, I decided to save it under The Asshole Fireman.

chapter 6

levi

The shift at my new firehouse went off without a hitch. We got a few calls in those twenty-four hours, but nothing huge or life altering. Scar and I texted a lot throughout the night. Mainly, I shared with her what my cock wanted to do to her pussy.

I'd laid the groundwork for my plan and had lunch scheduled with the good doctor tomorrow. But before I tried anything, I wanted to make sure Scar was on board. At eleven p.m., after a false alarm, I sent her a text.

Me: *Hey beautiful, you awake? I want to run something by you.*

Redhead Seductress: *Yeah, I'm awake, waiting to be with you.*

I didn't respond. I dialed her number, and she picked up

on the first ring. "Fuck, Scar, you're making it impossible not to yank myself off to your words."

"Um, whatever it takes, LT," she flirted. And with the two letters she called me, I smiled at her nickname for me.

"Hey, speaking of tomorrow night, I wanted to run something by you." I waded carefully in the shallow waters, not wanting to rock the boat. But when in the fuck did I really care about rocking a boat?

"Um, that sounds ominous. What is it?" In her tone was a tease, and shit, I wished I was near her. But I began to unravel my plan. Her inquiries and understanding had me just questioning one other variable—him.

Sleep did not come to me after leaving the fire station. If I had been able to grab a couple of hours of rest at my place, I would have been lucky, but the idea of having the hot doc in my house had me wound up. At eleven, I was hustling around, getting my house cleaned up for him. When I moved into my sister's condo after she moved in with her men, I had to dude it up a bit. Ell had her place too girlie for me and too fucking packed tight with all her shit. Mainly, it was all books that now occupied an entire room or three in her boyfriends' penthouse.

After buying a black comforter to cover up all the fucking white around the place, I also bought new furniture and a bigger television. Ell wasn't much for TV, so her eighteen-inch television would not cut it for me to watch the Cubs.

With the dishes from several nights finally done and the trash taken out, I felt the house was decent for the good doctor. Without a dining table, we'd most likely sit at the bar top island or on the couch. Fuck, I was nervous.

A chirp alerted me to a text, and I smiled with anticipation.

The Good Doctor: *I'm near Vinnie's Sub Shop. Are you good with a sandwich?*

Me: *Fuck, yeah, love that place. A Reuben please with everything.*

The Good Doctor: *You got it. Running ten minutes late.*

What should I say? Looking forward to it? Can't wait to see you? Get ready for me to freak you the fuck out? No, none of those would do.

Me: *Okay, see you then.*

———————————

Sliding my door open, I remembered how Ell was adamant about a barn door when she moved here. It was a little too girlie, but it was different, and I was always about being different. Jordan was in front of me in a pair of jogger shorts and a black V-neck T-shirt. His expression was not one I could read, but he smiled, handing me a six-pack of beer. I knew I liked this man, but now, he was perfect.

"Hey, Doc. Welcome to my humble abode," I said, moving out of the way for him to pass. I wanted to look at his ass in those shorts, but I didn't. I'd have a hard-on in a matter of seconds.

He was looking around my home, which was wide open even into the bedroom, when he gave me the beer. "Hey, I like what you've done with the place. Was wondering if Ell's girliness would rub off on you."

He was ribbing me, so it was a good sign he wouldn't go all territorial about Scarlet, but there was more to this meeting of the minds. I wasn't holding out hope, though I wouldn't ever shy away from what I wanted.

"Yeah, I had to tone out all the white a little, and I got a fucking decent television finally. Gotta keep up with my Cubbies."

I grabbed a beer out of the pack when I put it on the counter and handed him one. A nervous chuckle escaped his lips. "Ah, you're a Cubs' fan. I finally found something about you I like."

Oh, I could tell him there was a lot about him I liked, but I only replied, "Thanks, but I'm sure we can do better than that?"

I tried not to deliver it with any flirtatious undertones, but from the look on his face, I didn't think I was successful. Moving into the kitchen, I grabbed plates for us, placing our subs on. "Want to eat on the couch?"

"Sure." But he sat in the big chair near the couch, and I sat on the side closest to him.

But he didn't grab his food to eat. He sat still with his beer in his hands. Finally, he said, "So, LT, what's this about? I'm assuming you want to lay claim to Red as much as I want to."

Oh, there was so much I wanted to claim right then. I moved my sub to the side, too. Apparently, we were talking first, not eating. "You care for Scar, don't you?"

He swallowed a swig of his beer, and his Adam's apple bobbed up and down. It was so sexy. Before I could ogle him more, he began, "I love her, Levi. And if I'm honest, I hate that she cares for you like she does."

Yeah, her feelings for Jordan had never bothered me 'cause I understood how she could fall for him. But I kept this bit of info to myself. "I love her, too, Jordan. And if we aren't careful, one of us or both of us will lose her."

His stare turned to confusion. "What? Of course, she'll have to choose eventually."

Rubbing the back of my neck with my free hand and taking a swig of my own beer, I finally said, "But does she have to? Do we want to make her choose?"

"Of course, I don't want to hurt her, but she can't have both of us." Jordan's words carried finality.

I leaned into his space. "Sure, she can have both of us. We make it simple for her. She loves us both. We love her. Let her have us together."

I'd expected him to fly out of his seat, but he only sat back, though his anger was not contained. "What the fuck? I'm not like Arden and Daimen. I'm not into guys."

Shit, I had known this already, but I was not here about my own needs. In a perfect world, I would have loved to have what Arden, Daimen, and Elliot had. But this was not even close to a perfect world. I leaned closer to him and began laying out my case. "I get that, but you don't know what you're missing." He gave me a stare down, almost like a challenge. "But that's not what I'm suggesting. I want to have a committed relationship with Scarlet with both of us being her boyfriends. She has so much love, so let us share her together. Let me assure you that doesn't mean you and I are together—sexually."

"What do you mean? This is humiliating for Red. How can you even think she'd be up for something like that?"

I shrug because this will push him over the edge. "I talked to her about this first. What I'm suggesting is the both of us dating her. The two of us sharing her."

"Like the opposite of sister wives?" His question was delivered with sarcasm, but it still made me laugh.

"No, not really. You and I'd take her on dates together. You'd be here when we made love, and I'd be here when you made love with her. And if I worked, I'd know she was safe with you. If you had a late shift at the hospital, you'd know she was safe with me."

"But not you and me?" His question loomed in the air, and I wondered how much I should share with him.

"Well," I begin, stringing along the one-syllable word. Waving my hands through my light hair, I take a deep breath as I continue, my voice a little shaky. "To tell you the truth, I'm bisexual. I never thought of you as a threat because I want you equally. But I understand you're not into that. I like you, but I can keep my feelings at bay for the sake of Scarlet. Let us become friends. Let's work together to give Scar the one thing she never had—security and love together." Scar never had a family, being bussed from foster home to foster home until Arden and Daimen took her off the streets when she was eighteen. They were the only family she'd ever known.

"But you want me sexually?" His question came out so casual and matter-of-factly. It was a loaded question.

"Whoa, Doc, let's put your ego aside. Yes, I could fuck you if you were into men, but you're not. So let's worry about Scar and make her our focus." His fists were balled together like he could take my head off. "What I'm suggesting is you join us tonight. She's coming over, and we have plans, but I'd like you here. Yes, the first time I take Scar, I want you to be a part of it — for her."

He stood, leaving his sandwich and beer on the table, and walked out the door. I wouldn't go after him because he would have to work this out on his own. And since he left without his lunch, I had another sandwich I could enjoy.

chapter 7

scarlet

My heart raced all day. After Levi asked my permission to approach Jordan about a threesome, meaning the two committed only to me, my stomach had been in knots all day. Quite honestly, it was brilliant. Levi was taking a chance on his heart, but I knew he only wanted to prevent either him or Jordan from being hurt when I made a choice. And I was nowhere close to being able to choose between them. Though Levi's heart was falling for both of us at the same time.

I had spoken with both men about how I was a part of the foster care system. I had never let them see the real hurt that lived inside me or given them a full understanding of the anguish and misery I had — growing up without anyone to love me unconditionally. And though poor Levi had been disowned by his parents for the life he'd lived, he still had his twin sister.

If I were discarded again at this point in my life by the two men who I'd fallen equally in love with, my heart would never recover. They'd both take half of it with them.

When Levi's text came through, I was hesitant to check it. I'd already deduced that if it were Levi, it could not be good news. Looking at the time on the clock that sat on my desk, it had only been fifteen minutes since Jordan had arrived at Levi's condo. My heart sank as I read the words.

My Hot Fireman: *It's out there. I told him my plan, and he walked out. But that's not necessarily a bad sign.*

Ah, my sensitive yet cocky fireman was so confident. His care for me, making this decision that didn't leave me brokenhearted, was one of pure unselfishness. He'd never lied to me. He wanted Jordan as much as he wanted me, but I knew this gesture was for me. Being with me, as Jordan was, would be hard for Levi. It was in his little sentiment that I understood how genuinely unselfish he was.

Me: *I'm sorry, babe.*

My Hot Fireman: *I got an extra sub from Vinnie's out of it even if it was just dull turkey.*

Always so positive, that one. I couldn't help but smile at his words. I fired off another text.

Me: *You know I love you, right?*

We hadn't said those words to one another, but in the three months we'd been together, the flames were as evident to me as the real fires he put out daily.

My Hot Fireman: *Yes, this isn't the way I imagined telling you for the first time, but, Scar, I love you, too.*

Me: *I know, but I will make it up to you tonight. Sorry, babe. Your sister just appeared at my desk. TTYL.*

With our goodbyes, I placed my phone back in my top desk drawer and watched Ell watch me.

"Was that my brother who put a smile on your face or Andrew's brother?" Elliot never judged me for dating both Levi and Jordan, who happened to be her best friend's brother. Ell had the best of both worlds, too, but her men were as committed to one another as they were to her.

"Your brother," I plainly stated. "And you know about his little crush on the good doctor, right?" I asked.

"Yeah, we'd talked about it. And I adore Jordan, but I think it's a lost cause," she deadpanned, pushing one of her blonde curls out of her eyes. "And I know Levi too well. He has this fun-loving nature about him. He's serious but playful at the same time, so I know he wants you both."

What could I say? She could read her brother like the back of her hand. "Um, Levi playful?" I teased back. It was funny how Ell had her own playful man. Arden was the fun-loving jokester whereas Daimen was serious ninety percent of the time. And though Levi was less serious than the good doctor, he was a good mix of easygoing and business.

Pursing my lips together, it wasn't my place to disclose the little conversation Levi had with the other man I'd fallen in love with. Cocking my head to the side, I gave a simple reply. "Yeah, I guess we'll see."

Having already agreed to meet Levi at his place, I hurried home from work and took a quick shower. I wanted to cook for him, but his exact words were, "I want to spend as much time with you as possible."

I knew what he meant, and I was just as excited. The entire way home, I contemplated reaching out to Jordan. The good doctor was so stubborn. And Levi's plan was all his own.

When he'd called me the night before and proposed the idea, it sounded too good to be true. I loved Levi. With him, I saw a side of life from his point of view. Where most things with Jordan were black and white, Levi was all gray. So of course with their diversity, I got the best of both worlds. Our conversation lingered in my mind.

"Scar, I have an idea. And I'm not saying this to sink my cock deep into the good doctor." He laughed since I'd known

Levi was attracted to Jordan from the beginning. "No, beautiful, I don't want you to get hurt. And I understand having to choose between us will cause you to hurt deeply."

I hadn't said a word, but it was the truth. "Anyway, Jordan isn't into me. I get that, and I won't push." I chuckled because I wasn't sure who he was kidding. "Okay, I won't push a lot anyway. But seriously, I want to date you, and I want you to date Jordan. I want a commitment from you, but I want you to be able to call Jordan your boyfriend, too. And because I know you care for us deeply, I don't want you to choose."

Now, I was back to reality, but his gesture wasn't without appreciation on my part. It was similar to Ell with her men. But unlike Arden and Daimen, Levi understood Jordan was unattainable. Levi didn't have to tell me, but at that moment, he loved me enough to make this sacrifice. And more so than sharing me with Jordan, he'd see Jordan in a way he only dreamed of.

With the warm water drenching my red curls in the shower, I massaged my tired head. Only one thing remained on my mind for now — being with Levi for the first time.

chapter 8

jordan

He didn't follow me, and I wasn't sure if it was a good or a bad thing. His words affected me, and I sure as fuck didn't like how they had affected me. There was so much I wanted to do, and sucker-punching Levi was at the top of my list. I also desperately wanted to call Red and demand answers. Staying with him was yet another thought I entertained way too much!

I'd somehow slumped home. Well, to my brother's old condo. He was kind enough to take me in after I returned from Doctors without Borders, and I took over the mortgage when Andrew was given an apartment in the same building where Red and Elliot lived.

With the crazy, sometimes eighteen-hour shifts I'd pull over at Mercy, I really only needed a place to lay my head. Plus, his place was more than I could have imagined when I moved back to Chicago. But in the five hours I'd been home since seeing Levi, I'd remained seated in the same place my ass fell when I'd gotten back to my house.

My mind couldn't get over his proposal or his words. Ell had let it slip once after her accident while leaving the hospital that Levi was bisexual, but I didn't put much stock into it because she had been heavily sedated. But when I told her I was going to ask Red out, she'd joked with me. "Yeah, Levi is into her, but hell, he'd take you in the deal, too." I shrugged it off, thinking her own relationship along with all the medicine had clouded Elliot Arnold's views.

His comments about wanting me caught me by surprise. He really wanted to share Red? Part of that pissed me off, but the part that had me fleeing Levi's condo was more desire than anything. Those emotions were what truly scared me.

I knew a little of Red's past. She was bumped from foster care to foster care and was basically homeless at eighteen. Arden and Daimen literally took her off the streets. The second they saw her, they had told her she was like a little sister. Arden and Daimen's net worth was less than ten dollars, but they gave her a place to stay even though they barely had anything themselves.

Her anxiety of being alone was awful to witness. She kept it under wraps, but when we'd had our first fight— appropriately about Levi, shortly after we first started dating— I'd walked in on her in a ball on her floor. It was the type of hyperventilating crying where one couldn't catch their breath. It was the most heartbreaking moment I'd ever witnessed.

Thinking of her in that fetal position made me recall the complete memory of when I asked her out. It was the entire interaction with her, and just not the small bit I remembered the night we made love. It was vivid. It wasn't like she hadn't been honest with me from the beginning. Ell was still in the hospital and out of harm's way when I'd cornered her at the vending machine.

"Hey, Red," I'd started. With her flaming red hair, I

knew it wasn't original, but it got her attention.

"Hey, Doc. Just getting some sustenance for the night. After a crazy couple of days, I'm sending the boys home to get some rest. I'm staying with Ell for a few hours. It's all her men have agreed to." She bent over to get a bag of Doritos and Skittles from the vending machine. It gave me just enough time to stare at her ass. It was a fucking fine one.

"Hey, now that we know Ell's going to be okay, would it be appropriate to ask you out?"

Shit, I'd seen her the second she rushed in the hospital the night of the accident. She was this vision, and I knew I wanted her—in every way. When she hesitated, I stated the obvious, "Shit, you have someone. I'm sorry. Of course, you're taken."

Her face blushed, and it was so fucking adorable "Um, I'd love to go out with you, but you gotta know I'm sort of seeing someone. We aren't exclusive, though, so if you're okay with it, I'd love to see where you and I could go." She continued, "But I'm not looking for anything too serious. If you're okay with it, I'd love to go out with you, too." Somehow, I knew who the other guy was. His eyes never left her ass either.

But I wanted to get to know her, to woo her, and win her over. I just knew she'd choose me.

Back in the present, I hated I had been so cocky. But with her past, never being first in anyone's life, I understood what she needed—what she needed from me. The ding of my cell alerted me to a text, and I grabbed it, my hands sweaty the second the name appeared on the screen.

Asshole Fireman: *I'm giving you space, Doc. I'm not one to push. (Okay, so I'm one to push, but I'm trying not to.) Dinner is at my condo tonight at seven. I will set a third place setting. You're invited. My code to get in the building is 3249. I hope to see you. If not, please know we'll miss you. Again, I'm not pushing you. But since we both love Scar, and she loves us – it's an option for her to get the love she never had growing up.*

Well, shit, the asshole knew where to sucker-punch me,

didn't he? The mention of Red's life in foster care was all it took. I grabbed my phone, then my jacket and wallet, and looked at the time. It was 6:01. I wasn't necessarily going to Levi's, but I needed clarity. I knew where I could get it in droves.

The doorman assumed I was there to see my brother. He already knew me by name, but when I texted Ell and asked to come over, she didn't ask why.

Elliot: *Sure. The boys and I were wondering if you'd seek us out for advice.*

Well, hell, news traveled fast.

Pressing the code for the penthouse, I was glad I didn't run into Red or my brother. The second I arrived at their luxurious home, an automated female's voice announced my arrival. It was some sort of security to the stars, and of course, these self-made millionaires had it.

"Jordan, we're in the kitchen. Come have a glass of wine with us," Arden called.

Peeking my head around the kitchen, I saw all three sitting at the bar top, playing a game of cards. It wasn't what I expected this triad to be doing—something so down to earth as playing a game—but what had I expected? Walking in on them fucking like rabbits?

"Red or white?" Ell asked as she stood to give me a hug. Daimen rose to shake my hand, but Arden stayed planted, his eyes fixed on his cards.

"You winning, Arden?" I ask, finding this serious side of him surprising. This man has only been serious one time since I'd met him, and it was when Ell was fighting for her life in the hospital.

"Ah, don't let him fool you, Doc. This asshole is a sore loser when it comes to games," Daimen added as I pointed at the bottle of red on the counter, and he poured a glass for me.

Ell's arms wrapped around Daimen's waist with

Arden's cards hidden from them. "Well, caveman, we do have a lot riding on the results of the game." She giggled as she whispered into his ear.

"Yeah, what she said," Arden teased.

"Ah, fuck, did I walk in on some weird sexual card game?" I took a long swig of my wine, hoping it would help with whatever came out of their mouths next.

All three erupted into laughter when Elliot was able to mouth out, "No, but he's on to something. I'm trying to get them to add some color to the white-on-white walls we have throughout our house. If I win, I get to choose the paint, and they're afraid it's going to be pink."

"Shit, I like Doc's idea better," Arden said, tossing the cards. "I amend our agreement. Strip poker. That really is a win-win for everyone, especially if I get you both naked." Elliot left Daimen's side to walk over to Arden and kiss him on the bridge of his nose. She made the whole threesome thing look so easy.

"Sit, Jordan," she instructed. "I know you're not here to play cards with us or to be entertained by all our sexy times."

"But if you are, that's cool, too," Arden deadpanned.

"Spill it, Doc. We know a little. Might as well bring us up to speed," Daimen, the man who was always business, began.

"Well, shit, nothing is sacred in your little tribe, is it?" I questioned.

All three shrugged, and I had my answer. Squarely looking at Elliot, I began, "So your brother admitted to me he's bisexual and would have no problem sleeping with me." I laid it out there, and by Elliot's expression, she was not surprised.

"Yep, it sure sounds like Levi." She took a sip of her drink and was so casual about all of this.

I thought she'd be a little shocked, but watching how comfortable she was with her two men, I now understood why she was not. "Um, but he knows I'm not bisexual. He suggested that since Red loved us both and we both loved her, we could commit to her together." I drank more wine, because this was an awkward as fuck conversation.

They were all silent for longer than what was comfortable. All three looked at one another like they had something or maybe many things to get off their chests, but feared saying it.

"Just come out with it, guys, I won't be offended. Tell me what's on your minds." It was all the permission they needed, and they began to talk all at once.

Elliot worked her way into the conversation first. "My brother is cocky but very giving. I know he cares for you, Jordan, but his offer was with the idea of putting Scar first, which very few have done in her life," she said, pointing at her men. "And Levi's been in a relationship, a committed triad, before. He was young. It was the first guy he'd been with. They found a girl they both loved, and they were happy. But when the guy and girl wanted more—a family—he wasn't quite ready to settle down. So he knows more about polyamorous relationships than I do. But his offer focuses on Scar."

Ell pointed at Daimen, who'd been ready to say his piece before anyone. "Scar has so much shit from her childhood, so to be chosen by two men who are willing to put their differences aside for her would demonstrate your love in a very real and raw way." His words were simple, and it was all he had to say.

Arden grabbed Daimen's hand, looking at me when he began. "I know you don't want to hear this, but for me, my sexuality is more fluid. I fell in love with Daimen because he's Daimen, my best friend. He's the best man I'd ever known. I'd never been with another man. Love doesn't have to have labels. You can love someone for them. I have found labels sometimes mess up the ability to be happy."

Daimen slipped his arm around Arden's neck, bringing him in for a sweet but sensual kiss. "Fuck, I love when you tell our story." Ell only looked at her men as if they hung the moon, and for her, they had.

I took my last sip of wine, watching them make this look so easy. "Well, you all gave me a lot to ponder. I'm going to let you get back to your weird sexual/painting card game. I'd say good luck, but I think it's going to be a win-win no matter who ends up the victor."

chapter 9

levi

Chapter 9
Levi
After Jordan left suddenly, I ran to the corner market to pick up some chicken, ham, potatoes, and green beans. My specialty was chicken cordon bleu, and being the optimist I was, I'd gotten enough for the three of us.

I texted the good doctor because I hadn't heard from him. However, I knew this man was the analytical type. In my mind, I could see him with his pro and con list debating the merits of what I'd proposed.

As I pulled out the roasted potatoes and chicken, I heard a delicate little rap on my door. Opening it for her, I found Scarlet. She'd mentioned she needed to shower, and boy, did I love the smell of whatever she'd bathed herself in. This redhead seductress smelled like pears and cinnamon as her intoxicating aroma filled my loft. She was dressed in a bright pink skirt and a deep purple V-neck shirt, exposing the cleavage of her supple tits. Her colors, outside of the office, were always as bright as her personality. The girl wore the biggest hoop earrings and some sort of necklace that called more attention to the fine as fuck rack she displayed for my viewing pleasure. I pulled her into my arms. The good doctor might not show up, but fuck, she was a vision, and nothing would ruin our first night together.

"Shit, Levi, I didn't think I'd want anything but you, but whatever you're cooking has changed my mind." She winked at me as she continued, "I'm a bit hungry." Her lips curved up into a slight smile, and it was all it took to bring my cock out to play. Pulling her to me, I wasted no time, swinging her around and gently pushing her to the couch. Leaning over her, I covered her lips with mine immediately, sampling the goods with my hands.

Sure, my fingers had brought her to orgasms a couple of times, and her own hands were talented, too, but right now, I needed more. Popping my head for the briefest of seconds, I narrowed my eyes in on the heat of her hazel ones. "Fuck, I'll feed you, but I need just a little bit to get me through dinner."

She didn't mention the good doctor, nor did I. At this moment, it was her and me, and if he was stupid enough to blow the chance—well, fuck him. Because this was all about Scar. I wouldn't let one stupid person ruin our moment together. Not even the sexy good doctor.

My hand roved to the hem of her skirt, and shit, I had that piece of fabric hiked up in record time. "Fuck, Scar, I don't want to feel rushed but shit."

I'd barely touched her panties, and the wetness had me longing for something more edible than my world-famous chicken dish.

"Levi, we have all night." I'd completely missed the bag she brought in, and when she pointed at it, and I looked back, a large smile covered my face. "And I don't want to rush either. Feed me so I have the strength to ride that mighty fine cock of yours all night long."

Her words put a hurting on me, but I stood, trying to tell my body we'd have to wait. I didn't like it, and I knew as fuck my cock wouldn't like it either.

Not having a dining room table or really the room for it, I'd pulled out my old card table. I covered it with a fancy tablecloth and used the china plates my sister had left me.

By the look on her face, it was not lost on her that I'd set it for three people. We had yet to discuss the elephant in the room or the lack of one. But when I pulled out the seat for her, she sat with a smile on her face. Should I clear that dish that reminded us both that he was not here, or should I stay ever so optimistic?

Before I sat down, ignoring the other place setting, I lit the candles. "Wow, Levi, you did this all on your own?"

I shrugged my shoulders. Being a fireman, it was bound to be my turn to cook at some point. I'd had enough shitty dinners at the firehouse, so I wanted to treat the guys who put their lives on the line to a good meal each time I was up for that duty.

"Yeah, it's my specialty," I replied and pulled at her hand, which happened to be on the table. "Scar, I know it wasn't romantic—saying it for the first time over a text, but hell, I needed you to know how much I love you. It's this intoxicating sort of power you have over me. I only wish I could give you your deepest desires." We both looked down at the empty plate in front of us, but her brilliant red smile, as deep as her hair, was all the indication I needed to understand she was here tonight for me.

"Levi, what you did, what you proposed, I won't ever forget. We knew it was a long shot, but hell, you did it anyway, for me. I know you care for him, too, but still, this gesture …" She didn't finish her sentence as a couple of tears fell from her eyes.

Bringing her hand to my lips, I smiled at the thought of the good doctor eating my girl's pussy. Shit, my cock thought it was time to come out and play yet again. "But it's not over. What I suggested to someone as straitlaced as Doc, it may take him a while to understand the validity."

Pursing her lips together, she turned them to a small smirk. "But you need to understand, with Jordan, everything is black and white to him. Think about it. In his job, there's zero room for the gray area. In his methodical and analytical mind, it's one or the other. Plus, having a gay brother and a lesbian for a sister make it more real to him. Does this make sense?"

"Kayla is a lesbian?" I asked, and a smile betrayed my thoughts.

Lightly giving me a small kick under the table, her laughter took over the room. "Yeah, but that's beside the point, you pervert."

"Hey, what can I say? I'm a guy." I paused, realizing she wasn't amused and I hadn't answered her question. "Yeah, it does make sense, and I get it. But it's not the way my brain works."

She sighed at me, continuing, "Anyway, to him, you like a guy or you like a girl, and there's no in between. He sees Ell with her guys. He thinks it's cool, and he's certainly not homophobic. He was the first supporter of his brother coming out of the closet. But to him, there's a clear choice."

I loved how she went to bat for the good doctor. It showed me how much she cared for him. Her love for Jordan had never bothered me.

But I mentioned the big difference in my scenario. "Beautiful, that's not what I'm suggesting," I began. "Sure, I laid my cards out today. It would have been unfair not to let him know I hoped for more, but for you, I want us to have you together. It's clearly what you want."

Nodding her head in agreement, she continued, "True. To pick between you and Jordan would be the hardest thing I'd ever have to do."

I pushed my chair back, scraping it against the flooring, but it didn't stop me. Walking behind Scar, I wrapped my arms around her beautiful neck and kissed her ear. "And that's why I wanted this, both him and me, equally desiring to please you." Her moans and her reaction to my kisses led me to believe we'd be skipping dinner for now.

My hand snaked around her body, and with her low-cut shirt, my fingers danced across the beauty of her breasts. Squeezing one nipple, I elicited a deep groan from this woman. Her hand found my free one and brought it to her thighs. "Scar, do you want this?"

Her answer was barely audible but nonetheless, I could hear her consent. "Yeah, Levi, so bad."

My tongue was still at her neck when a small tap on the door stopped us for a moment. Without a thought, I called out, "Who is it?"

We waited for a second or two, and when I thought we must have imagined the tap on my door, a voice that sent shivers down my spine, answered. "Um, it's Jordan, Levi." Bringing my face around to Scar, I didn't move but answered, "The doors open." I had no intention of moving from this scene he was about to walk into. I couldn't have planned it more perfect if I'd tried.

Sliding my door open, he was face-to-face with Scar and myself in the midst of foreplay. Giving him a slight bro nod, my tongue was in Scar's ear and my one hand was on her tit while the other one was right below her pussy.

With Scar in her seat, and with a clear jerk of her body, she wanted to run to him to let him know how much we both needed him with us. With a little whisper, I warned, "No, Scar. Let him come to us." With a nod of her head, she agreed with me.

My eyes locked on the good doctor. "Hey, Doc, looks like you're just in time."

All he'd done was shut the door. He was motionless, watching Scar with either a slight smile or a grimace. I wasn't sure yet. "If we do this, it's for her, just her. Nothing between us. You got it, LT?" He was direct and to the point. Why had I expected anything less from the good doctor?

His direction changed, and his eyes were only on me. Fuck, he was so adorable standing there, his frame resting on the door and the bulge of his pants showing me the outline of his cock with each second that passed.

"Okay, Doc. I won't push. Just know ..." He cut me off by raising his hand. He indicated we wouldn't be discussing this any further. I grinned because when one protested this much, it made me wonder.

"Levi." It was a deep warning, the tone that made me want him more, but as I promised Scar, this arrangement was only for her.

"Yes, Doc, agreed. Now get your ass over here. This girl is on fire." I liked how he took my command and came when I beckoned.

He got as close to Scar as he could get. When she pulled at his belt buckle, he didn't resist her. "Is this really what you want, Jordan?" she asked. Her tone was so breathy with need that I could barely resist picking her up and placing her on my bed to have my way with her.

"LT?" Jordan stopped me. "Are you sure this is okay for your first time? I mean, I've had her to myself already."

Scarlet's body was reacting to our touches, our voices, and my commands. "Look at her, Doc. Look at how she wants us both together. Believe me when I say I think there's enough of our redhead seductress to go around."

I kneeled by her knees, which left Jordan's crotch in my face. Hell, my own cock strained, and I wanted to unzip him and take him in my mouth. But shit, this was about Scar, and we'd make it only about her.

Pulling at her chin, I took her gaze and moved it to the belt area of Jordan's. "Show him, Scar, how happy you are that he's here. Give him your appreciation."

Taking an extra-long time to spread out every bit of

anticipation for him, Scar unbuckled his belt, unbuttoned his pants, and slowly pulled his cock from his boxers. I'd always been very pleased with my own cock. In my opinion, it was pretty glorious. But hell, the good doctor's dick was like Picasso's masterpiece hidden in his underwear.

chapter 10

scarlet

Both men I'd fallen in love with were here. I had only been able to admit to myself how much I loved them in the past couple of days. Each man was the full picture of what I wanted. Levi was indeed more relaxed. I wouldn't call him a complete funny man, but he was so comfortable in his own shoes. He made it possible for me to accept this arrangement he had worked out.

To say he was in love with Jordan would be an overstatement, but the chemistry was there. On his end anyway. But every once in a while, I saw Jordan's eyes roam over Levi. I knew what it looked like—I'd been around it my whole adult life with Arden and Daimen.

But as comfortable as Levi was in his own skin, Jordan was the exact opposite. He was not a control freak, but he certainly was wound up a bit more than Levi. He could be so funny — when he let loose and didn't let doubt fill his mind. But now, Levi had kneeled at my feet, and Jordan's cock was in my hand.

My mind overtook the passion that exploded around us. "Should we talk?" Both men looked at one another — as if Jordan's mind was playing catchup with everything. I wanted this — fuck, I sure as hell wanted this — but I never wanted him to regret it the next day.

Jordan looked down at Levi, and I couldn't see what they shared between their gaze. He grabbed my chin above him, and said, "Nah, Red, we'll talk afterward. If you are worried I'll regret this, sweetheart, I'll never regret putting you first in my life."

"Doc, I couldn't have said it better myself." Levi stood, moving behind my back. "I need you, baby, but first, the good doc should get something extra sweet for being here with us. Want to give him a treat?"

I didn't wait for Levi to coordinate what he had in his mind he needed to see. And shit, I knew Jordan's cock was that of legends. It was large, and I already knew my mouth drove him crazy. My lips worked around the tip of his cock as I sucked the pre-cum. A hiss released from his mouth when Levi's arm twisted around my body, working his hands in my bra to bead my nipples through his fingers. Every once in a while, he squeezed them, and a small pleasurable pain coursed through my body.

"Fuck, LT, whatever you're doing to her, continue. Her moans are music to my ears."

Levi bent over, whispering, "You're beautiful with his cock in your mouth. You know, right?" Between the chemistry, the feels, and the words, my pussy was soaked and in need of one or both men inside me.

"Shit, Red, I'm going to come. You need me to pull out?" I shook my head, and Levi released a long and loud groan. Though Jordan was here for me and me alone, I knew Levi got off on Jordan coming. And that did something to my already sopping panties.

"Doc, you ready to take this to the bedroom?" he asked. Not like we had far to go — this place was Elliot's at one point, and it was open — so his bed was basically behind us.

"Yeah, LT, but I've had her. I think it's only fair. This was supposed to be your own night with her by yourself." It was not regret that accompanied Jordan's words. Hell, it was his unselfishness, letting Levi have this. And though I loved Jordan, he was certainly the more selfish of the two men — always wanting me for himself in the past. Yet in this exchange between the two men, I saw a difference in him.

"Um, okay, but you're here with us for Scar, so by all means, work our girl over in every and any way you can think while I bury my cock deep in her." We hadn't moved yet, but his words had both Jordan and I grasping for body parts and trying to lose clothing. I turned to unbuckle Levi's belt while Jordan unzipped my skirt. As soon as I was free, I jumped into Levi's arms, and he caught me. But I turned, holding Jordan's hand while he followed us to the bedroom. "By her head, Doc," he demanded, and Jordan obeyed. It was not in his nature to do as he was told, yet he did with Levi. I filed this away for future investigating.

Levi placed me on my back, but my head fell between Jordan's legs propped up slightly by pillows. Looking up, I was lost in the hazelnut hues of Jordan's chocolate eyes. I mouthed, "Thank you."

When he leaned down to kiss me, his words melted my heart. "I'd do anything for you, Red." I got this, and I loved him for it, but I didn't miss the out of character way he was acting in the presence of Levi. Part of this scared me to death. I never wanted to make Jordan something he was not. And if he ever felt pressured by us to change, it would ruin what we were about to partake in. But could he let go of the stigma of sexuality? Could he love the people he was with for them and not based on the idea he might have bisexual tendencies? I wanted all of that for him. I wanted him to be free. I saw this so much in my life with Arden and Daimen until Arden finally accepted he loved Daimen. It didn't make him anything but a man who loved another man. And in Arden's mind, the world be damned for making him ashamed of it.

"Doc, you do whatever you want to our girl to make this good." He turned to me. "And Scar, this is real, pure, and true. So hold on tight, beautiful, because I'm going to make this feel so good."

Jordan never flinched. And with his propensity to overthink, I thought he might worry I'd compare them. In my mind, one was not better than the other. They were different, and I would always crave what they each gave me. One on one, each man was an eleven out of ten, and together, they multiplied everything tenfold. Looking over at Levi and up at Jordan, I understood that as a package deal, they were a hundred out of a ten.

Levi kneeled at the end of the bed, my legs open for everything and anything he wanted to do to me. "Hell, Scar. Your pussy is gorgeous. Don't you think, Doc?"

I loved how he included Jordan in every aspect of his seduction. Jordan's groan was not subtle, and when Levi's eyes locked behind me, they shared a silent exchange. "The fucking best, LT."

I didn't see his face, only the top of his head, and I anticipated his touch or the slightest lick. My gaze fell to Jordan's. "Relax and let it happen. In his own time, Red. Let him make you feel so good."

Jordan caressed my hair. This small experience was so erotic. I couldn't take my stare off him. Our eyes communicated in silence when Levi lightly stroked my clit. A long hiss of pure pleasure met both men's ears. With a small chuckle, Jordan yelled to Levi. "I think she likes whatever you're doing to her. Keep it up."

"Oh, I plan to. I fucking plan to." His tongue concentrated on the top of my clit. Whereas most men circled that area, he wanted all my sensation focused there. One finger worked the lips of my pussy as another worked its way inside me, deeper and deeper. As I writhed, Jordan moved his free hand to my nipples. Levi liked to evoke pain, but with Jordan, it was the soft little brushes over my nipples that competed with where Levi's tongue was working me overboard for my attention.

His head popped up, and I could see his face, though now more than one finger was inside me. "Doc, what do you think? I'd say she tastes like maple syrup and cinnamon. Any other suggestions?"

My eyes remained closed in the hope I wouldn't open them to find this was only a dream. When I did look at the beauty of Jordan, a slight grin met me. "Yeah, that's fair, LT. Just wait, soon you'll have some whipped cream to go on those pancakes."

Levi's snicker could be both felt and heard on my end. These men could elicit pleasure in me I never knew existed. Right now, I was only getting a glimpse, but I waited for more.

Jordan moved slightly toward the end table on the side of the bed, interrupting my concentration. In one solid motion, he tossed something toward Levi, and his head popped up just in time to catch. It was almost scary how in tune these two men were with each other, but it made me wetter for them both. "Thanks, Doc. Great minds think alike." I loved their nicknames for one another. Part of me loved the idea of Levi being called LT. And although Levi was a LT, due to his position with the Chicago fire department, it was still a fucking turn-on. And then there was the Good Doctor Levi called Jordan in my presence and just plain Doc to his face.

"Scar, you want me to make you come now, or would you like to come with me inside you?"

There was a choice? Well, shit, there was an easy answer to all of this. "Both. Levi, I need both."

Jordan's laughter was music to my ears. "You have your work cut out for you, LT. Think you're man enough?" Jordan teased, and the easygoing banter had me wanting so much more from both men.

Levi didn't dignify his response with a verbal answer, but he lifted his hand to flip Jordan off. Another laugh was his reply, and fuck, this was fun. Just not sexy as hell—which it was—but fucking fun!

I didn't have much time to think because the challenge only ramped Levi up. I slipped into my pre-orgasm flutter, summoning my body to ride out the ecstasy being delivered to me right now. "Let it take you over, Red. Let him please you." Jordan's words broke through the pleasure, and my hands moved to Levi's head, threading my fingers through his hair.

"Ah, fuck, Levi! Keep … doing … whatever … the … h … e … l … l … you … are … doing," I uttered.

My eyes flew open, and his head popped up. "See, Doc, I knew I could do it."

Jordan's words surprised us. "Yeah, I had a feeling you could, too, LT. Just giving you incentive."

chapter 11

jordan

It was hard to believe Scarlet's entire body was between my legs while I watched Levi feast on her. It was fun to mess with him and push him like I had. In Red's eyes, I sure as fuck knew what it did to her. And now, I was sitting here, staring at his condom-clad cock. Why couldn't I admit the three of us in this intimate predicament turned me on? But it did. Sure, a good portion of it was Red, but I'd be lying if I didn't admit Levi's presence wasn't a part of it, too.

I was watching Red come down from her orgasm, and my own cock had to be pushing into her ass. It was rock solid hard, and if I didn't get relief soon, watching them fuck would sure as hell make me come.

"You still with us, Red?" I asked.

Her eyes were heavy, but her lips had a smile adorning

them. She finally mouthed, "Hmm, yeah." She popped her eyes open, and with her gentle hand, she caressed my face. "Thanks, Doc." I didn't reply because I couldn't. Something had come over me, instantly choking me up. Something leading me to this moment, in the bed of another man, with the girl I loved had me at a loss for words and a little emotional. Running my fingers through her fire engine red hair, I felt a grin tug at my lips. "I love you," she said, rubbing the scruff of my five o'clock shadow.

I needed to reply to this, so I said, "I love you, too, Red."

Moving my face, I saw Levi straight ahead. Sitting in silence, he watched all of this transpire. He looked happy—happy for us and happy to be a part of it. Never did he have a twinge of jealousy in his eyes. I wanted to look away, but I couldn't. I was surprised when he winked at me, and I returned his gesture with a smile. But it was too easygoing with us. I didn't want what I knew he wanted. His cock might turn me on, but hell, I still didn't want him like this. I changed my tone quickly. I rapidly replied, "Well, whatcha waiting for, LT?"

He looked conflicted by my harsh words.

"Scar, sweetheart, you ready for me to fill you up? To feel me throughout your body. And as I come, know I love you and only want what's best for you in life."

Fuck, LT was so wordy. All I wanted was action. I needed to get out of my own mind right now and watching pure passionate fucking would get me out of my own head. Get him out of my head. Or so I hoped anyway.

Levi leaned forward, kissing Red. "Taste yourself. You're fucking delicious." As he gave her a kiss, his eyes locked on mine. "You want a taste?" he teased, and I averted my eyes from him.

"Levi," Red warned.

"Just kidding—um, sort of anyway." Giving Red another kiss, he moved farther down, and I saw him position himself. "You want long and sweet or hard and quick? And don't worry, I recover fast. We can go all night long—either way you want it. But lover boy gets you next."

Shit, the way his lips formed those two words had me harder, and it had nothing to do with the redhead I loved with all my heart between my legs, sitting against my chest.

"Hard. Fuck me hard, LT," Red said, and I was stone hard with her declaration.

I couldn't take my eyes off the love these two were sharing. Sure, it was rough and hurried, all qualities I saw in Levi, but shit, when he pushed into her so deep, his face was within a hand's reach of mine. I could stretch my arm and caress his five o'clock shadow if I wanted to. Shit, what was wrong with me? I didn't want to ... did I?

Red's and Levi's moans were mesmerizing. My mind was on them and them alone. Levi's movements were hurried, but he stopped briefly to kiss Red, and his hand reached for mine, touching it quickly. He mouthed, "Thank you." Then before I knew it, he was provoking screams from Red. "Hold on, Scar, I'm almost there." One more push and he slowed.

"Holy shit, Scar. You're everything worth waiting for. But thank fuck, I don't have to wait anymore." He pulled out quickly, taking off his condom and tossing it in the wastebasket near his bed. He sat next to me, and I moved to make room for him and Red as he cuddled in close to her. "No need to move, Doc." But I was standing, watching the way she fit in his arms and the way he'd kissed her forehead, whispering, "I love you, beautiful."

Red leaned over, just enough, and grabbed my hand. "I can take care of you." I looked down at the wood I was sporting due to what had occurred between them. I was freaking out a little after witnessing something so sensual, so powerful, and a fucking turn-on.

"Um, no, that's okay, for now." I felt I delivered my tone too shaky when both pairs of eyes were on me.

Her hand was still in mine when Levi called to me. "Doc, get out of your head. We've done nothing wrong. It's okay. We're here for Scar and Scar alone."

"Lie with me, hold me? Please, Jordan," Red pleaded. How could I deny this from the woman I loved? I snuggled into her back as she faced Levi. My hand was squeezed briefly, but the calloused fingers told me it wasn't Red. I looked over toward Levi, and his smile was bright. He winked again, but I found myself both mad and confused. I made a mental note to discuss this arrangement again just man to man when we got a chance.

———————

My stomach woke me up a little later. Turning to the alarm clock on my side, it was almost nine at night. No wonder I was hungry. I hadn't eaten since this afternoon, and if memory served me right, I didn't eat then, either. Fuck, I'd left my favorite sub here with Levi. I saw how he ate food, so the fucker probably ate my sub.

I tiptoed out to the kitchen to rustle up whatever Levi had cooked for dinner, remembering the wonderful aroma of his home cooking and how it had filled the house earlier. I found Levi in his boxers, sitting on a stool at the island.

I was aware that I, too, only had my underwear on and had become a little self-conscious. It was as if Levi sensed this when he softly spoke. "Bro, you saw my cock, and I'll see yours, too." His smile reminded me I needed to have that talk with him and quick. "It's okay to walk out here in your boxers." He stepped out of the chair but left it out for me. "Here, have a seat, and I'll fix us something to eat. You gotta be hungry," he began.

"Um, yeah, I just remembered that I didn't eat lunch today," I reminded him, but I was sure he hadn't forgotten.

"Oh, I ate it. It was good." He smiled, shrugging his shoulders. I was right; the fucker had eaten my favorite sub.

"Shit, I've never seen anyone eat quite like you," I replied as I playfully flipped him off. I'd been to dinners at Daimen, Arden, and Elliot's home. I couldn't believe how much the fireman ate. "But whatever you cooked for dinner, is there enough for the three of us?"

When he turned to the kitchen, I was left with the view of his ass and back. Shit, the muscles on this man had me both envious and wanting to grab them at the same time. When he pulled the dish out of the oven, I saw three pieces of chicken cordon bleu. I raised one brow, a question to the number of servings.

"I was optimistic you'd come around," he mused, that gorgeous smile of his never fading from his face.

"How'd you know this is one of my favorite dishes?" I asked while he turned to grab plates for us.

"I didn't." He pulled a pot off the stove and added some diced potatoes to our plates along with green beans. "It's still warm. I was heating it up and didn't want to use the microwave. I don't want to wake Scar."

Handing me my plate over the countertop island, he continued to stand, cutting a piece of chicken.

"Hey, Levi ..." I began.

Glancing up at me, he replied, "Yeah?"

Pulling at the base of my neck, I started, "I want to make it clear that this is for Red. We're here together for Scarlet and Scarlet alone. I'm not sure what you're trying to do with the flirting, but as much as you want this, you and me won't ever be anything more than two men who love the same woman."

He shook his head, but by the way his mouth flattened and his eyes widened, I didn't think he believed me. "Okay, whatever you say, Doc."

"Now, see—you're goading me. You're so cocky ..." My voice was louder than I meant, and Levi pointed at the open bedroom space. I began to whisper again. "I'm serious, Levi."

He brought his hands up, saying firmly, "Okay, Jordan. I get it. But we need to get along, hell, even become friends if we truly do this. You know where I stand, but I won't push."

"Never gonna happen." My voice elevated. "No winking or touching me just to touch me," I insisted, every syllable harder than the last.

His lips turned up at the ends. "Um, okay, whatever you say, Doc."

"Levi, I need you to promise you won't push this. This is only about Red."

He lifted his hands up, and said, "Scout's honor, Doc." He stopped for a second, turning around to his fridge and pulling out a couple of sodas. Twisting off the cap, he gave me one, and continued, "But I know I'm not your favorite person."

Shrugging, I conceded, "Yeah, well, I thought we were in competition for Red."

Taking a swig as I shoved potatoes in my mouth, he replied, "I never saw you as competition, Doc."

I now knew that after his endless flirting with me. "But I mean it when I say I'm not pushing you. But with that being said, if we're going to put Scar first, maybe we should try to be friends and hang out some. I never want her to be the referee between us."

I needed alcohol and not soda for this conversation. "Okay, so what do you propose?"

"It's simple. Let's just hang out, do bro things that guys do, and put Scar first in this. She loves us, and we both love her. Let's get to know each other—I promise just as friends—and if something comes up, let's talk about it before it becomes an issue."

"I can get down with that." Before we could exchange anymore ideas, Red was behind me, wrapping her arms around my waist. In seconds, Levi placed himself near her back with his hands around her body, touching me. I knew it wasn't intentional. As we shared Red, we'd have to touch. But why did his touch feel so good?

chapter 12

scarlet

They looked like sin and honey sitting across from each other in a hushed conversation. Without a doubt, I knew what they were discussing. Jordan wouldn't let it go that he was not into Levi. But I also knew that Levi wouldn't deny Jordan anything, as he wouldn't me. But I recognized Levi was going to push Jordan a bit, too. Or as I had witnessed, probably a fuck ton.

I assumed by the whispers that Levi conceded to keep things just about me, but Jordan didn't fool me. We had been around each other enough even before we made love just a couple of days ago for the first time. I recognized when he was turned on, and Levi did something to him. But only Jordan could cross the bridge when he was ready to accept it.

"Did I miss anything?" I asked with both men

surrounding me.

"Nope," Levi began. "Well, besides Jordan and me are going to become friends." I heard the smile in his answer even though he was behind me.

"Oh, is that right?" I asked.

Jordan twisted his face around me. "Does that make you happy, Red?" he asked, a smile on his face, this one I could see.

"You two make me happy." I grabbed a bite of whatever was on the plate in front of me, Jordan's, I think. "And sure as hell, this food makes me happy, too." In a split second, Levi was back in the kitchen and had a plate down, heaping a large helping on it.

He put the plate in front of me, and I scooted Jordan's over to him. "I guess I can give yours back now," I teased while continuing to eat, standing up on the other side of the island across from him.

"So, um, that was pretty, intense," I began, never one to shy away from a difficult conversation.

Levi looked up from where he'd been watching his food and smiled. "Yeah, it was. Doc?"

"It was, well … more than I … uh … it was … shit, I can't come up with the words, but hell, Red, seeing you pleased at the hands of another man was a turn-on." His cheeks reddened because my good doctor was normally so articulate. He wasn't able to convey his emotions in a way that made sense. It was because he was allowing himself to be vulnerable.

"So how is this going to work?" I shot straight because I saw a lot of little hiccups in Elliot, Arden, and Daimen's relationship early on, but it was different than what we were attempting to build. This would be harder for many reasons. Levi would push. Jordan and Levi were not sexually committed to one another, and my relationships with Levi and Jordan were all still new. Plus, up until twelve hours ago, Jordan hated Levi because he saw him as the competition.

"I thought this whole threesome thing might go smoother if Jordan and I became friends. I think we need to be on the same page to make you our number one focus."

I nodded my head in agreement. "And so is it all three of us or none of us?" I asked boldly, setting the ground rules early on.

Jordan looked like a deer in headlights when Levi answered, "Oh, lord, I hope not. I work a twenty-four-hour shift every three days. And Doc works odd hours. I say if we're both off, then let's be all together, but if I'm at the firehouse, you two can be together. Fuck, eat her out for me." His stare found Jordan, and he laughed. "Having her safe in your arms will give me comfort at night."

Jordan was quiet but nodded in agreement. "But you have to be honest, both of you, when it gets uncomfortable and especially if you feel pressured." I turned to Jordan because I meant this more for him.

He grabbed my hand and took a swig of his drink. "I appreciate it, Red. Levi and I'll work it out. We love you, and this is for you and you alone," he said, kissing me on the cheek.

"All I know is we better as fuck hurry and finish this food because it's the good doctor's turn to have his way with you," Levi said, shoveling food into his mouth and downing his drink. If I were to wager a guess, I'd say he was more excited to see Jordan inside me than being inside me himself. And because I knew Levi very well, the odds were completely in my favor.

The guys actually moved to the couch, while I grabbed my overnight bag and disappeared into the bathroom. They were watching some sort of sport. I never really bothered to learn much about sports. The athletes who played with some kind of ball were the ones busting their asses, yet my men thought they were actually playing the game, yelling at the television.

My men—it was hard to believe, and they were actually

getting along. But I was about to up the ante with a very hot little number I'd run out at lunch to pick up. Looking at the bright orange lacy nightie that played well off my hair, I'd fuck me, too, if I were into girls. I laughed at my thoughts. I brushed my teeth, the last thing I had to do before I presented myself to them.

Shutting the door behind me, I cleared my throat, and Levi turned to me, smacking Jordan as he, too, finally turned. "Fuck baseball." Oh, good to know now what they'd been watching. "I'm ready for our own balls to get some action."

They attacked me, rounding the couch to Levi's open loft. He stepped back, giving Jordan first dibs on me. "Fuck, Red, I may have to change your name to that new color. You look amazing in orange, but shit, it won't stay on long."

"No, it won't," Levi agreed. Moving behind me, Levi slipped a strap from my shoulder, exposing my nipple. "Doc, where do you want us? Want us like you were before?"

Jordan's mind had to process this. His inner thoughts were deafening by the way he fixated on me, and Levi holding me tightly. His eyes shifted to Levi and then me. "Um, no, lay her flat and then kneel on the bed at her hip."

I was curious. Levi wanted Jordan near his junk, but I didn't think Jordan would want the other man near him in that way.

"I can't be gentle, Red, but I'd never hurt you," Jordan began as Levi handed him a condom. He sheathed himself and looked at Levi. "You're in charge of keeping her wet."

Levi turned to me, and I only shrugged. "Um, Jordan?"

"We're in this for Red. We'll inadvertently touch, but I won't freak out over it." The smile on Levi's face had Jordan backpedaling a bit. "Lieutenant, I said inadvertently, okay?"

"Yeah, whatever you say, Doc," he replied. Leaning over my left hip, Levi twirled his tongue in and out and all around my clit.

"Okay, Red, quick, that's what I need tonight," he explained, and I was about to come undone at the thought of them in close proximity.

"Yeah, I'm okay with that, Doc," I pleaded, needing both release and relief at the same time.

His cock penetrated me, and even with his force, he was a completely different lover than Levi. Jordan was more methodical. Not that Levi lived by the seat of his pants, but he certainly did compared to Jordan. With Levi, there was an ease in the air, and with him, his number one concern was making sure it pushed the boundaries of what he'd done before. With Jordan, in his mantra, there was always room for improvement, analyzing how to make it great now and better the next time.

Every thrust drove harder and harder into me. Levi moved his tongue and his fingers, talented and artistic in his motions, and he made the spasms hit sooner. I wanted to pop my head up to watch them and their interactions. Were there any touches, looks, or expressions that could give me an indication of what was going on in Jordan's mind?

But the spasm raked through me so hard, and Jordan's voice permeated my pleasure, but just a little. "I'm not quite there yet, Red. Want another?" he crooned.

I couldn't answer, and it was Levi's voice that split the silence in the room. "Ah, Doc, you've made her speechless. I think she has another in her."

His tone was playful, and Jordan only chuckled, plunging in me harder and deeper to stimulate me again. "Oh, fuck, Jordan, I'm about to come again."

"See, Doc, look at her squirm." His fingers, I swear, were in me as was Jordan's cock. I wanted to look. I needed to look. I caught wind of Levi's face, the way he looked at me, gazing at Jordan. I wanted to stop him because this could get bad, but I couldn't think of anything but Jordan inside me. The idea of his fingers on Jordan's cock pushed me over, and I screamed, the pleasure almost too much to bear.

"Shit, Doc," Levi said.

"Yeah … thinking … you … had … something to do … with it … too." Jordan was breathless, and after one more thrust, I heard his release from his lips in a moan, remembering the first night we were together.

He was still inside me as he collapsed on my stomach, and my arms immediately encased him. "Fuck, Red, I love you so much."

"Back at you, stud." It was my reply when fingers intertwined with mine. I looked up to see the green eyes of Levi, staring at me, and mouthed, "I love you, too."

The smartass mouthed, "I know." Jordan pulled out of me, removing his condom and throwing it in the same trash can as before. With Jordan on the side of me that Levi was on earlier and Levi on the other side, they both bookended me. I had so many things rattling through my mind, and I was surprised when the one thing I chose to say, to mark this momentous event, was, "If we're going to do this, Levi, you're going to have to get a bigger bed."

Both men laughed as the security of them surrounding me lulled me to sleep.

chapter 13

levi

I watched smugly as they rushed around the loft at 6:30 a.m. trying to get ready for work. Jordan, who didn't bring a bag, said he was heading straight to the hospital. I offered him a clean toothbrush and a change of clothes, and he happily accepted. To save time and water, he and Scar showered together. I was too fucking tired to get my ass out of bed to be a part of them, but quite honestly, my shower barely held me, let alone the three of us.

I was taking in everything about these two and had a full view from my bed into the kitchen as Scar brought me coffee. I had no plans for the next two hours other than to fall back to sleep after they left.

My firehouse notification beep filled the room with Doc and Scar in the kitchen eating bowls of cereal. Shit, I knew what this meant. Picking up the phone, I listened to the other lieutenant on duty today.

"Arnold," he started. Almost everyone in the firehouse called me by my last name, as did Matt Shirley who, without a doubt, was ruining my plans for an early morning nap. "My kid got sick at daycare. My mom is an hour out, and the wife is in New York today for a business meeting, so I can't get to the firehouse first thing. I don't need you to cover all day, just for a couple of hours until my mom can get here." Shirley and I relied heavily on one another for this, but I didn't have a wife and kid like he did, so I barely used him.

"Yeah, give me an hour."

"Okay, Driscol will stay until you get there." I hated Kevin Driscol—he was a douche and not a great fireman either, but he happened to be the other lieutenant on our rotation. He always took over for me, and that was about the most I could deal with the man.

"Driscol is staying?" He never wanted to help his fellow brothers out.

"Um, Chief gave him no choice. He actually told Driscol to stay until I got my little girl settled, but you know Driscol."

I looked up briefly to see both sets of eyes on me, now smiling. They seemed pretty excited about my nap being interrupted. Back to Shirley, I began, "Yeah, I sure as fuck know Driscol. Let me brush my teeth and I'll just shower at the house." I ended the call with both of them laughing.

"Ah, does our tired little guy have to go in today and work?" Scar teased. She thought I had such a cake schedule except for the fact I ran into burning buildings. She didn't like that part one bit.

She crossed the room as I got out of bed stark naked. "No, seriously, LT, please be careful." I loved that she started calling me what Jordan did. It made this whole thing feel like we were really building something even though it wasn't all I wanted. The other person I wanted was staring at Scar and me.

"I'm out of here," he replied coldly. I wasn't sure if his

quick departure had anything to do with my naked body near his clothed body. My gaze followed as he walked toward the door.

"Wait," Scar crooned. She almost ran toward him, pulling him in tight. "I love you, please know that."

Ah, Jordan must be a bit insecure right now. I pulled on a pair of athletic shorts and started toward him. If we were going to build something, even if it was only for Scar, we'd have to be close or at least good friends.

I started toward them, and it was the first time since he walked in the door last night that I saw hesitation on his face. "Friends," I began, reminding him of what we promised one another. Scar released him, and I brought him in for a bro hug. I whispered in his ear, "Thank you. See you tonight, I hope." I looked down at his arms, and they were filled with goose bumps. I smiled, hoping I put them there.

"Yeah, sure, I guess. My house?" He stumbled over his own words, and I continued to smile.

"Sure. Scar, you okay with this?"

"Definitely. Seven. I will bring a bag and you should do the same, LT," she added, and then she and Jordan left. He looked over his shoulder, and I winked at him. He began to glare at me, but fuck, it only got me harder. His little pout was almost as cute as the pout Scar wore at times. Both did the same thing to me.

———

I arrived at the firehouse just in time for turnover. The asshole, Kevin Driscol, barely had to stay five minutes longer than he needed to. He'd never liked me and always had a chip on his shoulder. As he left, he'd always say the same phrase upon departure, "One day, brother, your luck will run out." Yeah, what a dick for another fireman to point out the fear we all carried deep down inside us.

I did what I told Shirley I'd do. I brushed my teeth and

changed. After turnover, I rushed to the shower in the hopes that I'd clean all the sex off me from last night before a call came in. Even thinking about last night and how my fingers were in Scar as he thrusted in and out of her made me hard. I sure as shit didn't need one of my guys walking in as I tried to dry off with a woody the size of a large cucumber. I stayed in the shower just long enough to control my erection and then got dressed. The second I put on my last shoe, the alarm went off.

I rushed outside, got into my apparatus in less than ten seconds, and hopped on the truck as Adams pulled out of the station. It was an abandoned warehouse building, which was good, but the apartment building next door had occupants.

Pulling up to the blaze, I saw the wind and flames could cause the building next door big problems if we didn't get this under control. Adams and Foster went in first. I referred to them as my two beers.

"Beer 1," that was Adams, "and Beer 2, you both are together. Call out and make sure no one is in there." It might be summer in Chicago, but fuck, the homeless people wanted off the streets regardless of the season.

"Torrin, Gallagher, on the hose." And these men, they were as loyal and hardworking as they came. Never questioned me even if I wasn't their ordinary lieutenant, but I worked with Torrin in Aurora before we both transferred to Chicago. He was one of the best firemen I knew.

When the flames began to dissipate with the hose, Adams and Foster had not come out of the building, and my calls went unanswered. On my call, Jackson, Wilford, and I entered the building. In the entranceway, I saw their bodies. They were so close to being out, and I watched Jackson grab Adams while I helped Wilford with Foster, a much bigger man.

The second we emerged from the building, the paramedics were on us, checking for vitals on both men. It was odd; as much as I had seen death and buried some of the finest, I was never okay with it. Never would be. I guess it was how I knew I was still human after all these years.

"Status?" I insisted of the medic working on Adams.

"A faint pulse." The next ambulance came barreling down the road, and they loaded Foster into it.

"Status?" I asked again, but this time it was the medic working on Foster. The CPR had not stopped while Torrin, Gallagher, Jackson, and Wilford were watching their fallen brother. The second the next set of medics arrived, Lanie Shore, the smallest human adult I'd ever seen in my life, standing no taller than four feet, seven inches, attempted one last time. A whopping cough escaped Foster's mouth, and we were finally able to breathe. All that went through my mind was how these weren't even my men. They were Shirley's, and I almost lost one of his men on my watch. That didn't bode well with me.

———

As I did with my own men from my standard shift, we followed the ambulance to the hospital. Beer 1, as I called him, was alert once the motherfucker started breathing. Shirley texted to tell me he was on his way, and just like that, my two-hour shift was over. It was an almost catastrophic day.

Rushing into the ER, I still had Beer 1 to check on. I opened the drapes just enough to see Adams was okay. He was sitting up in bed, his face still black from the smoke.

"Shit, man, don't do this to me," I began. "What the hell happened, Adams?" How were they so close yet didn't make it out of the building?

"Foster?" he questioned, and though I didn't know Adams well, he seemed groggy.

"Yeah, he's okay," I answered, his other brothers crowding in the room.

"Fuck, Lieutenant, we were hit from behind." I was expecting a whole myriad of reasons of why they hadn't gotten out but being attacked was not one of them.

"What?" My pulse slowed, and beads of sweat broke out under my uniform.

"Yeah, I saw someone with a shovel come up behind Foster. I tried to fight back, but another person came at me from behind, too."

My eyes had to look the way I felt. "You mean, two men did this?"

"Yeah, at least two men," Adams began, but the ER doctor walked in.

She was short with spikey blonde hair and turned to us. "Okay, guys, I'll take good care of this one. I just sent the other one up to CT since he was hit. This one is next."

Shirley rushed in the room as we were getting ready to leave. When I filled him in, he had patted me on the back, assuring me his guys were always in the best of care with me. "Want a ride back to the house?" he asked on our way to the rig, which was blocking a majority of the ER entrance.

I'd turned to him to catch him up on what Adams told me, when I ran smack dab into someone. "LT?" I looked up into Jordan's dark, chocolate eyes.

"Hey, Shirley, I'll catch you back at the house. I'll ride back with one of the medics. Let them know to wait for me." Shirley nodded, and I turned around to Jordan, who saw me in a way I didn't want him to. These men almost died on my watch, and I'd never take it lightly.

"Shit, Levi, you okay?" He pulled me into a triage room, closing the curtains behind him. "Shit," he started, pulling at my arms, inspecting them for burns, then taking out this annoying as fuck bright light and shining it in my eyes.

"Doc, I'm okay. I really am." I attempted to walk away from him, but when he grabbed me, I wasn't sure if it was his strength that stopped me or how adamant he seemed.

"Let me check you out. The fireman who came in? I examined the first one, your man?" Somehow, he had me sitting down on the exam table, and he was checking my reflexes.

"Yeah." I looked down, just now realizing how bad it could have been, and shit, on top of it, they were ambushed.

Was the fire set intentionally?

"Hey." He tipped my chin to look at him. "Friends, right, that's what we are? Now, seriously, tell me, are you okay?" His tone, the words, and the way his pitch fluctuated told me he was as worried for me as I was for Foster and Adams.

There was so much bullshit in this job, and I'd never been able to be honest about what I did. Serious relationships were not a part of me, though not for lack of me trying. I had one when I was younger but I wasn't ready to commit. As I got older, I'd wanted more. I'd wanted more for a long time. Nothing had worked and though Jordan and I weren't together, we were starting a relationship, too.

"No, I'm not okay, not one bit," I began, and in one fluid motion, he had me up and in his arms.

I wasn't one to cry, though I didn't think I would cry in the arms of a man who wasn't even mine. But he was comfort and home all rolled into one. The corner of my eyes leaked just a little. I could hold onto my balls for another day, so I let go. He squeezed me tighter, and with every little bit, I moved in closer to him, and my heart surrendered to this. Whatever this was. If it had been a weird as fuck friendship where I wanted more than he was willing to offer, I'd take whatever he could give and be thankful for it.

He backed away. "I now have someone who's important to me in danger, running into burning buildings. Just know, LT, I'm here for you." And I knew this time, in a creepy triage ER room, he meant it, and it signified a change in our friendship.

I somehow made it back to my loft, and after a crazy number of texts from Scar, my mind could not stop drifting back to the images of the men on the ground or how long it took to revive Foster. I'd thought I'd lost him, but more, what they said, a vicious attack was the only reason they could have been killed.

Picking up my phone, I called my chief, not able to get this whole picture out of my mind.

"Arnold, thought I'd hear from you. You okay?"

I took a deep breath. "Yeah, I'm good as long as Adams and Foster will be all right." He didn't say much, but my chief had been around so long, he, too, was processing what happened today and the what-ifs. "Look, I've been thinking. I know I'm on tomorrow, but in Aurora, I worked arson."

"Yeah, I knew this was coming. Take your men in case there's a call. I'll let special investigations know you'll be there. They'll be glad to have you."

When I decided to move to the city to be near my twin sister, there was no doubt I'd go back to the firehouse. Though special investigations wanted me to take a position with them, I needed to get back into the thick of it. I turned down lead arson investigator, but I had an inkling about the fire today. Something the investigator in me couldn't ignore.

"Thanks, Chief," I replied, hanging up the phone. The day had not gone as planned, and as much as I wanted a nap earlier, every time I closed my eyes, all I could see was what could have happened. I couldn't handle it, not then, and with the quietness in my house, it still was something I wouldn't think about. The what-ifs were too deafening.

chapter 14

scarlet

My hands would not stop shaking, nor would my mind stop playing out the horrible images of him blaming himself for his men who were injured on his watch. Levi hadn't picked up his phone when I called, but he finally texted me.

When you lost two of the most important people at an early age like I did, you wondered if life would really be cruel a second time. In my opinion, life was a bitch and hell-bent on causing me pain.

My Hot Fireman: *Sweetheart, I know you're worried, but I was never in danger. It was my men. It would have been easier if it were me. Anyway, I'm fine. I'll see you tonight at Doc's house. I love you.*

His words, It would be easier if it were me, hadn't done much to comfort my overactive imagination. I never liked the idea of falling in love with a man who ran into burning buildings to save strangers. It was selfish, but I couldn't lose him. And it was one reason I didn't want to choose between Jordan and Levi—of course, I hadn't bargained on falling in love with both of them equally either.

In my thoughts, I looked up into the same eyes as Levi's, his twin sister's. "Scar, you okay?"

I didn't want to worry her. She was anxious enough about her brother's safety. "Um, yeah."

"I know what happened to Levi today. Jordan called his brother." She sat on the edge of my desk. "I get it. Levi is my twin, and we have this connection. Understand, I go through the fear, too. So if you need to talk." She made herself at home, apparently without plans to go anywhere.

I rubbed at my face, a tear or two filling my eyes. "Isn't it selfish to hate a job that gives him so much joy? It scares the shit out of me," I confessed. Not like it was hard for Elliot to see the worry etched in the wrinkles on my face. This call and the accident of his men aged me ten years.

"Yeah, I get it. When he told me he was going to be a fireman, I begged him to find anything that would help me sleep better at night. But this life, it's part of him, engrained in his soul," Elliot explained, taking my hand in hers.

I'd seen it the first time we dated. It was his calling, and it suited him. I continued to discuss this job that gave me sleepless nights. "I know. It would be like taking a vital part of him away."

"Yeah, exactly. It's scary as fuck, but it's him. Just know this," she explained, empathizing with every word I shared.

She opened her mouth as though she had something to say. But she stopped just as words were about to form on her lips.

"Ell, by that smile on your face, you have questions but are afraid to ask."

"You caught me. Jordan came over last night to talk to us. I wasn't sure what he'd do when he left our home, but we gave him advice concerning a polyamorous relationship and his misconceptions of them. Especially the fear of giving up his own ideas of his sexual identity." We were in the middle of the executive offices talking like two girlfriends as it was merely makeup and nail polish that we had in common and not our desire to be wanted by two men at the same time. She took a deep breath. "It was a struggle for him because he thinks this will lead to him falling for Levi. Arden addressed the inner struggle that he went through when he admitted he loved Daimen."

I wished Jordan would have told us this, but he was so fucking proud. "Well, that explains a lot."

"So he came over to Levi's?" She arched one of her brows.

My smile was all the answer she needed, but I continued, "You know, your brother is pushing him. Not much but enough. Levi wants what Jordan may never be able to give him."

Nodding her head in agreement, Elliot countered, "Yeah, Levi likes to push the boundaries, so I see it. But I think Jordan may have feelings for my brother."

I rubbed my temples. This conversation taxed me because there was truth there. Loving someone who couldn't be his full self because of stereotypical shit made me hurt for Jordan. I stopped to take a sip of my coffee, then continued, "Yeah, I get it, but Jordan has to come to this conclusion on his own." My eyes met hers, and I knew she understood. It wasn't too long ago she, also, had to decide between her happiness and the opinions of others.

"If anyone gets it, I certainly do." She stood when Daimen exited his office and entered my domain. "Little Girl?" It was his pet name for Ell. She hated it at first, but now she loved it as she did Daimen. "Coming to see me?"

Standing to embrace him, Ell answered, "Will the ego be crushed if I said no? I was checking on Scar. Levi had a close call at work today." Daimen, who was like the big brother I never had, turned to me.

"Scar, why the hell are you still here? Go be with him. Even if it's to hold his hand, it's fine. I'll grab Karen from HR to man the phones." I didn't have to work. Wise investments and five percent stock in this company made me overly comfortable. But I was there for Arden and Daimen as they'd been for me so long ago. Plus, I was more than their secretary. Truth be told, I ran the everyday operations of the business, and they'd be lost without me. Although those were my words, they said it every time I was gone. So Daimen shooing me out of the offices meant he understood how much Levi needed me. Or maybe it was how much I needed to see my hot fireman.

I turned to Ell to get her opinion. "Go. He tries to act tough and in control, but he's never had someone there to put him back together after something like this happens. He may push you away, but it won't be for long." Grabbing for my purse, I was out the door before I had a chance to say goodbye. In the elevator, I shot Jordan a text.

Me: *I'm leaving work early to check on Levi. Text me when you get home, and we'll head over.*

The Good Doctor: *I'm not here much longer either. I had some patients to check on and got roped into triage. See you this evening at my house, and if I'm not there, you have my extra key.*

That was right. I totally forgot this, and I smiled at the turn of events, even in the past twenty-four hours. These two men were mine.

———

I slid open the door to Levi's loft without bothering to knock. He had me as a fixture in his life, and if that meant being a bit invasive, then hell, it was exactly what I would be.

The television blasted some sports channel. Go figure. The water was running in his bathroom. I knew I'd scare the shit out of this man in one way or another, so I opted for the good kind of surprise. Stripping out of my clothes, I quietly opened the door to his bathroom. After I pulled back the curtain, he screamed like a girl, but then a large smile covered his face. Especially when he saw I was naked as a jaybird.

"You can give me a heart attack every day if this is what it takes to get you naked in my shower." He pulled me in quickly. "Shit, Scar, I should have known you wouldn't leave me alone. And I'm not the only person happy to see you."

Not saying a word, I fell gently to my knees. The second my lips touched the tip of his cock, his hands were in my hair. "Ah, shit, Scar. I love your lips around me like this."

My eyes averted to his, watching me swallow him farther and farther. As I deep throated him, I was amazed at the size of his cock and how it fit so perfectly in me. I hadn't been with many men, but it was like both Jordan and him were made to push tightly inside my cunt and my mouth, too.

"When I tell you to pull out, Scar, pull out, okay?" I nodded, obeying him, but I tried to burn his flavor to my memory because I loved the taste of him in my mouth. "Now, Scar." I pulled out, and he came so hard. The water was off, and he had us wrapped in towels, drying me off. Pushing me farther and farther out of the bathroom, he kept walking until I fell backward and landed on the bed. "Fuck, now I get to taste you, my redhead seductress."

"Taste me, eat me, have your fill," I teased, and it was all the goading it took when he spread my knees wide and buried his face in me. I hadn't been with Levi by myself yet. Last night was out of this world hot but I required this one-on-one time with my strong fireman.

"Do you feel like we are cheating on Jordan?" His eyes were full of hunger but guilt at the same time.

"You're so sweet, LT, but no. We agreed to this." He leaned over to give me the sweetest kiss on the lips. "But if your tongue isn't in my cunt in the next ten seconds, I'll make sure it's not for a while."

"You and your demands." A crooked smile greeted me. "But I think I can comply." His face met my pussy, and with one circle of his tongue, he had me writhing. "Shit, beautiful, you're fucking perfect."

"As much as I love your tongue on my clit, your mighty large cock had better fill me up soon." I was bossy when I knew what I wanted and needed.

A chuckle greeted me when his face met mine. "I love your dirty little mouth, Scar. I fucking love it."

His cock was at my entrance when he pushed in slowly. Every little stroke of his cock against my sensitive walls had me on overdrive. I loved Levi's slow, methodical pace. His green eyes never left mine with every deep thrust within me.

"I love you, Scar," he said.

My orgasm hit me quickly, and when I came, I almost yelled, "I love you, too, LT!"

chapter 15

levi

I couldn't lie, sex with Scar was amazing. But afterward, holding her tight to me with her red hair draped over my naked chest, I was content with our bodies fused together like one. My hand rubbed her stomach as I snaked it up at times to pebble her perfect tits.

"Red, I'm so in love with you." My heart tightened in my chest because this girl was taking over my thoughts at every point in my life. She was the first face I wanted to see in the morning and the last when I turned out the lights at night. "You're really okay with this? With Jordan?"

She pulled away briefly to prop herself up with her elbows. Adjusting her head and cocking it to the side, she placed her other hand on my cheekbone. "Shit, Levi, no one has ever put me first. Do you get this? I mean, you going to Jordan with this plan was everything. And then, him accepting it. Shit, I know how much I love you two, but now I know you both love me just as much."

A tear fell down her face, and I brought her into my embrace. I had to hold her. Seeing her this way broke my heart. I needed to know more. "Scar, you know my parents pretty much disowned me, but I had a good childhood. I guess what I'm saying is I need to understand a bit more. I need to understand what it was like for you. I know you don't talk about it much, but shit, give me something. It will better help me to love you better."

She didn't move or speak. When I thought this conversation was over before it began, her shaky voice assaulted the room, her head still in the crook of my neck. "When I was thirteen, I had gone from the best foster home to the worst. My favorite foster mom got sick, and they couldn't keep me. My next foster parents were awful. But in it all, I made a friend at my new school. Our rations barely kept us fed, and I was always hungry. Jessica would invite me over to her house. The assholes who were charged with my care didn't give a shit. And when I was with Jessica and her family, it wasn't even the food I missed out on. No, the one fundamental need I desired was love. The family dinners, the time her mom would sit down with her to work on homework. She had a younger brother, and the dad would pull him up on his lap and read to him. To this day, I see the book that Jessica's dad used to read in a bookstore, and my heart aches for what I wanted so badly. Silly, right? The Giving Tree by Shel Silverstein still gives me anxiety. My favorite meal is still beef stroganoff because it's what Jessica's mom cooked almost every time I was with them."

She stopped, and her tears soaked the side of me. "It was all of those things I missed. I didn't care I was hungry all the time or that my clothes were rags. I never had a birthday party or presents to open. No cake or balloons. None of that mattered. All I wanted was to be held, read to, and told I was special in someone's life."

I wasn't able to say anything as I held her tight for the life she deserved and the life I was hell-bent on giving her.

chapter 16

jordan

I was at my house early, hopeful both Red and the LT would be waiting for me there. Watching Levi come apart today was more intimate than I could have dreamed of. The malicious intent, his men, and his vulnerability were all things I hadn't been ready to witness.

It was odd, but I was as excited to see him as I was Red. The second they had let themselves into my apartment, they were holding hands. Before last night, this had made me mad, jealous, seeing green, and many more emotions. But now, it only made me stupidly grin—watching them both so fucking happy.

It had been close to six by the time they got to my house, and through it, I was getting worried. If this had been yesterday, it would have made me question Red's commitment to me. But today, I'd become anxious about them both getting to me safely. The second they crossed the threshold to my place, their closeness told me they'd been together. And as much as I thought I'd be jealous, I wasn't. A switch had flipped, and I put them first over what I had wanted.

"I wasn't sure what you'd like for dinner," I started, kissing Red and bringing Levi in for a bro hug. He held me a little longer, and after today, I allowed it. It was a shit day for him.

"We stopped and got groceries. I'm cooking," Red began, marching straight to the small as shit kitchen that sat behind my living room. I watched her for a brief second. Hell, this woman was stunning. I loved the vibrant colors she wore. With her hips swaying from side to side, her ass looked perfect in the orange skirt with large black polka dots, sitting right above the knees. I hadn't missed the way her tits looked in a tight black tank top. Her three-inch heels made her long as fuck legs look sexy as hell. Not only was she knock-out gorgeous, but she was also caring and loving. It was obvious she wanted to take care of us by the way she sorted through my kitchen as if she belonged there. And hell, I wanted her in my condo. I wanted her as a fixture in my life.

Levi started to follow her when I pulled at his arm. Stopping immediately in front of me, he began, "You want a hello kiss, too, Doc, all you have to do is ask." This guy was never going to relent from his intentions. I had to be the one to stand strong.

"Nice one, LT," I returned and averted my eyes. I wanted to know, but I hadn't wanted to come across as the jealous third wheel. "Were you two together?"

With his face turned down, he didn't look at me. "You mad?" His hand was caressing my arm, and again, I allowed it.

"Um, not at all. We agreed to it, but tonight, it's on. Last night was a dream, knowing I can call her mine." This time when our eyes met, neither one of us looked away.

"It was the best," he agreed, his hand still on my arm.

"Jordan, you have to know, I—"

I cut him off because I did know. "Yeah, bro, I wish I could reciprocate. I do." Did I? Could I? Should I? I knew the answers to these questions but buried them deep inside my mind.

He pulled his arms away, shaking his head, leaving me to my thoughts. My mind was equally on him and Red today. Those emotions Levi stirred inside me were not who I was. I didn't find men attractive. Then why did I watch his ass as he walked away in disappointment?

***

I'd run upstairs to straighten up my room and put new sheets on the bed. Red and Levi cooked something for dinner that smelled amazing. The aroma permeated my entire apartment. When I turned the corner from the staircase, I saw Levi setting my table, and I couldn't help but rib him. "Ah, she has you trained already."

"You got that right," Red answered for Levi when coming out of the kitchen with a skillet full of ground beef and a plate of corn tortillas in her hands.

"What the hell smells so good, Red? Besides you, of course," I added, swinging her around after she had set down the food.

"It's my famous barbecue tacos," she called, heading into the kitchen and coming back with the rest of the condiments in her hands. "I'm fucking starving."

"Yeah, I heard about your extra-curricular activities," I teased, "but you better get some food in your system because if last night was any indication, tonight will be out of this world."

Handing both of us beers, Levi clinked his with mine. "Yeah, I'm down with that."

"Me, too," Red agreed, and although the barbecue tacos were amazing, I knew the sex would be intense and out of this world.

———————

Meals were never something that constituted anything but a time to refuel since I'd been in medical school. There was always too much to do—a test to study for or a book to read. Even now, there was that next call that could come in. However, as we laughed, joked, teased, and flirted over Red's incredible barbecue tacos at my little dining room table, the sexual tension was palpable.

Levi's accounts of his stuffy parents and sheltered upbringing had us cracking up so much. Of course, with Levi, even the things that pissed him off as a child—and there were many when it came to the Arnold patriarchs—were relayed in a humorous way. "They got so pissed off at me when they caught me with a girl in my bedroom. Yeah, when I brought Dane, my first boyfriend, home with me, my mother, of all people, told me she wanted a redo. The girl was not a big deal after all." In Levi's animated ways, he turned the hurt that his parents doled out into a funny story.

I didn't know why the mention of his first boyfriend caused an ache deep within me. Just his name, Dane, those four letters left me understanding that others had laid claim to his heart in the past. Why did it piss me off so much? And as with most things me, it must have been evident from my body language. Red squeezed my knee, and a smile on her face helped to ward off the green bitch of envy. I wouldn't let it ruin my good mood.

We clinked our beers together each time we opened a new one, and between the many beers and our crazy harmony of bonding, I understood right then, the sex would be crazy and adventurous, and with these two, I'd expect nothing less.

chapter 17

levi

"Hell, Scar," I began, "those tacos are almost as delicious as you." That earned me a laugh by both Jordan and my redhead seductress.

"I know, I'm awesome like that." She smirked. "You should see what else I can do with my hands."

"Is that supposed to be a challenge?" Jordan asked.

"I meant in the kitchen, boys. Get your head out of the gutter." Scar stood, grabbing the plates to clear the items from the table.

As she attempted to snatch my food from in front of me, I spun her around and pulled her onto my lap. "Nope, you aren't clearing the dishes, Scar. You cooked. Anyway, I think there's something more important we might need to take care of. You with me, Doc?"

He looked around at the dishes on the table. I should have known the type A personality of our doctor wouldn't let him concentrate with a mess. "Doc, work with me here."

He stood, moving to where Scar was sitting on my lap, her skirt offering easy access. "Um, yeah, I can let a dirty kitchen slide this time because I have many dirty thoughts of you on my mind, Red."

I loved his analogy. It was something a control freak would say to make him feel better about leaving a mess. And it was cute. Fuck, I wanted to dirty him as much as he wanted to dirty Scar. "Good one, Doc. Let's get our girl upstairs."

"Nope, I have plans for her right here." His hand worked up the loose skirt she'd put on after our afternoon fucking session. It wasn't as tight as the pencil skirts she wore to the office. "I can't wait the thirty seconds it'll take to get to my room." He pushed up the skirt, his fingers falling on her upper thighs. "No undies, Red?"

Well, hell, how did I not know that?

"Um, yeah, I thought it might be a nice surprise," she countered.

This time, Jordan winked at me. In the hazelnut hues of his chocolate eyes, I winked back at him. I didn't want to push him, but fuck, his body wouldn't stop giving me mixed signals.

He laced kisses up her thighs until he landed between the little curls she kept trimmed around her pussy. It was the same wild fire color of the hair on her head, and his mouth on them caused my own cock to grow hard underneath her sweet ass.

"Fuck, that's sexy. What do you think of the little tiny curls?" Jordan asked. I'd been with many women in my time — some who went natural, some with a landing strip, and some as bare as a baby's ass — but this was the first time little red curls caused me to want to explode without stimulation.

"Fucking perfect, like our redhead seductress." I loved how she was ours. But as much as I loved Scar, and that was never in question, the doctor was claiming my heart every second I was around him.

I only imagined her cunt was sopping wet because I could hear it from my vantage point. "Fuck, Doc, make her orgasm. We're both going to take her tonight at the same time."

My challenge didn't stop him from causing the longest orgasm to rock through her body. "Want a taste, man?" he asked, and if Scar had not been on my lap, I might have fallen over. Was he going to give me a sampling from him? His finger glistened with her juices, and he gave it to me to lick.

I didn't wait to see if we were on the same page before I placed my tongue on his finger, soaking up every last lick of her scent. Scar had to feel my already hardened cock come alive with his finger in my mouth. And when Scar moaned, "Shit, that's sexy," I knew I needed to be in her and soon. I opened my eyes that had remained closed during this time only to see Jordan mentally withdraw from me.

I didn't give him a chance to work it out when I pulled Scar over my shoulders—making my way to his bedroom somewhere upstairs. "Coming, Doc?" I asked.

"Yeah, right behind you." It was a small step, and I fucking hoped it was not going to be a step backward.

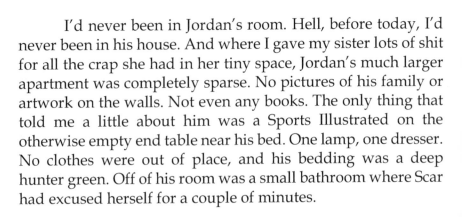

I'd never been in Jordan's room. Hell, before today, I'd never been in his house. And where I gave my sister lots of shit for all the crap she had in her tiny space, Jordan's much larger apartment was completely sparse. No pictures of his family or artwork on the walls. Not even any books. The only thing that told me a little about him was a Sports Illustrated on the otherwise empty end table near his bed. One lamp, one dresser. No clothes were out of place, and his bedding was a deep hunter green. Off of his room was a small bathroom where Scar had excused herself for a couple of minutes.

"Doc," I tried to probe, "you okay?"

He shook his head, turning from me. "Yeah, this, the three of us, is still a new normal I'm trying to get used to."

He didn't want me to see the worry or uncertainty written all over his face. "I get it. I understand." I wanted to comfort him and offer him some words of wisdom, but I remained quiet. The demons, his fear was only something he could work out. In my own thoughts, the creak of the door alerted me to Scar's presence. I turned to see her in a long black lace nightie with a slit up the side, reaching to her ass.

I didn't wait on Jordan. I would share with the good doctor, but I still would worship this girl in front of us like she was the only girl in this world for me. It sure as fuck was the truth.

"Not sure why the hell you get dressed because we'll just take it off, right, Jordan?"

I was pleasantly surprised when I turned and found him behind me.

"Yeah, Red. You're sexy in this but more so out of it." Jordan sank to his knees in front of our redhead seductress, placing his mouth near her pussy. Of course, the fabric would not hinder this man. They were stunning together, her red hair and ivory skin a complete contrast to Jordan's olive complexion and dark head of hair.

"Are you going to help, LT?" Jordan inquired, his hands snaking inside the material and up her succulent thighs.

"Um, I happen to love this view. Continue to please our girl, and I will take over in a second."

My words didn't startle him or stop him. When I imagined his fingers entering her, Scar's eyes reached mine, her words putting us both on notice. "Fuck, you two are unreal, hot, and all mine."

I closed the space between us, moving to Scar's back. I took her hands in mine as I wrapped my arms around her waist, kissing her back all the way down.

"You're fucking right about that, Scar. We're both

yours."

She had opened her mouth to say something when the full force of Jordan's hands sent her into a tailspin. The orgasm quaked through her body when I locked in on Jordan's gaze. He smiled at me, he didn't look away, and our eye lock continued through Scar's orgasm.

My grin quickly tugged at the edges of my lips. I knew when I was happy and I showed it. I only asked, "Want to move our girl to the bed?"

"Fuck, yeah," he replied when we both walked her over to it. I had turned briefly to grab my bag. I'd hoped we'd both experience Scar at the same time. With the lube and condoms in my hands, I threw them to Jordan.

A large smile plastered his face when he tossed the lube back my way. "It's only fair you claim her ass since I had her first."

Yeah, I wouldn't complain. "Great idea, Doc."

Scar was coming down from the mind-blowing orgasm Jordan had given her. "Scar, honey, you okay with this?"

"Yes. I. Need. More. Orgasms." Smirking at the good doctor, I laughed.

"Greedy little thing we have, Doc."

He was stroking his glorious cock when my mouth dried at the sight. "So fucking greedy," he countered, not registering I was in awe of him¬ — all of him.

"Okay, Doc, lie down. We're doing the double stuff method." He cocked his head to the side. "I've given you the best visual, didn't I?" We high-fived each other as Scar rolled her eyes at me. Leaning down, I kissed her cheeks. "Let the doc work himself deep in your wet pussy. Let him get moving, and I will inch in little by little. It will hurt at first, but you know what they say about double the dick?"

My words had her reddening, but I knew her greedy look. She was ripe and ready for the taking. "I have no idea."

"Once you have double the dick, you'll never want to go back."

My comments elicited a laugh from Jordan, and I chuckled back.

"Then hurry up. Let me impale myself on him while both of your cocks ruin me for all other men."

Her words stilled us both and it was then we realized she was ribbing us. "Ah, you bring up another man in our presence again, Scar, and we will both spank you."

"Okay, but I'm positive I would love your spankings, too!"

Jordan set out to do what she dared as she impaled herself on his cock. Watching her work herself up and down on him with ease caused my heart to swell. Sure, it was hot, but it wasn't all from the sexual nature of the act. It was the sensual love shared between these two.

"Fuck, LT, you get to break in her sweet ass. But I'm next."

"Anything for you, Doc. It'll be such a chore for me."

With her sweet rear in the air as she worked the doc's cock, I added two fingers in her. "Scar. This is going to feel good."

Her moan told me she was ready, but I wouldn't enter her until I stretched her a bit more. When I got two more fingers in, Scar's patience ran thin.

"You get that mighty fine dick of yours in my ass, or it will be off limits soon." The sweet redhead would never deny me, but she wanted me so much, I was done teasing her.

She slowed her pace, stilling on Jordan's dick. He moaned. Could he feel my own dick through Scar. "Fuck, LT." I think he answered my question. I pleased my doctor. I was in a world of bliss, and the more I inched into my redhead's ass, the better it was.

Scar started her rhythm with the good doctor as I started the in and out motion. The quicker I went, the more she sped up. And through it all, the moans of Jordan spurred me on. Fuck, when I thought last night was out of this world, this night topped it.

I came first, and the murmurs of Scar told me she was close, too, but when Jordan came, it was a good thing I'd already come because he would have done me in.

chapter 18

jordan

I didn't physically still at his words from earlier when we were both in her at the same time, but my mind couldn't get over what he had said. "Fuck, Doc, make her orgasm. We're both going to take her tonight at the same time." And just when I thought he surely couldn't mean double penetration, I realized I was wrong, terribly but wonderfully wrong. I was still getting used to all of this, yet his words undid me so much I let him suck my finger dry. And I wouldn't even get into what that did to other parts of my body.

Growing up with Andrew, he'd always known what he wanted. He'd come out and confirmed his sexuality after telling us he was dating the boy next door. It wasn't a big deal. With my sister, it was the same way. I'd suspected early on. She was proud of her sexuality, and my parents wrapped their arms around her in support. In my world, you loved one or the other, not both. And I loved women, and it would be that way until the day I took my last breath.

But why did Levi's challenges and innuendos affect me so much?

As we laid with Red in the middle of us, Levi's fingers were only mere centimeters from my shoulders when he had said, "You have a bigger bed than I do, so that'll be a little more comfortable." Yeah, never thought that much about the California King my brother left me. He made a good point.

I had a reply on the tip of my tongue when Red beckoned us. "Um, guys, we can talk HGTV and home décor another time. You both gave me so many fucking orgasms, this girl needs her sleep. Unless you want to fuck me again."

With Red on her stomach, I was able to look over her naked body and straight at the bare chest of Levi. It was strange. With Red's soft curves, it was the opposite of what drew me in with the fireman. His chiseled chest scattered with light hair caused my heart to pitter-patter for him. I don't pitter-patter for anyone. What the hell?

"Like what you see, Doc?"

Fuck, I did like what I saw, but how the hell could I answer it. I rolled over, covering up with the blankets. "Night, LT."

I thought it was over until a calloused hand hit my hip bone. "Night to you, too, Doc." Well, shit, even with his touch, I couldn't deny what was beginning between us.

I wasn't able to sleep, not one wink, so I unwrapped myself from Red's limbs and grabbed my boxers. I wasn't sure if it was the two beautiful people in my bed causing my mind to overthink or if all the dinner dishes beckoned me to clean them. I told my heart it was the second, but I was pretty sure it was actually Red and Levi cuddled up next to one another causing me to have a restless night's sleep.

Downstairs, I put all the leftovers up and poured a glass of milk. With my kitchen neat and tidy, I sat down to watch Jimmy Fallon when I saw feet descend the stairwell behind my television. I knew right away it was Levi and not Red.

"Can't sleep, Doc?" he questioned the second his face was in view.

"Dirty dishes," I replied, pointing at now the clean dining room table and a kitchen free of a cluttered sink.

"Ah, so you're that kind of guy? Doesn't surprise me." He plopped his ass down next to mine, both of us still just in boxers. He was going to see my semi hardness if he got any closer. Grabbing a pillow, I covered myself as if I was just merely uncomfortable with my almost nakedness next to his almost nakedness.

He didn't comment, not one time about my attempt to cover myself. He only continued, "So, that was pretty hot, the two of us claiming her at the same time."

At least chatting about Red, I could blame my boner on her. I only answered, "Yeah, it was pretty hot."

"Question for you?" Levi waited for me to nod my head before he continued, "Could you feel me through her? Could you feel the motions of my back and forth in her sweet cunt and wonder?"

I stood, breaking any sort of physical and emotional connection. "You know what? I'm not playing this game with you right now." I tried to almost run, but his parting words had me reeling.

"Okay, but you're the one who let me lick Scar's essence off your finger, and you're running for the hills at this little mention. Try to deny it, but you feel something for me."

I flipped him off, then headed upstairs. The second I walked in the room, Red was covered with a blanket but still shivering. The girl was always so cold. I crawled into bed to warm her up, and she woke to my touch. Moving her hand down my stomach, she silently told me she was ready for round two. I obliged, fucking the hell out of her while trying to remove the image of Levi licking my finger from my mind. When I turned around, and he smiled at the sight of me taking her hard and fast, I understood it would almost be impossible.

———

The next morning, after more sex than I might have had in my entire life, I laid in bed a little longer than I normally did, considering I was a morning person. Levi and Red had exhausted me. As I thought of them, they appeared and were dressed, poking at me. "Come on, we're going out for the day."

I wasn't sure how it would work. Red and Levi were affectionate people. Would we hold hands? Would we both kiss her? Did it matter in this day and age? Yeah, I already knew it was a stigma that was hard at first with Elliot, but they got over it eventually.

Before I knew it, we were out in the late morning air with Scar between us on our way to the Navy Pier. Red pulled at our hands at the same time, proudly holding them. We got many looks. Actually, we got a fuck ton of attention. It was anywhere from, "Ah that's disgusting" to "Way to love who you want to love, dude."

It was odd being as public as we were. It wasn't something I was ashamed of, not of what others thought. It was my own notions of sexuality causing me to fight what the three of us could truly be. In my scientific black and white brain, you loved a man, or you loved a woman. In my mind, there wasn't room for anything else.

———

When we got home from the Navy Pier, Levi pulled me aside as Red headed upstairs to return a couple of business calls for Arden and Daimen.

"Hey, Doc, want to run an errand with me?" he

whispered.

"Sure," I stated in the same tone. "Where to?"

"I'll tell you on the way. Let's leave a note for Scar. She'll be a while." I shrugged my shoulders and followed him blindly outside the condo. Once on the streets of Chicago, I waited for an explanation while he looked for directions on his phone.

"Okay, now I'm curious, LT. Where the hell are we going?"

He had a grin, one which lit his whole face. "We're going to the closest Barnes and Noble."

Now I was confused. "Um, a bookstore? Really? Care to share why?"

He put his arm around me, and I allowed it. "Let me tell you a story on the way there."

As he spoke, my heart broke with each word he uttered. Shit, my poor Red. I had no idea.

chapter 19

scarlet

Looking at the clock in Jordan's room, I was shocked to see I'd been on the phone for two fucking hours. I'd planned to run to the little grocery store down the street to pick up something I could cook fast. Jordan never had groceries in his house unless you counted beer, milk, and granola bars.

Making my way down the stairs, someone was cooking dinner. Once I got a view of the entire living room, I was accosted with at least a dozen balloons, a cake on the table, and a present wrapped in birthday paper.

"What is this?" I asked, but in my question, the memory of opening up to Levi hit me.

"Listen, Red," Jordan began, "we never want to diminish the pain you have from your childhood, but hell, we're in this for the long haul. We'll build new memories; ones when you think of what you didn't have as a child will lessen the pain with each passing day — because now you have us, and we'll move fucking heaven and earth for you."

My hand was at my trembling lips. I was shaking so much. This was one of the sweetest gestures I'd witnessed, but my brain had not allowed my mouth to form the words I needed to express my gratitude.

Levi approached me with Jordan behind him. "I hope you're not mad, Scar. I thought the good doctor deserved to know. We only want to love you. And fuck, we love you so much."

I hadn't realized it, but I wasn't crying, I was sobbing. Levi put his arm around me, bringing my emotional self to the couch. "I'm so sorry, Red. We didn't mean to upset you."

"No, it's not ..." I tried to get something out, anything. "I love it. I'm crying because no one has ever done this for me." Arden and Daimen had wrapped their arms around me and were my family. They had made thoughtful gestures for me in the past, but it was different coming from the men I viewed as my future.

"So you love it?" Levi's vulnerability was so cute.

"Yes, I love it so much. Someone better get me my present so I can open it." Jordan was off the couch so quick. In a split second, it was in my hands.

Pulling the wrapping paper off, I was face-to-face with a very familiar green colored book. I looked over at Jordan, then over at Levi. "You got me this?"

Levi cupped my face. "From now on when you see The Giving Tree, I want it to be your sign of hope. We will read to you, help you with your work, hold you, and give you everything you never had but needed so desperately as a child. We'll give you everything."

Opening the book, I saw an inscription on the white backing of the cover.

Scar,

We are always here for you. Don't look at this book and see what you never had but look at this as what you will always have with the two of us in your life.

Forever yours,

Levi

I moved my eyes to the other inscription.

Red,

You will always be my future, and with that, this book should remind you that I will always fill any voids others left in your life.

I love you.

Jordan

Each inscription was part of these men. Jordan's was sensible and down to earth and methodical like my good doctor. Levi's was passionate and daring like my hot fireman.

"Say something, anything, please?" Jordan asked.

"You're really mine, forever?" I almost hadn't wanted to hope for something this grand, this perfect.

Both stood, pulling me toward them. "Of course. We aren't going anywhere," Jordan answered.

Levi kissed the back of my neck. "And the night of surprises continues because we cooked dinner for you, just for you, Scar."

"What the hell smells so good?" I wondered out loud.

With a broad smile on his face, Levi replied, "It's beef stroganoff."

The night was perfect, and as I sat with my men, making new memories for the future, my hope for a real future, a real family overtook me, and at times, I almost had to pinch myself.

———

I found myself sneaking out of bed later that night. It took a lot of concentration not to wake my men, but I had to hold their gift. I'd settled on the couch, with a glass of milk, holding the book, looking at what both men had written for me.

"Red?" Jordan's voice pulled me out of the trance the book and their gift had done to me.

"Ah, you caught me." I put the book down and opened my arms, hoping Jordan would come and keep me warm. He kept his house so cold. Walking over to his closet, he grabbed a blanket, bringing it to me.

"You don't need to ask. I'll always hold you," he said, sitting on the couch and pulling me up against his warm body.

I didn't let much time pass between us when I said, "Listen, Jordan, I hope you're not upset I didn't share my foster care story with you."

Placing a kiss on my forehead, he squeezed me tight. "In a short amount of time, I've realized Levi is not my competition. We both complete you. Red, you have so much love—I never have to worry about being excluded."

This was a radical change for Jordan. I wanted to give him something, anything to show him how much I loved him. "When I was sixteen, my foster parents went on a binge. The cabinets were locked. But it wasn't only me in the house. There were an eight-year-old and then ten-year-old twin girls. I was the oldest, and they looked at me for help. More than anything, the hunger pains in the eight-year-old broke my heart. I tried to get the keys, and I couldn't. It wasn't the steel locks because fortunately those motherfucking foster parents were cheap. I found bolt cutters out in the garage and cut the lock housing the peanut butter, crackers, and boxed mac and cheese." I had to stop because this memory was one I tried to never relive.

"It happened to be two days later, after the bender, the shitheads came downstairs to the broken lock. I knew I'd get in trouble. And I'd admit to it being my fault. I could take anything as long as the three younger ones were fed. But when the foster dad found food missing and the lock removed, he took the same bolt cutters and cut all of our hair with them. We were all girls and already dressed in horribly ugly clothes. We went back to school with our hair cut as short as a boy. And as he'd cut the hair, he'd purposely pull on it, making the little ones scream."

Like with Levi, I hadn't known I was crying. Jordan picked me up and placed me on his lap. "I got you, Red, and I'm never letting go."

chapter 20

levi

One week with all of us waking up in each other's arms was all it took to solidify those two were my future. And it was safe to say not only was the attraction still there on my end with the good doctor, but I was falling in love with him. The solemn look he woke up with daily until my wink made him smile along with a million other things that were unique just to Jordan Peters was all it took. He had this way of staring into his coffee as if it was his daily calendar that put a smile on my face. Or the way he'd take in the sweet aroma of our girl when he hugged her tight. Every time our eyes met and he gave me that bro nod, my stomach tingled as though I was some teenage girl. But what really put a smile on my face was when I would catch him smiling at me when he didn't think I was looking. I saw the same want and lust in his eyes when he looked at Scar. He wasn't fooling anyone. But trying to convince him to take a chance on me was a whole other story. I wasn't sure how to make that a reality.

All these thoughts rattled through my mind as Driscol, the motherfucking jackass, was rattling on and on about all the indiscretions of one of my men who had been filling in for one of his men on his shift. It wasn't even his turnover. He didn't work last night. No, he came in specifically to bitch and moan about my man.

"We're different bosses, that's all. Jeffers did nothing wrong, and I run my team differently. It was the first time he worked with you, so just let him know how you run your team next time if he ever has to cover for your man again," I explained. Poor Jeffers—his indiscretion? Taking a shower after a pretty awful call to calm his nerves. Apparently, Driscol expected a sit-down with his men to discuss the call. It wasn't a bad idea. I did something similar after my men have a chance to decompress. No one told Jeffers, and he missed the meeting. You'd think by the way Driscol was moaning and complaining that Jeffers missed the fire itself.

Leaving the meeting that included my chief and Jeffers, I took my guy aside and told him not to worry about it. It took every little fiber of my being not to call Driscol an asshole to his face, but I was calm, as calm as I could be.

Thirty minutes after the turnover, I was doing paperwork in my office when a call came in. As was the procedure, we were all on the truck heading to our first fire of the morning. This time, it was another abandoned building, not far from where the men were attacked the last time. Ever since that call, I'd been more aware of my surroundings—never wanting a repeat. My men, Landon and Forge, manned the hose when I paired myself with Torres. Between us and Harrid and Shankly, we searched for anyone within the abandoned warehouse.

"Watch your back, men." It was all that needed to be said to register in their minds. It had only been a week since Foster and Adams had been knocked out. Luckily, no other reports of similar incidences had been filed throughout the other firehouses.

Entering the warehouse, I had an eerie sensation of déjà vu. The entrance was similar to the fire when Shirley's men were ambushed. "Be careful, boys," I instructed, and we parted ways.

Torres was in front of me, and I had my hand on his shoulder. We called out for victims trapped in the warehouse. No one called out, and after five minutes, the structure and the ceiling were about to collapse. On the radio, the chief ordered us out. "Harrid, Shankly—get your asses out of here." We didn't hear a response. "Harrid? Shankly? You copy?" There was still no answer.

"Arnold, get your ass out of there now," my chief ordered. Yet I had the same sick feeling as last week with Shirley's team.

"On my way, Chief." Of course, I continued through the radio to get a hold of my guys. At the entrance, like before, the bodies of Harrid and Shankly were sprawled out, but this time, their apparatuses were removed, and their bodies had the full effect of smoke inhalation. "Fuck!" My scream was heard by Torres, who was still near me. "Chief, Harrid and Shankly— same thing! Same fucking thing as Foster and Adams." At the door, we were met with the engine's team—all of us trying to grab Harrid's large frame where Torres was able to grab Shankly like a sack of potatoes. With both medics in house working on the men, I took off in one direction around the warehouse, searching for the person who was hell-bent on killing someone in my house.

———

Garner Blakely was in the ER when we arrived. Both Harrid and Shankly were breathing, but the amount of smoke they inhaled had our lead medic concerned. I'd only met

Garner a month ago when he was transferred from Springfield to be closer to his family, mainly his brother. Garner was a detective with a special unit within the Chicago Police Department. It shouldn't surprise me he was waiting for my statement. One time was just that, a one-time thing, but with the second occurrence on the same house—it was more than a coincidence.

"I see they sent the best." I knew very little about Garner Blakely besides being Arden's brother. But what I knew of the man, he didn't put up with bullshit or red tape. He was here to investigate. Being one of Springfield's best homicide detectives, transferring to this elite unit was a no-brainer for both him and the police department.

"Fuck, man. When I was told it was your house, I was hoping it wasn't your unit," he started, shaking my hand.

"Yeah, the first time was not my guys. I was there, though, filling in for another lieutenant in the house." To my knowledge, I wasn't aware of this happening in other houses throughout the city.

Garner took a deep breath. "Okay, I know you want to go check on your men. I'm going to be conducting interviews for a couple of days. I'll be in touch." He handed me his card. "You need anything, let me know—you got it?"

"Yeah, thanks, bro." Rounding the corner to Shankly's room, I passed none other than the good doctor.

"Levi." Though I was trying to avoid him, his words stopped me. The last thing I wanted was this to get back to Scar and my sister.

"Hey, Doc." I attempted to act as if this was an everyday thing for me, but honestly, when a fireman was in a hospital, it was never good.

"Shit, LT, it happened again. Didn't it? I heard some firefighters were brought in. I came down to check in and saw you with Arden's brother."

I turned from him. "Can you not tell your brother or Scar? She and my sister will go out of their fucking minds," I began.

"Come here." He didn't wait for me to answer and pulled me into the nearest room, which happened to be a supply closet. His hand was still in mine. "I won't tell Red for now. You can't keep this from her, though." His hand grabbed my head. "It's me. We're more than just Scar's boyfriends. You're important to me. It's the three of us, so talk. Don't go all macho on me. Tell me, are you okay?"

I looked down at where our hands were still intertwined and felt his other hand on the back of my head. "You know, we are in enough danger without someone purposely trying to hurt my men," I admitted.

His head rested on mine. "I know. I get it. I may not run into burning buildings, but with this job, I see the shit in people at times." The second my hand went to grab his neck, the moment was over, and he backed up, aware of our proximity. My eyes turned to his, and he looked like a deer in headlights. When I thought he was finally giving in to stereotypes, he clammed up. I didn't want him to kiss me. I needed a friend, someone to tell me it would be okay.

I rushed past him. "Don't worry, Doc, I won't let others know that for one second you let your barriers down, thinking of me for once and not your fucked-up preconceived notions. You can't give me comfort although I'm in desperate need of it." Slamming the door open, I made my way to my men's rooms to assess their condition. Jordan called after me, but I didn't turn around. I only flipped him off on my way down the hall.

chapter 21

jordan

I'd tried to give him comfort. Solace and friendship were all it had been at first. But I freaked when Levi returned it as affection. If I had continued, I was afraid my comforting actions would turn into more. Of course, he needed to be cared for, but even if the feelings of confusion weren't building up in me, Levi was more than just any friend. Even if I was fighting what part of me wanted, our relationship would be stronger than that of my other everyday friends. I mean, we shared the same person, after all. He was close enough to my dick each night to suck it.

And that vision had me excited as evidenced by the hard-on in my scrubs. Watching him storm away from me, I half-assed tried to get him to stop, but the part of me fighting this between us didn't want him to.

He'd flipped me off before but always in a fun banter

sort of way. No, this time he basically told me to fuck off. And yeah, I deserved it.

Having retreated to my office for a needed break, I reflected on the past week and how Levi had worked his way into my heart. "Fuck, Peters, what have you gotten yourself into?" I wondered out loud. Yeah, I was losing it, and if that wasn't bad enough, these were all things I understood couldn't be denied for much longer.

———

I'd gotten home that night to a slew of texts from both Levi and Red.

Red: *I need a day at my place. I haven't done laundry, and my house needs a good cleaning.*

Red was a millionaire and could afford to hire a service to clean, but she was very specific about her cleanliness and didn't like anyone doing it for her. I would have thought it was a blow-off since Levi's and my little disagreement this morning, but knowing Red, she needed to get shit done on her own. But then I got another text from her, and I understood a little bit more about her decision to stay at home.

Red: *BTW, could you stop being an asshole? I'd tell you how I really feel, but I don't have enough middle fingers.*

Okay, so she wasn't pissed. She was angry as fuck. And I got it. I thought of myself and not the fact that Levi's men had been attacked. I grabbed my phone to call Levi when a text came through. It still had the original name I'd programmed into it several days ago.

Asshole Fireman: *Since Scar is taking a break tonight at home, I am, too.*

My fingers hovered over the key pad for several minutes when I finally decided to own my mistake from earlier.

Me: *I'm sorry about this morning.*

I fell back on my couch, waiting for a reply. After a couple of minutes, I stopped staring at the phone and turned on the baseball game. It would only be me for the night. I called in a medium pizza and headed to my fridge to grab a beer. Sitting my ass back on the couch, I still had no reply from Levi.

After the second inning and my first beer, the doorbell rang and I popped up from my seat to answer it. On the other side wasn't my medium pizza, it was Levi standing with his hands in his pockets. For being the second week of September, it started to get chilly when the sun went down. His eyes were turned down at first. He looked up, and I could see a different man in front of me. The cocky jerk was gone.

"Levi, you okay?"

"Did you mean it—you wished you'd given me comfort this morning?"

I stilled in the moment. I wasn't sure what he wanted, but I answered honestly. It was what I owed him. "Yeah, LT, I wish I would have been the friend you deserved." He sidestepped me, entering my house. He sure was at home here, and part of that made me smile. The other part had me sweating bullets.

I turned around where he waited for me. In one fluid motion, his arms were around me. It took me a second to understand he wasn't putting the moves on. No, this time, he was vulnerable.

I pulled him tight to me, and that strong, hard muscle fit perfectly against mine. The more I tightened my hold, the more he tightened his.

"I'm not trying to cop a feel with you, Doc. I just need …" He trailed off. He didn't have to finish his sentence because I got it.

We fell into dry and witty banter between us, watching the Cubs game. Since hanging out with him, I started drinking a fuck ton more beer than I normally did. Reaching down for the last slice of pizza, I turned to him watching me.

"Sorry, did you want this?" I teased, taking a bite to claim it as mine. He grabbed his beer, laughing at me as I continued, "By the way, LT, you're a bad influence on me. I never drank this much beer before you."

He placed his hand on his stomach. "No, you're the one to blame. Thanks to you, I'm going to have to work out more."

I shouldn't think it, but his body was in tip-top shape. And then images of his abs came into play. To ward off all sensations this man caused me, I playfully smacked him. "Why do you need to work out? You get enough exercise pushing your luck with me." It was delivered in my dry tone, but even I cracked a smile.

Levi slapped his leg. "Shit, Doc, look at you! That was funny as hell. Who knew you had it in you?"

"Hey, how about a walk? I like them especially when they are taken by people who annoy the fuck out of me." Again, a smile accompanied my comeback.

"Hell, you're on a roll, Doc. We should do this more often." Yeah, the problem was I wanted to do a lot more than just tell witty jokes.

After the Cubs beat the Yankees, Levi stood. It was nearing eleven. "I better get home."

My eyes locked on him. "Don't you have clothes here? It's stupid to go home when you have a change of clothes and there is a spare room upstairs."

"Well, yeah, um, it's just that ..." His eyes darted down. Then as they found me again, I felt the heat in them as if a thousand suns were powering them. "Shit, Jordan. It wasn't supposed to be like this. My idea was to be there for Scar, which I always will be, but fuck, through this, us both loving the same girl, you've grabbed my heart, and I don't know how to get it back."

He took his wallet and his keys, heading to the door, and I didn't stop him even though everything in my body told me to.

chapter 22

scarlet

Over the past month, sex with these two had been everything. But in it, we were foraging a deeper relationship. There were kinks and little problems that came up. Mainly, it was Jordan pushing his feelings for Levi aside. Levi, of course, pressed Jordan a little more every day. Well, hell, he pushed him a lot. And in my time alone with Jordan, we talked about Levi and the apparent feelings they had for one another.

"I'm not into men. If I could will myself to love in that way, I would." I was not convinced, but with what I'd learned about Jordan Peters, I knew he couldn't be forced into this lifestyle.

I'd been skirting my family dinners with Arden, Daimen, Ell, and Andrew. This had been so new and out of Jordan's comfort zone, I didn't want to push. But Levi, in his typical way, brought it up, and Jordan didn't stand a chance against Levi Arnold. If anyone could push Jordan, it was my fireman. I was so afraid that one day he'd push too hard.

"It's just your brother and Levi's sister. It's going to be okay," I said, holding his hand for the short ride from my apartment to the penthouse where Arden, Daimen, and Ell lived. Levi got called in to support his findings on the arson cases but promised he'd meet us later.

The second the doors opened, enough noise met us to justify more than the four people who were supposed to be there. Jordan didn't want to walk off the elevator, but with my hand in his, I pulled him out.

He was not quite out of the elevator yet when a tall blonde came around the corner from the living space. "Jordan Peters. You get your ass out of there and give your sister a hug."

Kayla Peters ran toward her brother and embraced him, squeezing him tight. "Hey, little sis." This was a surprise. I'd been around her a lot since Elliot's accident. To my understanding, she was more of a little sister to Elliot than any of Elliot's real sisters. Releasing her brother, she hugged me like she'd known me her whole life.

"I knew she'd pick you over the fireman." She didn't attempt to whisper, yelling behind her, "No offense to you and your brother, Ell." Everyone erupted into laughter with Kayla looking around the room. "What have I missed?"

Andrew was behind us, giving his brother a bro hug when Jordan observed, "I see Kayla didn't get the memo."

"Even I got the memo." A large bulky man appeared behind Andrew, wrapping his large arms around my friend in an intimate way. I had a feeling something was going on with our new CFO, Brock Spaulding, and Andrew. Brock had been flirting with him for weeks. It looked as if the man had finally worn my friend down.

"Well, this is new." Jordan pointed at his brother and Brock.

"What the hell? I know nothing," Kayla almost shouted,

stomping her foot. "Would someone tell me what's going on with Scarlet and Jordan?" I couldn't have planned better. As if on cue, Levi stepped off the elevator with Garner Blakely.

"Well, shit, what's he doing here?" I was not sure if she'd meant Garner or Levi, but before anyone could say anything else, Levi came up to me and kissed me on the lips.

Garner, who I knew well, laughed, looking at Kayla as if he could eat her. Kayla would have certainly been his type if she were into men. "Um, you do realize he's Elliot's brother?" The way Garner spoke to Kayla surprised me. He'd always been sweet to most girls, but with Kayla, there was an odd tension. Hell, with this group, I was starting to have a hard time making all the connections between everyone. We really needed to be on some sort of daytime talk show.

"You know what, asshole, your parents are living proof that two wrongs don't make a right," Kayla almost spat on Garner.

Garner chuckled at her insult and patted Jordan on the shoulder. "Good luck with this one." Something was going on there, something I wanted to dig deeper into, but for now, I was content to let Jordan deal with his sister's little tantrum.

"Now, I really need to know what the hell is going on." Jordan's little sister was stomping her feet, again. Kayla had always been a wild card with no filter. What Kayla thought was always said without consideration for others' regard. Not that Levi could get his feelings hurt by Kayla. He took most of what the popular world said and ignored it. It could be one reason he could live a carefree lifestyle where he openly shared a girl with another man. Or how he'd been in committed triads before.

"Hush, brat," Jordan retorted, and for Jordan, his feelings could get hurt simply by telling him he wore too much gel in his hair. Although he acted aloof, he wasn't. And brat was more of a term of endearment as both brothers called their little sister that.

During this exchange, Jordan had been looking at the

newly painted light turquoise walls in the penthouse. "Elliot, you won the card game?" I had no idea what he meant, but it elicited laughter from Elliot, Arden, and Daimen. "I love the color," he added as his hands found their way around my waist while Levi placed another kiss on my lips. Yeah, Levi was a little bit of a shit stirrer. And he thrived on it.

"She loves us both," Jordan began, back to the matter at hand. Kayla's bright blue eyes bore daggers at Levi, which only made him laugh. "So we decided not to make her choose. Red has enough love for the two of us, and neither of us want to give her up."

Kayla's lips pursed as she cocked her head to the side. "But you two?" She pointed at both men. "You two aren't together."

"Um, no." With Jordan's adamant reply, I felt Levi stiffen. Stepping away from me, Levi gave me another kiss on the lips, then went to Kayla, leaning over to her ear.

Just loud enough we could both hear him, my little shit stirrer whispered, "Not yet, but don't worry, Kayla, your brother will admit what he wants. Eventually."

Kayla's eyes locked with her brother as I left him to undo Levi's words. If he wanted to deny it, I wasn't pushing it. Though I'd called bullshit on him several times. Sure, Levi was making this difficult, but he wasn't wrong.

Turning the corner to the living space that was now a makeshift dining room, the number of people shocked me. But our little group, the family I chose, was growing by the second. Andrew was there with Brock Spaulding. From the second Brock began as the new CFO for the company after Spencer Alders died, he'd had his eye on Andrew. At first, Andrew denied all his advances. Andrew hadn't wanted anything steady. He was into one-night hookups—something to do with an old boyfriend of his. Jordan and Andrew alike were very hush-hush about it. Even Elliot didn't know what it was about. So if Andrew brought him here for the night, it signified the seriousness of this new relationship between the two men.

Kayla, who had moved to Chicago before school started to be with her new girlfriend who was transferring to the city next month, was a bright spot in my day even though her third degree was a little taxing. But she was protective as fuck of both her brothers. I understood it ... a little. I'd be the same about the two men in the room who I called my brothers.

And before I knew it, I saw Arden's doppelgänger, his little brother by only three years. He'd transferred from Springfield to the police department in Chicago. Our little dinners were getting bigger by the second. It was okay because I'd never say no to more family. I could use it. I never understood what I missed until Arden and Daimen had welcomed me with open arms.

Jordan was in the main living space with his sister. I didn't miss the way Garner's eyes followed her everywhere. Every once in a while, he'd tease her, and she'd turn around to flip him off.

"Kayla, if you'd go out with me, I'd show you a real man. You'd never go out with a girl again." And I knew Garner well enough to know he was not diminishing her sexuality. He loved to mess with her.

She turned one time as we made our dinner plates. "Yeah, the only problem is a guy like you is the reason I fell in love with pussy to begin with."

Most of us, who'd been drinking wine or beer, spit out our drinks at her comment. I turned to Ell. "What the hell is up with those two?"

She shook her head. "A long fucking story. Believe me, this looks funny, but it gets old really quick. I wish they'd just fuck like rabbits and get it out of their system." Ell got closer to me and whispered, "Is my brother behaving himself around Jordan?"

She knew Levi as well as I did. Hence, she laughed at her own question.

"Not even a little," I replied, and she shrugged.

"Do you think Jordan cares for him?"

When I nodded my head, she smiled. "Yeah, I figured. Fuck, I can read it on him. Of course, I denied it, too, but it was different for me. I didn't have my own sexuality to face. It was two men, which I'd always known loved each other. But hell, I get it. He's letting the world dictate his happiness like I did."

She told me nothing new, but yeah, if anyone understood Jordan's plight, it was Levi's twin sister. But before I knew it, my men were on either side of me, making me their priority, and as shitty as my past had been, I would take it and never question it.

My apartment was in the same building as the one the guys and Ell owned, so we chose to stay at my place for the night. With just enough wine in our system, we were overly handsy on the elevator ride down to my place.

Jordan was in front of me, kissing me as if his life depended on it, and Levi was behind him. I knew there was video feed in the hallways and elevators, so the security was getting a front row seat to our foreplay. But that was all it was because the second we exploded into my apartment, both sets of hands were on me, almost tearing off my skirt and blouse.

"Fuck, Scar. I can't wait. We aren't getting to the bed right now." Levi lifted me up, placing me on my table like I was merely a feather.

"Glad I bought an extra sturdy table." I was pleased I opted against one with glass.

"Yeah, you and me both." I watched him turn to Jordan. "Doc, pull down your pants. Let her take you all in."

This was how I found myself scooting to the edge of the table to where I had access to his cock. The table was just the right height that not only did I have the ability to suck Jordan's thick erection, but Levi was also at the right height to have easy access to my pussy.

"Fuck, Scar, I think we need one of these tables at my

place along with the good doc's house. What do you think, Doc?"

I looked up from where I was taking all of Jordan's large cock. His eyes rolled back into his head, and I understood I was achieving what I set out to do.

Between the pleasure I was giving one of my men and the pleasure my other man was heaping on me like it was Thanksgiving dinner, I was just given an extra slice of pumpkin pie. I was letting myself go, ready for the whipped cream that was sure to top my metaphorical piece of pie.

With one last thrust from Levi, I came the same time Jordan let go and exploded in my mouth. It was harmony, and we all worked together, causing the melody to play in each of our hearts, making us get lost in one another at the same time.

With both men on either side of me, I floated to sleep, feeling their love and devotion at the same time. It was something I hadn't experienced in the past, not like this. Levi's calloused fingers I loved so much were on my ass, and Jordan's delicate surgeon hands were on my back.

All of a sudden, I threw my body up in a sitting position from a deep sleep as tears pooled in my eyes. It had been years since I'd had a nightmare like this. Ms. Maizie was in front of me in my dream, telling me my parents had died. A social worker was yanking me from the comforting arms of my surrogate grandma while I screamed. Then the sequence of the dream moved quickly to my twenty-second foster home. Yeah, I kept track of the thirty-one homes I'd been in, plus a few group homes along the way. Being taken from the one home, my twenty-second home when I was twelve, the only home I'd ever been loved was what woke me up.

Before I realized it, both the calloused hands of my fireman and the delicate hands of my doctor had me encased close to both of them. Yeah, it didn't take a Freud to figure out I'd dreamt this particular dream because I was afraid these two would be yanked from my life.

chapter 23

levi

The days when I was off and I surprised Scar were the ones I looked forward to the most. Well, of course, I included the "friendship outings" the good doctor and I went on, too. I didn't know what to call them, but they were a way we could get to know one another. Plus, I thought he liked them just as much, especially as he used the time to bitch and complain about something I had done — he had deemed inappropriate. And nine times out of ten, he was right, and I pushed a little too much. But at those times, I saw something — he wanted to reach for me as much as I wanted to reach for him — but he stopped right before he followed through. His rational and stupid thoughts got in the way of what could be the three of us. I'd texted him earlier, inviting him along to surprise Scar. I'd never heard back but hoped he'd show up to take Scar out for lunch.

The elevators opened to the offices of Torano, Blakely, and Arnold, LLC. The first thing I saw through the glass partitioned doors was the straight shot of Scar sitting at her desk. My mind focused solely on her, and I didn't see anyone else until a voice from my past pulled me from my thoughts. "Levi Arnold, is that you?"

I turned to the side, and he was older but still as handsome as ever. Standing right smack in front of me was Dane, Dane Gregory. His hair had a sprinkling of gray, and the sexy bastard was in glasses and a three-piece suit, but shit, this was the same man I'd fallen in love with all those years ago.

"Come here, you good-looking asshole," I exclaimed, opening my arms as we'd embraced. "Shit, it's been, what …?"

"Seven years," he answered, and my arms were still on his. It'd been a long time since I'd loved Dane Gregory, but seeing him brought back the memories of the first time I'd been with a man. Plus, he was part of my first committed triad.

"Are you still one of those smooth-talking lawyers, you handsome devil?" I wasn't flirting with Dane, but because of the relationship I'd had with him, it was easy to remember why I had loved him at one point.

Nodding his head, he said, "Yep, I'm still working for the devil as you called it all those years ago." He holds up his ring finger. "And Cami and I are still together. Two kids, Maggie and Bridget."

I shouldn't ask, but I did. When we ended it eight years ago, after being in a committed relationship with him and Cami, I wasn't ready for the forever like they were. I bowed out, and they understood. They were a good seven years older than me, and they wanted more, needed more. I'd run into them a year later, and even though it hurt to see them, they were happy in a committed triad with someone willing to say forever like they had deserved.

But I couldn't help myself. After all, this was Dane and Cami. If I was just a little older, done more things, and experienced life, it could have been very different. So I asked anyway. "And Jack?"

He looked away and shrugged. I shouldn't have asked. "Yeah, well, Jack—after Bridget, our youngest, was born, he said he wasn't cut out for family. He never wanted to commit to us. It was like he regretted it. When we'd talked about children, he was adamant he'd never be the biological dad, and he never bonded with our girls." Dane's face grew pale. I'd known him so well and for so long that this was his sign of hurt, and it was evident on his face. "So two years ago, he left us." He placed his hand on my chin and rubbed it. "Fuck, we miss you. Any chance …?" I didn't let him finish because there wasn't.

I mimicked the gesture with my hand on his cheek. "I'm in love. It's not what I expected or wanted, but I am."

He smiled, shaking his head. "Should have known." His touch on my shoulder was intimate but not over the line. We'd been lovers, so of course, a little bit of the spark was still there. "So tell me? He? She? Both?"

There was not a clear, easy answer, so I gave the standard, "It's complicated." Out of the corner of my eye, I saw Doc open the door from the stairs. Of course, the crazy heart healthy doctor climbed thirty floors, and the handsome jackass was probably not even winded. His eyes locked on mine with Dane's hand on my shoulder. Shaking his head in disgust, he turned back to the stairwell. "Ah, shit, Dane, one of those complicated situations just got the wrong idea," I started. "Can we get together? I'd love to see Cami and meet the girls."

I was rushing to the stairwell when Dane called out, "Yes, Arden Blakely's secretary has my phone number."

I shouted behind me, "Ah, good. That's my girl."

"You don't do easy, do you?" It was what he'd always said to me in the time we were together.

I waved as I opened the door to the stairwell. "You know me, have I ever?"

I saw Jordan, already three floors below me. "Doc, wait." I knew the bastard could hear me because it echoed like crazy in here. "Listen, you got the wrong idea. Just stop."

"Why? You don't owe me anything. Certainly not an explanation!" he yelled when he finally stopped. If this was not him being mad, then I didn't know what was. "And me being upset over you touching another person is not for me; it's Red I worry about. What if she were to see you?"

I did this weird thing with my lips when I internally questioned how I could respond to people in an adult way. I pursed them as I moved them to the left side, gently biting the inside of my cheek. Doing this, his eyes narrowed on me, and I wondered if he got it—that I was officially pissed off. He might in the tone I was about to unleash on him. I got close to him, very close for him to understand my words.

"Well, Doc, I actually hope that if Scar questions my commitment, she'd come to me, like I wish you'd done. All this shit would have been a lot less dramatic." Oh, he got that I was pissed. But in his eyes, I saw his own anger brewing. "Listen, what you witnessed was a man I used to love sharing five minutes of his life with me. Just because I loved him once doesn't mean I still do. And just like anyone I care for, I'll be there for them, as I'm now with you—trying to resolve this before it gets out of hand." When I reached for his hand, he didn't pull it away. "Doc?" My hand rested in his palm, and his touch, though different from Scar's, did the same thing to my body. "Are we cool?" I asked.

"Yeah, we're cool." He pulled his hand away, heading back upstairs. I stood dumbfounded. We were sharing a moment, and he bailed on me. "Coming, LT, so we can take our girl out for lunch?"

He was a fast son of a bitch, already an entire floor above me. "Yeah, yeah, I'm coming," I answered and wondered what in the world happened between us right then.

"Did I see you speaking to Dane Gregory earlier?" Her question was innocent while she took a bite of her chicken salad sandwich at a diner down the block from her building. Jordan's intense stare could not be ignored, but Scarlet had no idea the can of worms she had opened with her question.

"Yeah, I know Dane. We go way back."

Jordan choked a little, and I knew it was forced. "Oh, yeah, way back? Like how?"

Scarlet still had no idea of the tone in which Jordan was baiting me, but as I'd known earlier, this bothered him too much. Oh, he wanted to act as if this truly didn't upset him, but I would mess with him so hard.

"He was the first man I ever fucked." I didn't have to be so crude, but for some reason, using the word fuck got his attention. It was then, Scarlet understood the conversation affected him deeper than she'd seen at first. But I wasn't done. "He tried to turn me from pussy to dick, which I always thought was sort of funny because he loved pussy as much as I did. Then we were a package deal, and we started dating his now wife. They're older than me and were ready for that American dream. But me—not then. So they started a life, and I wished them the best."

Scarlet continued to eat her sandwich with a small smile pasted on her face. If we could have talked telepathically, she'd say, "I know you're messing with him, but pull back a little, though this is funny as hell." My response would be, "Yeah, he's so fucking cute when he's jealous. Just let me have a little more fun with him."

Jordan threw a french fry down on his plate. "Well, he sort of seemed like a douche."

I raised my one eyebrow, almost silently questioning him. "You mean, for all of the ten seconds you watched us what, talk? And then hug?"

I had rendered him speechless. It was yet one more indication he was fighting what was clearly there between us—all three of us.

chapter 24

jordan

He tried to walk with me, but I increased my pace, and somehow, the fucker kept up. It shouldn't surprise me. After all, he was in tip-top shape as a fireman. But I didn't want to talk to him after lunch. Sure, I put on a happy smile for Red, but I'd iced him out. I gave her a quick kiss on the cheek and left immediately, but the asshole had caught up to me.

I had my keys in my hands, hoping to slip into my condo before Levi could join me. No such luck. As I opened the door, he barged in with me.

"Jordan, what has climbed up your ass?" he asked.

"You." And as soon as I answered, I regretted it.

An incredulous smile plastered on his face told me what he was about to say. "Yeah, I only wish. And quite honestly, Doc, you do, too."

We were only in the entrance of my place when I turned and grabbed him by his jacket, pushing him up against the wall. "This shit stops now, Levi."

He didn't fight me, and I didn't expect him to. This was his MO, the way he was. Laid back in a way, pushing the boundaries. Oh, that was Levi, for sure.

"What stops now? The fact you're jealous of a previous boyfriend of mine. You watch my dick slide in and out of Scarlet's pussy. You get as close to me as you can, yet you never touch. You watch my ass as I leave the room and adjust your hard-on when I accidentally touch you when Scar is nowhere near us."

His hand moved down my arm, down my stomach, toward my crotch. "Who's this for right now, Doc? Because I'm the only one here, and your jolly roger seems like it wants to come out and play with my Peter Pan."

"You're ridiculous." I let him go, but his hand had not released my cock. "Unhand the family jewels, will you, asshole?" I instructed, but his hand remained on my dick.

"You think I'm ridiculous, Doc?"

"Yeah, I know you are." It was not very convincing, but fuck, I needed away from him before I did something I'd regret, so I wiggled out of his grip.

As I walked away, he continued, "Well, if you want to prove this to me, pull down your pants." I was close to the kitchen when his instructions stopped me in my path.

"You're out of your fucking mind, LT," I began, intending to put space between us. But he was behind me with his hands wrapped around my waist.

"Prove it, Doc." His whisper in my ear had my skin breaking out with goose bumps.

Twisting my head to his face, I squirmed out of his reach. "I don't have to prove shit to you."

He allowed my freedom from him for a moment, but then he grabbed my head with so much force, I couldn't stop him. He kissed me on the cheek. "Keep telling yourself that,

Doc. You're only punishing yourself by not being honest." He walked past me. "Want a beer?"

As though this was a normal occurrence, he was back in front of me with a brew. Making himself comfortable on my couch, he turned on a Cubs game. "Come on, Doc. Stop contemplating the world, take a load off, and watch the Cubbies with me."

As if the past five minutes of him cupping my dick or kissing me or causing my jolly roger to harden hadn't happened, I sat down a good arm's reach from him to watch the baseball game like it was any typical day.

I had a dozen Coronas in the fridge when Levi and I started watching the Cubs. "Doc, how pissed do you think Scar would be if we asked her to stop to get us beer?"

"We drank all that beer, LT, already?" I called back to the little kitchen sitting behind the large living space. My home certainly gave us more room than Levi's little condo.

"Yeah, but shit—we never texted her to let her know we're here for the night, did we?"

"Um, we're here for the night?" I questioned.

"Yeah, I have a change of clothes I left last time and a toothbrush." The bastard. Of course, he did. From behind, he handed me a glass of what I thought was Coke until I took one swig and tasted more rum than soda.

"Shit, LT, some warning you laced it with poison would have been nice," I retorted, and this man only laughed. Leaning forward, I grabbed my phone. I hadn't checked it since my mind had been on getting my raging hard-on under control. Six texts from Red and three missed phone calls. Levi played his message for both of us to hear.

"You both better be dead. I'm worried about you assholes."

"You should call her back, Doc. She's worried about us."

His tone was playful.

His little command made me chuckle. "Yeah, nice try. You can call her back."

He placed his phone down. "Oh, I'm not touching it with a ten-foot pole, you asshole." A small smirk escaped his mouth, and he grabbed my cell from the coffee table, tossing it at me.

"There's no way you can make me. I dare you." I didn't see it coming, but Levi's hands grabbed my sides and started tickling me.

"Yeah, Doc. Say Uncle, and I'll relent." I was laughing so hard because I was ticklish as fuck.

But as strong as he was, I could match him. My hand found his side, and I started tickling him. Through laughter, I squeaked out, "You're just as ticklish."

Levi's hands forced down my shoulders, and he was over me, trying to pin my body and continue the torture at the same time.

"I think I have the advantage, Doc." And I was beat.

"Fine, I'll call our girl back. Just stop punishing me."

His body became almost flush with mine. "Oh, Doc, I haven't even begun."

Speechless, that was what I was with his face so close to mine—he could smell the rum on my breath.

"Doc, your jolly roger has come out to play again." But it was not a tease, it was a whisper and a fact. "Doc, I know you want this. Why can't you admit it?"

I remained speechless, his lips so close to mine, his one hand on my thigh, one of the ways he still had me locked in. But I didn't move. I wasn't sure I wanted to.

"Doc?" He licked his own lips, and because he was so close, he licked mine, too. "You want this. I want this. Scar wants this. Why fight it?"

The ability to make words was gone. "If you don't stop me, I'm going to kiss you, you stubborn asshole." And I didn't. I couldn't. His lips touched mine just as I heard the front door open.

Red couldn't be through the door when she yelled, "You assholes better fucking be dead, or I'll kill you myself for worrying me."

Without thinking, I flipped Levi off me, and he landed on his face on the floor between the couch and the coffee table. "Fucker." I heard him say.

Red rounded the corner from the entryway to the living room as Levi peeled himself from the floor. "What the fuck? What were you doing on the floor?" she asked Levi.

He smiled at her, straightening his jeans, then he turned his head to look at me. "This conversation is not over, you fucker."

I stood to try to smooth things over with Red. On my way to her, I whispered, "Yeah, you asswipe, it's over and won't ever be fucking discussed again."

chapter 25

scarlet

It was as clear as the stars in the sky, I had walked in on something. I didn't question Jordan because his feathers would become more ruffled and his attitude would be just as bad as a peacock. The one memory of the only foster family who cared for me, the twenty-second family, was them taking me to the zoo. It was a wonderful day I remembered vividly, but that day, I'd realized that what I thought was one of the most beautiful creatures on this planet, the peacock, could be the ugliest as it charged me. My foster dad picked me up and placed me in his arms just in time, but hell, the pretty bird could change from that of beauty to ugliness in a matter of seconds.

I could see Jordan's feathers getting riled up when he and Levi had words I wasn't privy to. With groceries in my hands and feeling my own anger from being ignored all day, I let it slide. I acted as if all was right with the world when I said, "Hey, LT, I got a phone call from Dane Gregory after lunch. He wants to have us over for dinner the Saturday after next. Apparently, you all discussed this."

If Jordan was not already up in arms over something, this agitated him more. But I ignored him. I was still rightfully pissed at all the missed phone calls from the afternoon. "You don't work on that Saturday, Doc, I checked. I made plans for the three of us for dinner. I guess his wife, Cami, is excited to see you." I could sense the run-in with Dane and Levi affected Jordan more than he cared to admit, but it didn't bother me. Maybe purely due to the fact I was not fighting my feelings like Jordan was clearly doing with Levi.

"Um, you two go by yourselves. This is a couple sort of thing. I won't be the third wheel." Levi opened his mouth to speak, but I waved him off.

I was just as surprised as Levi when the words I uttered were in tune with my own attitude. "You wouldn't be a third wheel if you'd get out of your own fucking mind." Both men stopped, blindsided by my tone and words. "And I made plans, and because I'm fucking pissed off at both of you for ignoring me, and since I know you aren't working, Jordan Peters, we're all fucking going out and socializing with this couple. And you don't have to like it, but you will have to fucking do it if you ever want to get lucky with me again." I exited the living room without another word, my hands still full of groceries.

Part of me wanted to drop the food and leave them to dissect whatever I walked in on. And sure, it needed to be done. But I quickly searched for a large pot and began chopping up veggies. I was left to my own thoughts for about five minutes until the hands that wrapped around me were all I needed to relax. I didn't have to see who it was because each man's touch was so different. After a month with both of them together, I knew it was Levi behind me.

"Sorry, Scar. I wasn't trying to ignore you. It's just ..."

I turned my head to him, dropping the knife on the

cutting board. "I walked in on something."

"Yeah." He didn't elaborate, and I didn't ask what it was. He would tell me when he was ready. "However, gotta tell you, you're sexy as sin when you are bossy. It took every ounce of restraint not to attack you then."

Twisting my body to his, I cupped his cheek. "Oh, yeah? Tell me more." I moved my lips to his as we crashed against each other. Our kiss was hurried but gentle at the same time. When our tongues met, I let him take charge. Running his hands up the front part of my body, he worked his hand into my shirt, breaching the bra to twist my nipples. I yelped into his mouth and his other hand found my ass, squeezing it tight. I pulled back gently when a smile appeared on his face.

"Am I forgiven?" he asked.

"Yeah, the foreplay was apology enough." He kissed my cheek one last time, and I turned around to continue with dinner.

"How about Jordan? What will he have to do to get out of the doghouse with you?"

With the onions, celery, and mushrooms chopped, I began dicing the chicken, placing it straight into the boiling broth. "Well, I love vintage purses, if you couldn't tell," I teased. It was the truth, though.

He chuckled. "Yeah, I don't think I've ever seen you with the same purse more than once," Levi added, placing a kiss on my forehead. It was sweet but intimate in nature, and my heart swelled at the love I had for this man. "You want me to tell the good doctor, he should buy you a purse to get out of the doghouse?"

"Yeah, I don't marry a purse. I only date them." This had Levi erupting in laughter. "No, seriously, if you want to help the good doctor out, just tell him to stop being so fucking broody and moody." I gave him a peck on the cheek. "Give me a sec, and we'll go find him. Let me finish up with the raw chicken first, and I'll wash my hands."

"Yeah, I can imagine the germaphobe is not down with

catching salmonella today." With his little joke, we were back on the same page. Tossing the chicken in the boiling broth, I turned to wash my hands. With Levi in front of me, my clean hands found their way to my hips, standing firm, and I was still attempting to figure out what transpired between my two men. "So you gonna tell me what happened?" I tried to stand casual, grabbing the spices I needed to make a chicken noodle soup that would taste like it had cooked all day long. With the fresh basil and parsley in my hands, I grabbed a new cutting board, waiting for his explanation. From the corner of my eye, he looked behind him, and Jordan was nowhere to be seen. Hearing the footsteps above us, Jordan had sulked to his bedroom upstairs.

Levi took a deep breath, standing in front of the refrigerator to grab a bottle of wine. We had made ourselves so comfortable in Jordan's space. It came naturally, but I wished Jordan allowed himself to be just as comfortable with Levi. Pouring red wine in both our glasses, he began, "He'd just given me permission to kiss him, and a second later, you walked in. He clammed up, disappearing to his room after telling me it wouldn't happen again."

My back had been turned to him. I twisted around so quickly with an apology on the tip of my tongue. "You know what?" He interrupted me before I got the sorry to form on my lips. "It's not your fault, Scar, not at all." He kissed me on the head, bringing me close to him.

"What the fuck happened? He was like a little kid throwing a fit at lunch, then on top of it, he continued with the dinner plans I'd made." I stopped to give him a chance to answer, and when he didn't, I continued, "If anyone should be jealous, it's me. I mean, we're going to have dinner with a woman you slept with."

He grabbed a large stalk of celery and turned around with a jar of peanut butter in his hand. Dipping the celery straight in the jar, I laughed. "You'd really get the good doctor going if he saw you double dip," I teased.

"Yeah, it's not like he hasn't already thrown a big enough fit." Levi paused, only to finish up with, "That fucker is so damn stubborn. But to answer what you said before, you're not jealous of Cami because you're mine. He's only jealous of Dane because Jordan's fighting his attraction for me. It's easier to treat Dane as the bad guy because he has had me and Jordan hasn't."

Still biting from the celery and dipping it into the peanut butter, he was only smiling. It was like he wanted Jordan to catch him doing something that would inevitably cause him more grief. Grabbing the dipped celery from him, I took a bite of it, nodding my head in agreement.

"Yeah, it makes sense. But I'm sorry you weren't able to experience the kiss of Jordan Peters. He's a good kisser, by the way," I teased.

"Yeah, rub it in." He leaned over, placing a soft kiss on my cheek. "I'm actually going to give the good doctor some space. We're out of beer. I'll walk to the store and replace his twelve pack. Need anything, Scar?" he asked behind him, grabbing his keys and wallet from the dining room table.

"Bread. Grab some bread to go with our soup," I added, watching him close the door behind him. With the soup on simmer, I went in search of my other guy who, without a shadow of a doubt, was letting his mind get the best of him. Rounding the corner of the stairs to the master bedroom, I was right. At the end of the bed, Jordan sat with his head in his hands, and he'd never looked so scared in his life.

He didn't react to my heels clinking on his hardwood floors. With my touch, he leaned into me, my arms circling his strong shoulders.

"Want to talk about it?" I whispered in his ear.

"I'm sure Levi told you." His face still was turned down. I couldn't read it, not one bit, especially since I couldn't see it. "But no, I really don't want to talk about it, Red." His fingers were in my hair, and in a second, he turned to me, his lips devouring mine.

I pulled back. "Jordan, it's okay, you know. No one will judge you for your unresolved feelings for Levi. He's easy to fall for. Believe me, I know."

I saw a little sparkle behind his eyes at the mention of Levi's name. "I love you, Red. Fuck, you know me better than myself," he admitted.

His hand roamed to my zipper, undoing the button. He pulled me to him, having better access to me. Once out of my slacks, he tossed me onto his bed, crawling up to hover over me. "This isn't about him, right now, Red. It's about you and me, and I need to sink myself so deep inside you. I fucking love you so much."

I stopped him. "It will always be about him. The three of us—we're embedded in each other's souls. Make love to me now, claim me because you never have to worry. I love you both so much, and I have as much room in my heart for him as I do you."

A smile on his face lit his beauty like a fucking Christmas tree. "Shit, Red. Were you reading my mind?"

I kissed him gently, sweetly. "No, I just know you, Doc. Now fuck me and make it hard."

He entered me with such force, my body hummed with the friction of him moving in and out. With my mind lost on him, I heard something, someone behind him. "Fuck, I could come home to this every day and be a happy man."

I was about to invite him into the mix when Jordan's deep and almost brooding voice answered him. "What are you waiting on? A formal invitation?"

It was all Levi needed—to come rushing at us. After all, he was a part of the both of us, even if Jordan wasn't ready to admit it.

From that night on, the sexual tension between the two men had been emotionally intense. It was odd, they were closer after the little fight they had. Sure, they hadn't talked about it because they were men and weren't as wordy as I was. But it seemed to work for those two.

When I got home from work the next day, they were at the door. I thought they were ready to pounce on me. I was wrong. With smiles plastered on their face, I saw theater tickets in their hands. I wasn't sure how the sneaky bastards knew I loved the musical Chicago.

"Red, you're too hot to keep home night after night," Jordan started.

"Yeah, we've gotta flaunt you so every motherfucker knows you're ours." Levi leaned in to kiss me.

"Want me to wear a sign?" I bantered back.

Jordan, the more jealous of the two answered right away. "Yeah, actually I think we would like that, very much."

After dinner and the theater, snuggled in between both men after they exhausted me, my heart was full. It was like they read my mind, and went on a recon mission to find out how they could treasure and spoil me. Yeah, it was what they did and I loved every minute of it.

chapter 26

levi

My text alerts were going off shortly after Scar left for work. The Good Doctor was at the hospital last night and though it was a hard job, I kept our girl company. I was still in Scar's bed, her aroma filling the air from her morning shower. I had one eye open but grabbed the cell when I saw Jordan's name pop up.

The Good Doctor: *Hey lazy. I'm sure you're still in bed. Lucky bastard. Anyway, I have tickets for the Cubs' game today. Want to join me?*

The good doctor had me at both Cubs and spending the day with him.

Me: *Fuck, yeah. What time?*

The Good Doctor: *It's at two, this afternoon. Let's meet there. I'll text you. Gotta grab some shut-eye right quick. See you* *then.*

Because I loved messing with Jordan, I was quick with my reply.

Me: *Then it's a date.*

He had sent me an emoji back — the middle finger. Yeah, I affected the man more and more each day.

He was in front of Wrigley Field at one thirty like he had texted me an hour ago. In a simple grey t-shirt and jeans, I almost hadn't recognized him with a ballcap on. My good doctor was laidback, so unlike his usual persona.

"Ready Doc?" I asked approaching him from the side.

He turned quickly, taking me in from top to bottom. I had on one of my favorite Cub's t-shirts and a pair of shorts. Was he checking me out like I had with him, without him knowing?

"Hey LT." He opened his arms and brought me in for our signature bro hug. I held on tighter and he had too. "Let's go." I followed him in comfortable silence. It seemed so normal to be there with him.

When we bought our beer and hotdogs, we sat in fucking excellent seats, two rows up from first base. Every once in a while, we'd touch inadvertently but it was never awkward. Jordan leaned in one time when he asked, "You having fun, LT?"

I grabbed his arm affectionately. "Yeah, I'm having the best fucking time."

He leaned in even further and continued, "Next time, let's bring Red. I miss her. I know she hates baseball but I'm sure we can make it worth her while."

He hitched an eyebrow higher than usual. Oh, we were on the same page. "Yeah, I miss our redhead seductress." I stopped, squeezing his knee. "But this is nice, hanging out with you too, Doc."

His breath on my ear sent shivers down my spine. "Yeah, LT, I miss Red too, she completes us, but this is...."

I thought this day had been so intimate. Sharing something we both loved, in the proximity and touching one another like we had—it had been everything to me.

He trailed off and when I thought he wouldn't finish his sentence, he said, "It's been so comfortable." He leaned in further. "You are so comfortable and I love being with you."

I wasn't going to ruin the progress we'd made today. I merely said, "Thank-you."

————————

My life had been full of two things. First, I had Scar and Jordan. They kept me busy and easily entertained. Second, the fucking arson case had become a mystery that evaded me at every turn. I had a twenty-four-hour shift ahead of me. On nights I wasn't home, Scar was in the strong arms of our doctor. Knowing she was safe made it possible to concentrate on the job at hand.

He might never admit how he feels about me, but I'd always claim him as mine. Just as if someone were to mess with Scar, I'd become overbearing if someone did the same to my doc.

I was looking over the reports in front of me concerning both fires when a siren filled the station, and I listened carefully, making my way to the open bay where our trucks were housed.

"Fire in an abandoned warehouse. CPD will meet you there." It was my chief, heading to his own vehicle.

Garner Blakely announced all warehouse fires would be linked through 911, and his unit would be called in. My gut didn't like it, not one bit. And after being a fireman for twelve years, I listened to it.

This deep unease felt like it did eleven years ago when I got called to a house fire. Once we arrived, we were made aware that a twentysomething young woman was trapped in her home. The structure was crumbling before us, and there was nothing we could do. Our chief ordered us to stand down. The father and his teenage son went barreling toward the house to save her. We tried to tackle them. I got the son, but the father was too quick. Both this young man's father and sister died in the fire. The brother swore it was my fault, claiming he could have saved them both. I'd never forgotten the name Cassie Deckland or the fact that she'd died in the fire.

The brother tried to press charges against me, but I'd been cleared of all wrongdoing. It took me years to get over the guilt and the what-ifs and everything I'd been trained for as a fireman. But right at the moment, I was back to that time and place.

"LT, you okay?" Forge asked, my second in charge.

"Gut?" I said only loud enough for him to hear. I could only be that transparent with my right-hand man.

"Copy that, let's proceed with caution," he replied, and we both exchanged that silent acknowledgment knowing as a fireman, we'd never ignore our instincts.

Pulling up to the fire, I saw Garner's unit beat us there. "Be careful, Levi," he warned.

Pairing my men together as the other truck pulled up next to us, we entered the building, calling out for anyone who could be trapped.

Torres was near me, his hand on my shoulder until I no longer felt him. I turned back, and through the smoke, I barely saw it coming until a thick rod of some sort hit my helmet. Even with all my gear, it fucking hurt all over. The beam reeled through my body, and I fell, my eyes on Torres who was next to me on the ground.

***

When I came to, I heard a frenzy of sobs and beeping noises. My eyes narrowed in on the flaming red hair in front of me, and behind Scar, my gaze found passage to long blonde curls similar to my own hair color.

"Shit, Levi. I've been fucking going crazy." Yep, that was the sassy mouth of my twin sister, and boy, was I happy to hear the f word fall from her lips. I narrowed in on the watery eyes of my redhead.

"Scar, baby, I'm okay," I insisted, but was I? First, I was going through the warehouse with Torres, and the next ... ah, shit. "Torres?"

Another hand squeezed the other side of me, and I turned to find Jordan's eyes next to me, holding my hand. "He's okay. It was touch and go for a while, but he made it."

I smiled at my doc even though the simple act of smiling hurt. "Ah, Doc, if this is what it took for you to hold my hand, then I'd have done this a long time ago."

"Levi Aaron Arnold. Don't you fucking joke about that ever again." My sister's voice was so loud, it hurt my already sensitive head. But Jordan continued to stroke my hand. With Scar on one side of me and the good doctor on the other, my recovery would be easy.

"Your middle name is Aaron?" Jordan asked, and I found it odd as did the others. I heard more voices in the room as they came into play.

Andrew appeared from nowhere. "Hey, man, welcome back." He gave me a pat on my shoulder. "Aaron is Jordan's middle name, too, by the way. Funny, huh?"

No, it wasn't funny; it was fucking fate. Like both Scar and Jordan, I'd always known it was destined to be, and this was proof.

"Don't do that to your sister again." Daimen's voice was one I'd know anywhere. Of course, Daimen was the type to order me not to die and took it as an insult if I didn't obey him.

"Yeah, I will try not to get hit over the head next time." Good to know sarcasm was still in me.

"Yeah, try to make sure you keep your promise," Daimen retorted, and everyone laughed. I tried, but it hurt too much. Behind him, I saw Arden, who had jut his chin at me, silently communicating he was glad I was alive. Yeah, him and me both.

"Now that everyone knows he's all right, the doctor in me has to ask everyone to leave. Except you, Red. You can stay. I'm pretty sure you wouldn't obey me if I told you to leave anyway."

"And I don't want you to." I hold her hand tighter. My sister leaned down and gave me a kiss, and then her men escorted her out of the room. She looked back one last time to make sure I was okay. I get it. I was the same way with her when she was in the hospital just four months ago.

But with Scar and Jordan on either side of me, I fell back asleep, grateful for one more day on this earth.

chapter 27

scarlet

My mind wouldn't get over the fact that Levi could have been taken from me. My nightmares increased at this thought. Plus, Jordan still denied his attraction to Levi. It was bad enough that I feared having Levi taken from me, but now I worried that the weird chemistry between Jordan and him would tear us apart, too.

After one more day, the hospital released him into our care. With his place too small to house all of us and Jordan's place having stairs, we chose to hole up in my home. I'd taken a couple of days off work to be with Levi around the clock.

"I got hit over the head, but I was given an all clear," Levi claimed, thinking he was going back to work. Jordan put a nix to it, and he was stuck with the two of us, come hell or high water.

Settling him on the couch, I'd even given him the okay to watch as much baseball as he wanted. I promised to sit next to him, learning all the rules.

"Um, I'll take you up on your offer as long as you're naked, too."

One look up at Jordan, and we both laughed. "Yeah, I'm thinking he's feeling better, Red." We embarked on a weeklong session of naked baseball watching. But I was not the only one naked.

Within a week, Levi was back at work, and we were rotating between Jordan's house and mine. "I don't have a home anymore. I'm always living out of a suitcase." I understood he was starting the beginning of a conversation about us moving in together. It made sense because the other two paid rent, and it wasn't like Levi made a ton of money as a fireman. My place was plenty spacious with three bedrooms and a huge living room. It was over two thousand square feet. And though I couldn't stand a day away from both my men, I'd wanted to wait until Jordan could come to terms with the unresolved feelings for Levi.

"Yeah, yeah, your full-size bed would barely fit me and you, let alone the three of us," I'd said, waiting for Jordan's reply.

"That's right. Sorry, buddy. It's sort of a wasted space."

The wheels were turning in Levi's head, and I knew he was going to push Jordan, but the second Jordan had looked away, I raised both eyebrows toward Levi. It was my way of letting him know not to rock the boat. Levi threw his hands up, silently telling me he'd give it up for now. I was aware this subject would be brought up again.

I arrived at Jordan's apartment after work one night. If we were meeting at Jordan's, I'd leave straight from the office. Like Levi, I left a couple of changes of clothes and a toothbrush at Jordan's place. I used my key to let myself in and heard Maroon 5 blaring through the speakers. Levi was sitting on the couch with a book in his hands, and behind him, Jordan was in the kitchen cooking.

I took a second look. Surely, I was not in the right home. First, I'd never seen Levi pick up a book. He'd often tease me about my love for reading. He'd ask how I could concentrate when there weren't pictures. And the whole time I'd known Jordan, he never volunteered to cook. Yet here they were in front of me, looking sexy in both positions. Then the idea of positions had me thinking of all the dirty positions I'd like to try out.

"Doc, our redhead seductress is home," Levi called, rushing toward me.

"Be right there. Working on the cheese part of the dish."

A large smile greeted me along with a deep searing kiss. "Hey, beautiful, we were getting worried, weren't we, Doc?"

When had we become so domesticated? Jordan was cooking, Levi was reading, and they were both waiting for me.

"What fifties sitcom have I walked into?" I asked as Jordan walked toward me.

"What do you mean?" Levi made his way back over to the couch, picking up his book. On closer inspection, I looked down to see it was one of my romance novels. "What are you doing reading this?" I pointed at the book Prelude I'd left sitting on Jordan's nightstand last night.

"First, a bride fleeing her own wedding on the cover drew me in. And the scenes and writing, it's fucking hot. I'm reading about how Lina's love for Julian is so deep, and I feel for her." He looked Jordan's way, who was oblivious to the fact Levi equated the unrequited love of Lina in Prelude to himself concerning Jordan. "Maybe I've been reading the wrong books."

"Yeah?" I question.

"Seriously, and that sexy as fuck scene with Lina and Julian? Fuck, I even read it to Doc. We've been waiting for you for a while." His hint was delivered with this wicked but sexy crooked smile.

I had just finished the first book and couldn't wait to get my hands on the next one. "I ordered Interlude today. Hopefully, I can start it tomorrow when it arrives. I even paid for overnight shipping. I've got to know what happens." My mind was still reeling over Levi reading the steamy romance book. "You can read book two, Interlude, after I'm done," I began, watching Jordan's fine ass in the kitchen being all domesticated. "And, Doc, you never cook, so what's up with all this?"

He even had an apron on. I'd always loved Jordan in his white doctor's coat, but now with him in an apron, my body was ready to go.

"I have one dish I can make. But it's the most fattening meal in the world, and when I cook it, I eat my weight in it." This would be the deciding factor for my health-conscious doctor.

I followed his voice into the kitchen and saw the same pot I cook soup in with enough homemade mac and cheese to feed a small troop. Hell, forget that, I think we could feed the U.S. Army.

"Holy Shit, homemade mac and cheese." I looked at the food like it was the beginning of life, and also, by smelling it, I gained twenty pounds. "Why so much?"

He leaned in to kiss me. "'Fuck, I missed you. Levi's afternoon reading session has made me horny as hell." He took a test bite of his dish. "Oh, and to answer your question, my mom's recipe calls for three pounds of macaroni. I didn't know how to make it smaller."

As I molded myself into him, I felt how horny he actually was. I leaned back and smiled. "You know, Levi would have helped you with that." I pointed to his erection.

"Believe me. He always offers to help me with my jolly roger," he teased back.

"Jolly roger?" I asked when Jordan only shrugged. I fell to my knees as I called for our LT. "Hey, Levi, I'm about to help Jordan with his jolly roger. Want to come watch?" I didn't have to see him to hear he was running to us. Turning behind me, I caught his gaze on Jordan's very erect vessel. "Enjoying the view?"

His own cock raised in his athletic shorts when he winked and then he looked past me to wink at Jordan.

On my knees, I took Jordan completely into my mouth, working his balls. "Fuck, Red, you're making this one of the best welcome home greetings ever."

I worked up and down his shaft when a moan escaped him, and he exploded in my mouth. After I turned my head to Levi, he had grabbed a hand towel to alleviate his own explosion. "Well, fuck, Doc, I'm not sure that can ever be topped again. Seeing Scar on her knees taking you in and knowing mac and cheese is on the menu for dinner. Fuck me, it's going to be a good night."

chapter 28

jordan

We'd been invited to Levi's old triad's house. I was not happy about it, not one bit. "I'm not going," I insisted when it was just Red and me in my room. Levi was called to the firehouse to answer more questions on the arson case. We were leaving for vacation the next day to Arden and Daimen's second home on Lake Michigan. Levi wanted to tie up loose ends before we left.

"What the hell is your problem? We're a couple. Or a threesome or whatever the fuck we decide to call it." She'd stopped getting dressed, debating the merits of this dinner with me in just her bra and panties. That sneaky little seductress. "We're going to do what normal committed people do."

"But I don't know this couple." Poor point and I realized it as soon as I made it.

Pursing her lips together, she countered, "And I do? What really is your issue with having dinner with some old friends of Levi's? If the roles were reversed, he'd do the same for you."

"Yeah, but to sit through dinner with a couple he'd been with? Isn't it weird?"

She cocked her head to the side. "So you're jealous? Is that it?"

"Fuck, no." I was quick with my reply, but I didn't believe me.

Pulling my hands into hers, she brought me forward. "Good, then the problem is solved." Kissing me on the cheek, she slid on her tight-ass jeans that hugged her curves perfectly up her thighs. "Okay, let's go. We need to pick Levi up at the firehouse on the way out. Are you driving, or would you like me to?"

I'd driven with Red a couple of times in her Mini Cooper, and beside the fact that both Levi and I barely fit in the front seat, I knew neither one of us would fit in the back. Plus, I always sort of put my life in danger when Red was behind the wheel. Patting her ass on the way out of my room, I replied, "No, let me drive. We'll take my Prius."

He wasn't picking up his phone, and we'd been out in the parking lot for ten minutes. "Let me run in there. Everyone knows me," Red offered.

I pulled at her like I was not going to allow her to exit the car, and honestly, it was exactly what I had planned. "Um, like hell you're going in there dressed like that with a fuck ton of horny firemen. Our man is the only one allowed to ogle you like that, not the others." With her tight as sin jeans and her fuck-me boots along with a shirt that showed as much cleavage as a swimsuit, I'd put my foot down.

A large smile formed on her face at my almost caveman

instincts. I waited for her to argue with me, but she only stared my way. "Um, what, Red?"

I readied myself for a tongue lashing. Red was very independent. She had to be, growing up in foster care and being bounced from home to home, but she continued to look at me like she was amused.

"Um, Doc? Our man?" She laughed at her own remark while I internally replayed the entire conversation. Did I really say our man?

No, there was no way I did. Clearing my throat, my attempt to backpedal was halted by her hand. "Hell, Doc, why are you fighting this?"

Putting the emergency brake on, I unlatched my seat belt and opened the door. When I was out, I bent over and said, "I'll be right back. If those fuckers stare at you in your tight as hell outfit, I'll have to hurt them."

She laughed at my protectiveness or my possessiveness. I didn't care what the title was. Only Levi and I were allowed to both mentally and physically undress our girl.

Going through the large bay to get to the entrance, I was stopped by a burly, larger than Dwayne Johnson man. Oddly enough, he looked like him, too. "Hey, bro, can I help you?"

The firehouse was what I had expected. A crew of evenly divided Sox and Cubs fans sat on the couch watching the baseball game. And the banter that went back and forth in front of the television was loud. Behind them was a large kitchen, and to the side, a huge table that could hold thirty men.

"Yeah, I'm here to pick up Levi."

The Rock doppelgänger looked behind me. "Ah, shit, I thought his hot girlfriend was coming to get him." He popped his head to the men yelling at the ump for a bad call when in his presence, they all stopped.

"Levi's hot girlfriend isn't coming in." Everyone all hemmed and hawed over it as the hairs on the back of my neck rose.

"Yeah, I'd be careful, Rock." I heard Levi's voice behind

me. "Scar is the good doctor's girl, too, and he's a little crazy over her. Where I'm just like, you MOFOs, she's mine and you can't have her, Dr. Peters gets a little jealous."

The Rock—of course, that's his fucking nickname— looked at me and shrugged. "Sorry, Doc, what can I say? She's hot. And how in the world did both of y'all get her? She's missing out on the real deal with one complete man—me." I couldn't take on this motherfucker in front of me, but at his words, I wanted to try. Levi grabbed me by the waist.

"Come on, Doc, the Rock is seriously a shit stirrer." Levi's touch had my body betraying me again. I jerked from him, and the Rock continued to laugh as he moved down the hallway, but he wasn't done.

"Fuck, not only does he get the hot redhead, but he also gets the cute and spunky doctor. Not fair, LT, not fair."

He was almost out of earshot when I decided it was time for a rebuttal. "Um, we're not together."

Levi, who was behind me, leaned in, and I could feel his breath on my neck. "Yeah, just keep telling yourself that, Doc."

He was out the door so fast, I didn't have a chance to reply.

chapter 29

levi

The suburbs — this could have been my life. All I needed to do was look at the duo on either side of me to understand it was not what I was destined for. Sure, I had loved Cami and Dane so much. Letting them start their life together was the hardest thing I ever did. But they were older than me and ready for the next chapter when I wasn't.

I'd known Jack and was happy they'd found love with him. In Dane's eyes from just a couple of weeks ago, I could see the deep-rooted hurt that still lived in him from Jack's departure. I was sure to see it in Cami's eyes, too.

I happened to be in the middle of Scar and Jordan as we walked up to the front door. Typically, if we were out together, Scar was in the middle of us. But tonight, ever since my words to Jordan, he hadn't given me space; he'd gotten physically closer.

When Scar knocked on the door, we heard the screeches of little ones. I had enough nieces and nephews to appreciate the sounds of kids, which I did want one day.

A girl about four years old, the carbon copy of her father, opened the door. "You Daddy's old boyfriend?" she asked so matter-of-factly. Yeah, this was Dane's kid. Down the hall, I saw a little girl toddling behind her sister.

"Sissy, who dat?" If the little girl who answered the door was her dad, this little one was her mom. Crazy curly black hair stuck up everywhere and large almost gray eyes adorned her face.

"Yeah, I was your daddy's boyfriend at one point." I kneeled to her level. "And what's your name?"

She extended her hand, giving me a firm handshake. "I Maggie Lynn Gregory. This Bridget Anne Gregory. You gotta name?" Oh, hell, like one Dane Gregory wasn't enough for this world, now there were two.

"I'm Levi, and these are my friends Scarlet and Jordan." Before I could say more, a voice called down the hall for Maggie.

"Maggie, honey, stop giving them the third degree." Cami came around the corner, and shit, she hadn't changed in eight years. "Levi, oh, Levi." She came to me and hugged me like her life depended on it. I looked at Scar, and she was as natural as ever, happy for this reunion. But behind me, a hand appeared on my back the second Dane came into play. From the size and the firm grasp, I knew it wasn't Scar. And fuck, it was intimate in nature. I loved it. When I stepped toward Dane, the touch fell away from me. I made a mental note because we'd be discussing this later.

"Levi, you handsome bastard."

"Daddy said a bad word," Maggie sassed from below.

"Yeah, remind me, and I'll add a quarter to the cursing pot." Dane held my shoulders, looking me up and down, but all I cared about were the stare and the little pout that came from Jordan's mouth in my peripheral. Why was the man fighting me? I pushed all of that out of my mind when Dane's once very familiar arms enveloped me.

"Hell, look at you!" He turned to his wife. "Our boy is all grown up, Cam." He laughed and hugged me again. Pulling back, he looked at Scar. "Shit, I'm sorry, Scarlet. I hope I'm not overstepping. But fuck, the way he looks when he talks about you, no one can compete." Dane pulled Cami tight to his body.

"Oh, I'm not the jealous type," Scar teased. "By the way, I'm Scarlet Reeves." She extended her hand to Cami, but knowing Cam like I did meant they'd be fast friends in less than a minute. And I was wrong because it wasn't a minute, it was five seconds, Cami had Scarlet in an embrace.

"Yeah, we're huggers. No way around it, hon!" While Scar and Cami were in some sort of friendly back and forth banter, Dane looked over at Jordan.

"Yeah, we're huggers, but you don't look like the hugging type." I wouldn't want to hug Jordan right now either, and that was coming from the man who seriously wanted to touch every part of his body. His glare locked on Dane, and his jaw was set tight. I would have thought if the man was going to smile or even move his face, it would crack. It was set like stone.

"I'm Dane Gregory." He extended his hand, and Jordan looked down, staring at it. Shit, if this wasn't some sort of show of dominance, I wouldn't know what was.

I leaned into his space, and whispered, "Knock it off."

My harsh words were all it took for Jordan to extend his hand, though a smile would be the last thing I would get from him.

"He's a tough one, this guy here," Dane teased, finally shaking it.

"Yep, a bit of a wild card." I began to cut the tension coming from the good doctor next to me.

"Um, yeah, and that guy is right here." Jordan's little comment only had Dane and I breaking into hysterics.

"Oh, this'll be fun." Dane turned around, his arm around me, and led me to the living room space. Another low growl could be heard from Jordan, but at least I knew he was following us. Yeah, tonight, I'd challenge him. Tonight, he was going to admit what we already knew. He'd fallen for me just as I had fallen for him.

———

Cami had not changed. Sure, she was older, but she didn't look it one bit. And the figure on this woman, after two children, hadn't changed. I could agree, just as I had back when I was balls deep in both her and Dane, that she was drop-dead gorgeous. But she did nothing for me now. Certainly not with the two people I'd fallen head over heels in love with on either side of me. I found it funny with the odd reaction of Jordan at the front door, he'd stayed close to me.

"So you're telling me you were there to take Dane's sister on a date?" Scar asked while Dane was telling the story of how we met.

"Well, yeah, his sister was hot," I countered.

My comment elicited a laugh from Dane. "Yeah, but apparently not as hot as I was." Dane winked at me, and I winked back. My body faced away from Jordan, but it didn't matter. His hand clamped down on my thigh. I tried to ignore it, but then he squeezed tighter. I was not going to let him ruin this. However, I would try like hell to prove my point. With his hand under the table and out of view of everyone, I took my free hand to interlace with his. For a moment, maybe five seconds, he relaxed into my touch, holding my hand, but as soon as I got used to it, it was gone.

The laughter and memories continued throughout the night, and Jordan barely spoke, even when Cami tried to pull him into the conversation. He was a little more receptive to her but not much. I'd tried to delve into the breakup with Jack, but they both clammed up the second I asked. It wasn't hard to see that they missed being in a committed triad. Some people were just meant for the number three, and Dane and Cami were certainly two of those people.

Jordan had close to seven beers by my rough estimate, and Scar and Cam had finished two bottles of wine between them. Regardless, I couldn't drink since I was on call at the firehouse tonight in case the arsonist struck again.

Watching everyone enjoy themselves—well, except Jordan—was all I needed. Even in his own way, Jordan was enjoying something, and I'd hoped it was my view since he barely took his gaze off Scar or myself.

Jordan, however, sulked to his car after giving me his keys as I said my goodbyes to Dane. "Fuck, that boy has it bad for you, Levi."

With Dane and me in a deep embrace, I admitted, "Yeah, I know that, you know that, fuck, the whole world knows that, but getting him to admit it to himself is a completely different thing."

I clapped him one time on his back. "Yeah, but if anyone is up for the challenge, you are. Levi Arnold, you're a persuasive guy!" Dane pointed out.

Nodding in agreement, I broached another subject that needed addressing. "You and Cami need to get out there and find that third that completes you. I see it in the way she watched us tonight that you need it. And if anyone is fucking convincing, it's you!"

His eyes were downturned. "Yeah, Jack screwed us up big time, but you're right. I have a call into Haven Dorn." Shit, I hadn't heard her name in years. She hosted upscale triad events, so if anyone could find Cami and Dane their third, it would be her.

"Yeah, I can't imagine what it was like to lose Jack." I'd only met him a couple of times, but Cami and Dane were deeply in love with him. It had to have split their hearts in two.

With one last hug, I took Scar's hand as she tried to tear herself away from their feisty children. They'd instantly fallen in love with Scar as she had with them. We went to meet Jordan in the car, who'd moved to the back seat.

I didn't have a chance to address his behavior before Scar turned around and began to chastise him. "You know what, Jordan? I'm not a proctologist, but I know an asshole when I see one." I tried not to laugh. It wouldn't help the situation, but her comment was fucking funny as hell. With my hand over my mouth, I looked in the rearview mirror.

He waved her off, but she was getting the last word. "We're heading to my apartment. And we're not going to bed, and we're sure as fuck not going to the lake house until we hash out what the hell is going on in your head."

The car remained silent until we reached the city, and my phone started exploding left and right with text alerts. Scar took the phone and read them as I drove.

"Um, there is some sort of emergency, and you've been called in." Her voice shared the same disappointment I felt. This conversation had to happen, but there was nothing I could do about it.

"Okay, I'll drop you two off at your place, Scar, since neither one of you are fit to drive." It worked out since I was a block from her apartment anyway. "But I won't be long." She leaned over to kiss me.

"Please be careful." It was something we all were mindful of, especially after what had happened with the arsonist.

Jordan turned to me, squeezing my shoulder softly. "Be careful, LT."

I nodded in a reply, but continued, "Don't go to bed without me. We aren't sleeping until we sort this shit out, got it?"

Jordan's hard demeanor returned to his face. "Loud and clear."

chapter 30

scarlet

I didn't say a single word to him on the entire way to the 37th floor. Opening my door, I walked in and didn't stop until I was in my room. I heard the television turn on in the living room. The man was obsessed with baseball. He didn't even change out of his slacks and button-up shirt. I didn't want to be near him.

Jordan was giving to a fault. But only those close to him saw it. I knew what he did for Kayla, his sister. As a teacher, she made barely enough to afford housing in Chicago. He paid her rent so she could move to the city to be with her girlfriend.

On his off time, he volunteered at the homeless shelter. He'd go in at night and treat those who couldn't afford healthcare. When he couldn't get donations for the medicine, he had often paid for it out of his pocket.

He'd been away for a year, volunteering in Ethiopia with Doctors without Borders. Plus, he was a tender lover, always considering my needs first. He'd get up and have something for me anytime we greeted the day together, even if it was just toast with jam and butter, because the man couldn't cook to save his life. But it was always the thought that counted. And it counted a fuck ton now—especially since I was pissed as hell at him.

Why couldn't he allow others to see the wonderfulness within him? With my arms crossed, blocking his precious Cubs, his eyes met mine, and in it, an understanding that we'd hash this out right now.

"Red, I thought we'd wait until Levi got back."

Part of my talking helped take my mind off the fact that Levi could be in danger once again. I tried to push this thought away when I began, "Why did you act like a version of Daimen Torano when he goes all caveman on Elliot? It doesn't suit you, and I sure as hell can't ever and won't ever allow you to treat us that way again."

Nodding his head, he began, still sitting. "Okay, so we aren't waiting until Levi gets home." It was a snarky statement I ignored.

"Dammit, Jordan." I threw myself on the couch, my hand on my face, and started crying. It hit me so fast, out of instinct with memories of being left alone as I had been most of my life. Sure, Daimen and Arden were always there for me, but they were beginning their own life. Same could be said for Andrew as his new man was quite possessive of his time.

The second his hand tried to offer me comfort, I shot up from the couch. I was not going to allow him to ease my pain when he was the man who caused this heartache in the first place.

"Red." His voice had changed, and it was a little less lippy. "Listen, I was a jerk. I get it. I don't know what came over me."

My back was against the wall of my living space as the lights of the Chicago skyline danced against the windows. But right then, I didn't care about the streets of Chicago. I was worried about protecting my already shattered heart.

"Yeah, you know what was wrong. I can tell you—you're fucking jealous. And I have no idea why. Oh, wait, I do. Where I'm secure with Levi around an ex-lover, the difference between you and me—I've admitted I'm head over heels in love with him and you keep fucking denying it."

He was still, his eyes fixating on a picture of Arden, Daimen, and me in front of the Sydney Opera house. He watched the picture as if it was pertinent for the conversation I was trying to have with him.

"So are you going to stare at that picture all day, or are we going to talk?" I questioned.

He stood quickly and charged at me. I was not scared or worried. He was emotional, sure, but I'd never worried for my safety around Jordan Peters.

He was in front of me, holding my hands, his fingers interlacing with mine. "What do you want from me, Red?" His eyes pleaded for me not to push him.

"I want you to be happy. I want all of us to be happy, and I want this—what you, Levi, and I have—to never go away. If we're not honest, I'm going to lose you both. At this point, I could never choose. If you and Levi don't come to some sort of understanding, I'd have to walk away from you both, and fuck, the idea sends me back to when I was seven—the day I found out my parents died."

His hand made gentle contact with my cheek. "Fuck, Red. I forget sometimes. Shit, of course you're worried, but I'm not going to let anything happen to the three of us."

A tear fell from my eye, and he caught it. Still gazing at me, I simply replied, "You can't promise me anything, not when you can't be honest with yourself."

chapter 31

levi

"What's so important it can't wait until after my vacation is over?" I asked, entering the chief's office with all the higher brass waiting for me. My chief and I had always had an open-door policy. It would have been nice to know everyone in my chain of command was present at ten at night before I barged in. Shit, this was bad—very bad.

In my view, Garner Blakely was present in the meeting. Shit, all I wanted to do was get home to my two forevers. Jordan was so close to admitting what I already knew, but this was going to be a while.

"Lieutenant," the fire commissioner began, "I'm sorry to bring you in so late tonight." They pointed at my outfit. Sure, it might just be a pair of jeans and a nice button-up top, but I looked like I had plans that were ruined. And I sure as hell had.

"I can't say I'm getting a warm and fuzzy being dragged in on a Saturday evening with all of you here. What's going on?"

Garner stepped forward. Hell, he looked so much like his brother except his hair was a little darker. "I hate to bring you away from your girl, but something was delivered here this evening."

I looked at my chief and the other ten men in the room, and they all had their jaws locked hard wearing a grimace on their faces.

"Listen, it's a little disturbing, to say the least. But just know, we've got this. I'm putting my whole unit on the case." Garner extended a manila envelope my way. "We've already processed this and have everything we need."

I hesitated as though a snake would pop out from it. Pulling the note out slowly, I saw those stupid magazine letters taped to a white piece of copy paper. I'd only seen this in the movies, but it was somehow creepier and more eerie in real life.

"What the fuck?" I asked, my eyes glued to the paper.

I didn't read it out loud, though I was aware everyone had seen this.

It simply read:

YOU ARE NEXT, LT ARNOLD

It was to the point and fucking sent chills down my spine. I was the target, me. And just like clockwork, an alarm sounded. The overhead speaker flooded the chief's office. "Three alarm fire, an abandoned warehouse." When the address was given, Garner's and my eyes met, silently understanding this was not a coincidence. It was three blocks from the last three fires.

I walked to the door. Shirley was on duty, but they'd have a ride along with them today. "Um, Arnold, where are you going?" It was my chief.

"I'm a fireman, first and foremost. If he wants me, then he can come fucking get me." I'd expected him to order me to stand down, but when he didn't, I looked at Garner. "Care to come along, Detective?"

"Yeah, I'll follow you and have my team meet us there."

The factory was almost engulfed by the time we got to the fire. Shirley ordered his men down because the building would collapse soon. And as he promised, Garner's crew surrounded the warehouse, ready to pounce on the clown who was messing with my life and, more importantly, the life of my men.

"Detective." One of his officers called him over as we stood watching the blaze; making sure it wouldn't spread.

I didn't think much about it until he'd summoned me. With Shirley on point, I walked to the other side of the street, near a phone pole.

"Um, Levi, we have a problem."

"Yeah, what is it?" I asked, gesturing to a piece of paper in his hands.

"This was on the telephone pole." He gave it to me, and it sent a shiver down my spine.

ARNOLD, I WON'T REST UNTIL YOU'RE GONE.

This time, it was a black marker. But the message was fucking clear. I. Was. His. Target.

chapter 32

jordan

Scarlet had practically cried herself to sleep on my shoulder. I'd scooped her up and placed her in bed, promising not to start anything with Levi when he returned.

Watching the extra innings of the ball game and drowning my jackass-ness in a bottle of beer for making Red cry tonight, I was startled when the lock clicked and Levi opened the door. I turned to him, and he looked like hell. With disheveled hair and wearing different clothes, I knew he'd probably gone out on a call, but I wasn't sure why. His buddy, Shirley, was there for the night. I wanted to stop him as he took a right that led into the kitchen. Opening the fridge, he grabbed a beer for him and an extra one, I guess, for me.

Giving me the cold one, I took it as he turned to sit in the corner of the room in the stiff upright chair we both normally hated.

"Was it a tough one?" I asked.

"Yeah." He pulled a taste of his beer. "You have no idea."

"Fatalities?" It was the doctor in me getting to the point.

"Um, no. Just another warehouse fire."

I straightened. Some fucker was trying to hurt firemen, my fireman. Fuck, did I just call him my fireman?

We sat in silence and didn't say anything when the Cubbies had men on both second and third base with no outs. He was not into the game, and I could tell, but it was reaffirmed when he asked, "Where's Scar?"

I turned off the television. If my Cubbies won, it was really invalid compared to the events of the night. "Um, let's just say she had a rough evening."

He stiffened more. I couldn't imagine anyone loving Red the way I did, but I ventured to guess Levi did. "What do you mean, Doc?"

Putting my beer on the table, I leaned forward. "How much do you know about her time in foster care?" She'd shared a couple things with us, but I don't think it scratched the surface.

Clearing his throat, he began, "She's only shared a little with either one of us. I know she was on the streets at eighteen, and Arden and Daimen found her and took her in. And what she has told us was fucking heartbreaking."

"Yeah, I'm not sure how I fucking missed it—how scared she is of being abandoned. She thinks we won't work out, the three of us. And she won't choose between us, and for that reason, she's convinced she'll be left alone again."

Levi stood ready to punch something. It was a shitty night for him, and I knew he was holding something back from me about the call, but I wouldn't push. "Fuck, Jordan. This was the last thing I wanted. Shit! Do you know how much I love her?"

"I would wager to guess you love her as deeply as I do,"

I replied coldly. His anger only remained under wraps because our redhead was asleep in the other room. "And I made it worse tonight, too," I admitted.

Levi's stone-cold eyes were replaced with a little grin that led to his eyes. "How hard was it to admit you were wrong?" I smiled at him, and something as simple as what I'd said changed things around.

"A little hard." I took a deep breath. "I wish I could turn it on and off like you."

His little smirk was gone, and I instantly was aware I'd said the wrong thing.

"What? Turn it on and off, that's what you think? Just 'cause I like both men and women, I turn it off?"

"Fuck." My outburst gave me a chance to think, but he wouldn't let me talk before he got in my space.

"I don't turn it on or off. If I could, this would be so fucking easy. But I can't—that's the problem. I'm falling for you. You think I want my heart to break for what we could have, but no—you're too stubborn to take hold of your own happiness."

He was in my space, his lips mere centimeters from mine. "I want you with every fiber of my being. But it's you who turns it off because I know you feel it, too."

Levi's warmth against my mouth and my face was everything. The smell of the beer on his breath and the aroma of his aftershave brought my body to life, as alive as Red's body did.

His hand cupped my erection, just enough for me to feel his touch on my groin. "This is not for Red. Not right now, anyway. This is all me." He pointed down at my hard-on. "This is all for me, Doc. How can you deny yourself something that brings you joy? And fuck, I could take care of you." He removed his hand from my cock.

He moved his head to my ear, whispering quietly, "I'm not talking about sex. You and Scar would be my focus. The two of you, me loving you. Me taking on your needs, your desires. You want breakfast in bed? You want me to bring you those gross peanut butter, banana, and chocolate chip rollups to work on my days off? You want me to massage your neck after a tough shift? You want to hold hands while we root for our Cubbies together." His face was back in front of me. "All you have to do is say the word, and it will happen."

In no time at all, he'd raised himself from my presence, and he was gone, exiting Scar's apartment. He wasn't going to coddle me anymore. He was going to make me do all the work.

chapter 33

scarlet

I woke up with no one next to me. Why? I glanced over at my nightstand. The copy of The Giving Tree was sitting on it, reminding me of the promise both men made to me.

I was positive I missed something when I walked to the living room space to find Jordan sprawled on my couch with about a half a dozen beers on my coffee table. He was in his boxers with a blanket kicked off him. Both men were such hot boxes, always complaining I turned the heat up too much.

But now, I needed to know where the other part of us was. Gently giving him a nudge by kicking the couch, I remembered I was still upset over the shit he pulled last night at Dane and Cami's house.

"Well, shit," he began when his gaze fell on me, looking me up and down. "You're still pissed at me for last night, aren't you?"

I turned around, making sure I didn't miss Levi in my space. Maybe he was in my guest room at the opposite end of my house. But I hadn't seen his keys or wallet on my kitchen table where he always placed them.

"Well, I wasn't still mad until I saw Levi wasn't here. What happened?"

He sat up, and I walked around the couch to sit near him. "Jordan?" I pushed.

"He gave me an ultimatum, and when I didn't respond the way he wanted, he went home, telling me to figure it out."

I crossed my arms. "And what do you want?"

He didn't stop to think. "I want you. Fuck, Red, I've only wanted you."

I stood, giving me space. "I don't believe you, not for one second. I'm calling Levi, and you better as fuck figure it out by the time he gets here because we will not survive if you're not honest."

He was now in my space. "Are you giving me an ultimatum, too? Are you telling me I need to pick him to have you both?"

I pulled at his hand, bringing him near me. "No, not at all. But the bottom line is you can't have us both when you're not honest with yourself."

———

"Red?"

I was mad. My nightmares were coming true. And it just wasn't Jordan. Instead of letting everything happen naturally, Levi pushed him. Maybe Jordan needed the push, but only time would tell, and it was more than I could handle—if this perfect life was taken from me. They were what I wanted—I knew it, but they didn't quite understand my fear of abandonment.

"What?" My tone didn't hide my mood.

"Can I come in?" Walking toward the door, I opened it.

Jordan held out his arm, and I let him hold me. "Red, I'm so sorry."

I couldn't say anything. I only cried into his neck.

"Is Levi on his way?" It was six in the morning, and we had plans to leave for the lake house, but first, I needed reassurance they wouldn't disappear on me.

"Yeah, he said he'd be over soon. Couldn't sleep."

Jordan tipped his head back and crashed his lips to mine. We didn't say anything. I let him lead me to the bed where he pulled up my nightie and started stroking my clit when his tongue began to lick my pussy.

"I love you, Red. I'd never purposely hurt you." He was taking breaks between his words. But it was our closeness I needed. It was this closeness I desired. Until I heard, "Well, fuck, isn't this a sight for sore eyes?" Jordan's head popped up, and I only watched him watch Levi.

"I was just getting her ready for us, LT. Want to join in?"

Levi was naked before he reached our bed.

chapter 34

levi

Scarlet lay on her bed, her ivory skin glorious to our eyes. I was on one side of her with her nipples between my fingers. My head was close to Jordan's with his fingers inside Scar. Though mine were working my girl's tit and his were working her clit and cunt, our eyes never wavered from one another. Through her moans, I could sense Scar's eyes on me, too.

A minute, maybe two passed as we stared at one another. Another second or two passed, until my lips found his. And for the first ten seconds, he kissed me back. His tongue dueled with mine. Once my free hand touched his shoulder, the kiss ended, and he pushed off the bed until the wall stopped his flight from me.

"Doc," I began. What was I going to say? Sure, I had a

shit ton on my mind, but before I could say anything, his body came barreling over Scar to get to me. It was not in the I need you now kind of way. No, by the rage of his gnashing teeth, this was the I'm going to kick your ass sort of attack. After the first punch to the face, I was on the defense, and my fist contacted with his jaw as he'd done with me. A screech from Scar didn't stop us when we rolled off the bed, taking her with us.

He was on top of me, the lucky bastard, and it was the only reason he got another sucker-punch in. I pushed him, and then I was on top of him, punching him in the face. I swung my hand back again when Scar's pleas stopped me.

"Fuck you, assholes! Stop it, stop it fucking now." With my body covering Jordan's, I stopped just before my fist reached his jaw again.

I turned around, and Scarlet was cowering in the corner, holding her wrist. Even from far away, I'd had enough experience with wounds and broken bones that my body stilled. Her face already had a bruise cascading down the left cheek, and she was holding her arm in a way which confirmed it was broken.

"Holy shit, Scar." I released Jordan from my clutches and hurried to her. She kicked at me with her legs.

"Stay the fuck away from me, you asshole." The tears on her face had to be from both pain and the sheer shock of watching Jordan and I beat the shit out of each other.

"Scarlet, beautiful, we need to get you to the hospital," I began when her long legs continued kicking me away.

"No, stay the fuck away from me." She went to stand but winced, trying to pull herself from the floor.

I raised my hands in the air. "Okay, I get it. You're pissed, and you have every right to be." I grabbed my cell, hitting the contact button. Jordan stood, trying to get to Scar, but she kicked him, too. I could call Elliot, but that thought had me pushing another number.

In three seconds, I heard an almost out of breath Andrew answer the phone, another deep voice in the background yelling, "This better be good, Arnold." I knew the voice, the new executive working with Daimen and Arden.

"Sorry, Andrew," I began, Scar still screaming at us in the background.

"Levi, is that Scar? What is wrong with her?"

What do I say? "Yeah, we screwed up, Andrew. Your brother and I, can you come get Scar? She needs to get to the hospital. Judging by the swelling, she broke her arm."

"What the fuck?" Andrew asked. "I'm in the building, but I'll tell you what. You and my brother better get the fuck out of the apartment before Brock and I get there, or I won't be responsible for what we do to you."

Tossing a pair of jeans to Jordan and grabbing my own, I looked at Scar. "Shit, Scar. I'm so fucking sorry."

Jordan hadn't said much, only watching on with the same guilt that was in my own eyes. "We better go, Jordan. Your brother is not fucking around."

"We can't leave her," he pleaded.

"Get the fuck out of my sight. Right fucking now!" Scar screamed.

I tried to pull him, but he yanked his arm back from my grasp. "We need to, just for now. I think we've done enough." I was out the door, looking at Scar.

"Just go, please," she pleaded. She turned her head to Jordan with the same request.

We were out of the apartment just as Brock and Andrew were about to knock on it. "You fuckers better get out of his sight right now, or I won't be able to stop him." Brock's message was clear. Andrew didn't look at his brother when Jordan hesitated to say something. Brock, who I'd come to find out was protective in his own right, placed a hand on Andrew's back to escort him into the apartment. When the door was opened just enough to allow both men access, I heard Scarlet crying. And although both Jordan and I were taller and broader than Andrew, in his rage and anger, I think he could have taken us both on.

"Jordan?" I questioned.

"Stay the fuck away from me, Levi." He headed to the stairs as I found my way to the elevator. What the fuck just happened?

chapter 35

jordan

I'd been home an hour, unable to sit, unable to think about what I'd just been a part of. My actions hurt Red. It was more than just the physical pain; it was the emotional pain, too. I was holding my phone in my hands, willing Andrew to text me to alleviate my guilt.

After ten missed calls and about thirty texts from Levi, I called my brother.

Brock picked up on the first ring. "I'm just saying, you don't want to talk to your brother right now. I had to convince him not to call Daimen and Arden. If he had, one would be in your face right now and the other in Levi's. Hell, his own sister might be more dangerous than those two." He stopped to let all this sink in. He was right. Elliot would take out Levi first, then come pounding on my door next.

"Don't you think I feel like shit for what happened to Red? I deserve your wrath and a beatdown. But, can you tell me if Scar is okay?"

He took in a deep breath, blowing it out into the phone. "Physically, she's okay. A broken wrist. And a nice shiner to the face. But emotionally, she's a wreck. You two—this agreement was to put her first. I know a little about her time in foster care. How could you two let it get this far?"

"Brock, I'll own up to my actions, but I'd been clear with Levi, there was no him and me. And he kissed me. He fucking kissed me."

He chuckled into the phone for a second and then was quiet. I waited for something, anything. Finally, he filled the silence. "You are fucking delusional. I know for you, it's black and white. You're a man of science. You over analyze everything and overthink. Plus, with Andrew gay and Kayla a lesbian, you think there is a clear choice. But being fluid is not a bad thing. As I grew up, I never could have imagined admitting to liking men. My dad was as masculine as they got. Hell, I'm rather masculine. It took me a long time to come out, and it shocked the shit out of everyone. But if I found a woman to love, I wouldn't fight it. Love is not always about genders and clean crisp lines. Fluidity is not a bad thing. That man loves you—I know it, Andrew knows it, Scar knows it. You love him, and again, we all know it. It's time you accept it."

His speech was delivered a lot less in the I'm going to kill you kind of way I thought Brock Spaulding worked. His concern would always be for my brother. And my brother was hurt I would damage Red the way I had.

"Listen, Jordan, I have a very clear opinion on this. Either you admit what you already know and accept you love a man and woman alike, or you let them both go. And don't try to act as if you haven't sent him mixed signals because I've seen it. Sure as fuck you have, so don't for one second deny it. Yeah, Levi shouldn't have kissed you, not without your permission, but did you pull away immediately or did you let your mind mess with you?"

I didn't respond, and my brother's boyfriend continued, "Yeah, that's what I thought. First things first, you need to be respectful of the fact that Levi is worried about Scar. You call him, don't text him, and tell him what I told you. If either one of you gets within a hundred feet of Scar or Andrew, you will have me to deal with. You understand me?"

"Crystal," I replied.

"Okay, I'd leave Scar be for now. She'll be in touch once she's ready to face you. And I'm telling you right fucking now, don't make me get involved." He ended the call without even a simple goodbye, leaving me with the phone in my hand — willing myself to do the one thing I know I should. Lessen Levi's worry.

Levi picked up on the first ring. "Jordan?" It was a question, but he knew it was me. It was awkward. Why wouldn't it be? We had been beating the shit out of each other three hours earlier, and the woman we loved was in the hospital — from our hands.

"Levi, I don't want to talk to you about what happened. But you deserve to know — I spoke with Brock. Andrew was back with Red. She has a broken wrist and a black eye. He said it was minor, and she was more upset than physically hurt."

He remained silent. Not even a peep could be heard on his end. I waited for ten seconds. "Well, I'll go."

"Wait, Doc." His words were rushed, getting them out before I ended the call.

"Levi, I can't right now."

"Just listen to me for thirty seconds." I didn't interrupt him. "We're both going to lose her if we keep this up."

"Yeah, if we haven't already," I agreed.

"You're right," he added. "Listen, I don't know how we recover from this, but I want to. I will stop, I promise."

My laughter had an almost deep, sarcastic tone to it, and in the way my voice hitched an octave or two, he had to hear it with my response. "I think we both know it's not that simple for you, LT."

"I know," he countered, and his voice dropped. "Shit, Doc, I'm so sorry. How's your face?"

I'd been so fucked up over watching Scar cower in the corner that I'd forgotten about my own injuries. "Um, haven't really given it much thought. I'm sure it'll hurt once the adrenaline wears off."

"Yeah, me, too. I guess you know a good doctor who can fix it up," he teased.

"Yeah, and you know a man who used to be a paramedic." Levi laughed at my response. "Listen, LT, I need to go, but be sure to put some ice on your face."

"I'm not as concerned for me as I am you. You took the brunt." The smug fucker was right. I hated it—not as much as what we did to Scar, but it surely bruised the ego.

"Yeah, I heard the guy who clocked me is quite the asshole." What was wrong with us? We basically put Scar in the hospital, and I was what, flirting? "Okay, gotta go." And I hung up the phone without a goodbye.

chapter 36

scarlet

Andrew had become my best friend. I knew he'd always been Ell's bestie, but she'd been a little occupied with her men. Though he still held that title, it was equally shared with me. I knew this when he was pacing my living room with every curse word escaping his mouth when it came to his brother.

"I want to kill him, Scar! I think I just might do that or at least break his fucking arm."

Brock was behind him with a small grin. Brock must have known, like me, Andrew could never or would he ever in his life take down another person. Though I would say Andrew had a hot body, I would have certainly sampled those goods if he had been into women. Andrew wasn't much taller than I was, and the man had never played a single day of sports in his life. And though he worked out and ran, Jordan was out on the court a couple of times a week playing basketball. In the spring, he was on a baseball team, and he swam as often as he could.

Yeah, as pissed off as Andrew was, even in a rage with his adrenaline pumping, he couldn't take on his brother, and by the look on Brock's face, we both knew it. But we'd let him believe he could. Now, Brock, would do it solely on principle because his man was pissed and hurt by this turn of events.

"And fucking Levi, I'll sic Arden and Daimen on him." He stopped for a second only to continue with his thoughts. "No, better yet, I'll sic his sister on him. That's a fate worse than death." It was certainly the truth.

"Um, you will not tell Arden or Daimen. I mean, it's bad enough you two are about ready to kill them. I can't handle the thought of Arden and Daimen in jail."

Brock pulled Andrew into an intimate hug. "Whoa, killer. Give the poor girl a chance to breathe. Of course, we have righteous anger for her, but you're typically the calm in the storm. The hurricane and earthquake known as Daimen Torano and Arden Blakely will only make matters worse for Scar."

I knew there was a reason I liked our new CFO. He was a ball buster, but he was also sensible. Looking at Andrew, I was not sure he could be called the calm in the storm, not at the moment. Yet Brock was right; bringing Arden, Daimen, and even Elliot into this would upset the already bad weather I was experiencing with Levi and Jordan.

"Andrew," I began, my voice low, controlled, trying to bring back his sensible side. "I'm okay. Sure, my wrist is broken, but physically, I'll heal. But that stubborn brother of yours and Levi's spontaneity are a combination I don't think I can handle right now." The idea of saying goodbye to them was what broke me and had my whole body erupting in a pain so intense I could feel it from the top of my head to the bottom of my toes.

A tear fell from my eyes when Andrew pulled me toward him with my good arm. "So what are you saying, Scar?"

"I don't know. I mean ..." And it hit me. Just as I was

bounced from home to home, I would be left alone again. "What is wrong with me? What do I do to be left alone?"

When Andrew brought me to my apartment, he'd started toward my bedroom, but I stopped and took residence on the couch. I couldn't go back in my room, not where the fight of the century had taken place and especially since that was where they'd split my heart in two.

"What can I do for you, Scar?" In Andrew's eyes, I saw something I witnessed in myself when Elliot was hurt or Arden found out that his former best friend tried to kill her. Sometimes it was harder to watch your loved ones hurt more than it was when you yourself were simply the one in pain.

"I can't go back in my room, not yet. The lamp is broken, there's blood on the sheets from one or both of the guys' noses. Can you pack me a couple of days' worth of clothes and get me my toiletries? I'm heading to Arden and Daimen's lake house, after all."

I watched the interaction between Andrew and Brock. Before I could say anything, Brock had it all planned. "We will do you one better, Scar. We'll take you up there."

My bags were packed, and Brock had them in his Yukon before I knew it. But I'd talked them into giving me a couple of hours before we left. More so, I'd finally convinced Andrew to give me some space. He didn't like my plan, not one bit, and he insisted he would be there for the showdown I'd plan to have with both guys, but in the end, after a stern talking-to, he'd given me my space.

I looked in the mirror I had hung on the wall in the hallway near the bedrooms. My left eye where Jordan's elbow had landed and the red scrape below my right eye where Levi's knee had hit me showed the outward damage of their fight. An inward destruction, my broken heart, could not be seen but it was undoubtedly the deeper issue.

When I heard a tap on the door, I smoothed my long shirt and leggings nervously. Behind the door, in the hallway, were both guys, with their bags packed as I'd requested in my text to the both of them.

I moved out of the way, motioning for them to come in. None of us had said anything when I turned to find them in the open eating area between my kitchen and living space. I didn't even want them to sit, not yet anyway. Jordan opened his mouth to speak, and I silenced them with my hand as if I was a traffic cop.

"No, you'll listen, and I'll talk." I stopped because I wondered if I had the courage to go through with this. Issue an ultimatum?

"This whole idea of the three of us being together started as a way to put me first." My arms were folded over my chest as well as I could with my wrist in a cast. Both men fixated on it, as they should, because it was their fucking fault. "Let me be clear. I want the two of you together, like you are with me. I want it so much." I closed my eyes, willing myself not to cry. They didn't deserve one more tear of mine.

It didn't work, and when I wiped a few tears from my face, I winced in pain thanks in part to them. Jordan's arm reached out for me, and Levi stepped forward to give me comfort. I backed up, my voice cracking when I began again. "You promised it was about me. I felt selfish having you two to myself. But you promised and I believed you." I looked at Jordan, then Levi, then back at Jordan. "I can't do this anymore. After what happened yesterday, I'm back to the scared girl in foster care who'd been placed in yet another home because I was not wanted."

"Shit, Scar ..." Levi began.

"No, shut the fuck up and let me finish. You pushed Jordan even though you told me that having the three of us together was solely about me." I looked over at Jordan. "And you're fucking lying to yourself if you say you don't want Levi."

A myriad of tears began to form in the corner of my eyes, I had to finish this quickly. "So here's the deal. You two are going to stay here at my place. You've taken the next four days off so we could get away for a while together, but I'm going, and you're not. You're stuck in my apartment, fixing the shit you broke and working out whatever the fuck is going on with you— together. You want to fight each other, have at it. You want to fuck like wild animals and get it out of your system, then do it. You want to ignore the chemistry you share, then figure out a way to avoid making me your punching bag. I'm giving you one last chance. Don't fuck it up because I'm not sure I'd know how to survive." I was at the door, my fingers gripping the knob, with my back to them. "To be clear, I'm not running from you. I don't ever back down from a fight. But shit, you two have pushed me away!" My words were final, and I had thought I was done until I turned back around, not looking at them. "And you better take this time to think about if you even want me to be a part of your life. Because I'm sure as fuck going to be doing the same." I slammed the door behind me, and before I could crumple to the floor, the strong arms of both Andrew and Brock scooped me up—leading me to the car and to the much-needed break I required from these men.

chapter 37

levi

With the door slammed behind her, we were both left in utter silence. Jordan had not looked at me, but I could see the beginning of a bruise on his face. It was still black and not quite purple yet. I'd clocked him good. But he got me, too. Mine was on my cheek, though, and it split but not deep enough to need stitches. I'd gone to see the medic on duty this morning just to make sure.

"I'm taking the spare room." It was what he said as he grabbed his suitcase, leaving me alone with my thoughts. I certainly wouldn't be sleeping in Scar's room. We left it a complete mess, and as she said, she expected us to fix it. Moving to her little home office, I put my suitcase on the floor next to the futon. Fuck, those things were so uncomfortable, but without Scar, I would not be sleeping in her bed.

It wasn't my style to ignore the fucking walrus, elephant, and rhino in the room. Yep, it was so bad — the whole elephant wouldn't be a good description of what had come between Jordan and me. Though the good doctor would probably camp out in the room he'd been smart enough to grab before I had.

When footsteps stopped at my door, I braced myself for anything. A little knock was all I got. "I'm ordering something. You want Chinese or Italian?"

"Um, how about Thai?" I suggested. It was his favorite, though I was not fond of it. But I was ready to extend an olive branch to this man.

With the door opened slightly, he asked, "Um, can I come in?"

I stayed seated on the uncomfortable futon and looked up at him. Pulling the seat from Scar's perfectly clean desk, he sat. "What are we doing? Did you see her? Not just the fucking bruises, but she was broken."

Yeah, Jordan could hit me a hundred times, and it wouldn't have hurt as much as it had to watch Scar today, ready to kick our asses. She'd put on a tough exterior, but it was evident we had broken her.

I shook my head, looking up at him. "We can't ever do that to her again."

Jordan's elbows were on his knees, his head in his hands. "Yeah, it broke me. I mean, fuck, I did this to her. Sure, it was the both of us, but I started it. Shit, I love her so much."

Watching this man break in front of me hurt, too. "It's hard to watch those you love in pain — regardless of what the pain may be."

Yeah, I said it. It was time to get rid of that fucking rhino, walrus, and elephant and deal with the matter at hand.

A small grin appeared on his face. "Yeah, that was a little underhanded, but I guess I deserved it."

"Jordan." His hand popped up, and he stood quickly. Always so fast to walk away from the tough conversations.

"Listen, it's a conversation that's apparently overdue.

I'm not avoiding it." My eyebrows arched in a silent question. "Okay, I want to avoid it, but I won't. Not after what I saw this did to Red. But if we are going to be honest, truly honest, I need food in my system. And the doctor in me needs to look at your cheek."

It was my time to wave him off. "I had one of the medics look at it today." I paused, walking by him. This tender side of him was one reason I wanted to pull him to me and give him the comfort he needed. Sure, sucking his dick would do it, too, if he would finally give in to what we shared between us. But no, I wanted to hold him. I wanted the hardness of his muscles against my own hardness, feeling that jolly roger of his come to life as only I could bring it. Well, Scar and me, that was.

No, I walked by, clapping him on the shoulder, and that little touch was enough to tell me I did not imagine this. Jordan cared for me as he did with Scar. But the question was would he finally give in to what all three of us knew would break us up if he didn't.

———

An hour later, we had our Thai food along with some much-needed groceries delivered to Scar's apartment. "Um, we need to make a list of all the shit we have to get at Home Depot. I'll borrow a truck from Foster at the firehouse. He's on tomorrow and won't need it."

When I took the vacation days, this was not how I imagined spending my time off. No, we were going to have the entire house on Lake Michigan at our disposal. I had planned on being naked the whole time with lots of sex, lots of fun, and yeah, a fuck ton more of sex. It wasn't in the cards for us.

"Um, I don't know much about home improvement," he admitted, grabbing his food and a soda on his way past me to the couch. "The Cubs are on. Want to watch for a while before we get to the hard part?"

Hard part? It wasn't hard for me. No, I was in love with

the good doctor. There was no doubt in my mind.

"Um, sure." With Jordan on one side of the couch, I planted myself on the other side. The Cubbies were playing the St. Louis Cardinals. I wasn't sure if we'd tear ourselves away from the game. Yeah, those fuckers were our rivals, and I imagined most bars were jam-packed with a ton of people enjoying a brewsky and the game.

"We're up two in the top of the third inning," Jordan began. Yeah, I saw the score the second I sat down, but fuck, what else could he say. And knowing Jordan, turning on the game would give him time to mentally prepare for the talk and the three large as fuck animals still in this apartment of Scar's.

At the bottom of the sixth inning and with the Cubbies up nine to three, I grabbed the remote and turned the TV off. The quick turn of his head and the out and out stare he gave me told me he was still working up the courage to chat.

"Look, we could ignore this all day long. For the next four days, with the time we took off to be with Scar, we could sweep this under the rug. But then we're going to lose her."

He stood but stayed planted. "You told me this was for her." It was the first thing he threw out.

"Yeah, and I meant it at the time." My hands found passage through my hair that was at least three weeks overdue in getting a trim. "But here's the thing. With even the best intentions, I could only be so good." I gave him that panty-melting smile that seemed to work on many women and men alike, but it wouldn't work with him, not this time. "Seriously." I changed my tone. "I'm sorry, but I fell for you like I did with Scar, Doc. I mean, I fell hard."

He turned away, and fuck, I had to battle everything within me not to go to him. "Can you honestly say you don't care for me, not as Scar's other lover but as more?"

He shook his head. "Is that a no, Jordan? In that you mean, you care for me more?"

He turned, his eyes down. "Yeah, you arrogant fuck.

You have affected me more than I care to admit." His admission was not a surprise.

I wouldn't go to him. I wouldn't make that mistake. This had to be all him. "Okay, so what does that mean for us, Jordan? If we don't handle this right, we'll lose Scar, and I can't lose her."

His eyes finally reached mine as I continued, "And losing her would be just as bad as losing you. It's the perfect number, don't you see that? She needs us just as much as we need her. But I need you, too, Doc. We both do. And if I've read it right, you need me, too."

"But what does it mean for me? Am I gay?" Ah, labels, they bit me in the ass every time.

"Why call it anything, Jordan? I mean, love is love. Attraction is attraction, and lust is lust. I feel all three with you, and I don't care. Even my first time with a man was hot and passionate, and I was not expecting it. Hell, I was there to fuck his sister. You know the story. But when she stood me up, and the handsome bastard answered the door and invited me in for a beer, our chemistry was out of this world."

He was still standing, and I was still sitting. The only thing that had changed was his hands were now balled in fists. "I don't want to hear about this." His words were more clipped than normal for the uptight doctor.

"See, the story would not affect you if you didn't care for me." Of course, he admitted it, but I had more of a point to prove. "Yeah, I get it. Hearing about this would be like learning about Scar's sex life before us. I don't want to know."

Jordan was still so quiet. I still had the floor, apparently. "The point I'm trying to make is love is fluid. It's not about body parts and gender for me. I love who I love. And fuck, I love you, Jordan." The second those words were out of my mouth, I regretted them. But he only stared at me.

"Fuck, Jordan, that was not fair. I'm sorry."

He continued to stare at me, but I stood by my decision not to go to him. He had to come to me. Right when I thought he was about to sit down, he took in a long, deep breath and then let it out. "I'm not sure what to do with all of this, Levi."

I stood, turning the other way around the couch that was in the middle of the room. "Well, now it's out there, so do what you will." I walked away. He needed time, and I needed time. Pulling the door behind me, I stood against it, hoping that I did the right thing by laying it all out on the line.

chapter 38

scarlet

I woke the next morning in my bedroom at the lake house with a view of Lake Michigan. It was almost therapeutic until I heard giggles and laughter and moans. Oh, no! Not the moans. I tiptoed out to the living space with my eyes closed.

"Whoever this is, I hope you're here to rob me because if you're having sex, I'm calling the cops." Of course, I knew Elliot's giggles. It was the guys and their gal, but I was confused because they knew I'd be here with my men.

"Oh, shit." Thankfully, the men still had pants on, and Ell had lost her shirt but not her bra. "Fuck, Scar. We didn't see your car here, and I saw Levi today leaving your apartment, so we assumed you all couldn't come." It was then that their faces turned to my cast and then moved to the bruise that was on my face. "What the fuck, Scar? What happened?"

The tears began to fall, and I couldn't stop them. Ell was next to me in a second. Both men were pulling their shirts over their heads. When I looked up, the tic in their jaws told me all I needed to know. Arden had keys in his hands when Daimen and he were almost out the door.

"Stop right there." I didn't have to say the words because Ell had their number. "Before you go kill both Andrew's and my brother, let's figure out what happened."

In a matter of minutes, they had me surrounded on the couch, and I spilled everything to them about Jordan denying his feelings and Levi pushing him. Ell was off the couch. "You two don't have to kill them because I'm about to do it."

Arden pulled at Ell. "Hold on, hot stuff, let's breathe." Based on the pulsing vein on the side of his neck, Arden was not calm either.

"Listen," Daimen started. He could be the voice of reason when he was calm. And surprisingly enough, he was. "Scar, we're pissed, but the question remains, if Jordan doesn't come around, it can't be forced. Sure, he took the first swing, but Levi promised this was for you. And I know a little about what's going on in Levi's mind." He leaned in, placing the sweetest kiss on Arden's cheek. "This stubborn bastard had a hard time coming to grips with it, too." I never tired of seeing the three of them happy as they were. "But I couldn't push him, or we wouldn't have what we have now."

I hadn't realized I'd been crying again until Ell gave me a box of tissues. "And, honey," Daimen in his business-like way continued, "only you can decide if this is worth it, but you do have to know that we aren't going to stand by and watch both men destroy you."

Yep, I understood he'd get to this point eventually, and I had a feeling these brothers of mine would be having a heart to heart with Levi and Jordan.

"I don't want to lose them. But if Jordan isn't willing to be honest, even if Levi backs off, how can we build on this?"

Elliot pulled me into her embrace. "You know what we

need, girl?"

Oh, it was an open-ended question, wasn't it? With one look at the same eyes that her brother had, she turned to her own men. "This calls for a carton of rocky road, butter pecan, moose tracks, and vanilla."

With Elliot's order of ice cream, both men were up, heading to the door when Arden turned around. "Hot stuff, when have you ever been into vanilla?" he teased.

Before she could answer, Daimen replied, "Certainly not in the bedroom." They both high-fived one another and were out the door to get us our creamy calorie-filled goodness. In their comradery, I missed my own men and wondered what they were up to today, and if we'd ever get anywhere close to what these three had. It made my heart ache because I wasn't sure I wanted to know the answer.

chapter 39

jordan

We stayed in our respective rooms last night. I'd gotten a text from my brother first thing in the morning, letting me know Red was safe.

The Ugly Brother: *I'm being generous. I'm still pissed as fuck, but Scar is at the lake house, safe and sound. Leave her alone. Let her work through this.*

Yeah, he was generous. Andrew wasn't known as the hothead in the bunch. That title was left for Kayla and me to share equally. I thanked him as I lay in bed with thoughts clouding my very black and white mind.

My thoughts turned to the man in the other room on that uncomfortable as fuck futon. A smile and a twinge of guilt pricked away at me. Why was this so hard for me? I liked him, his body warmed my own even if we were not physically close, so I was fighting the inevitable. I understood that to give Scar what she needed and deserved, I had to be honest with myself. And I couldn't keep Levi at arm's length either in this scenario. It confused us both, especially after my bitch attack at Dane and Cami's house the other night.

I'd heard the screech of Red's office door and then movement out in the hallway. We needed to get to Home Depot to fix Red's room. Me in Home Depot? I didn't think my hands had ever been used for home repair. Body repair, yes. Bodily enjoyment, hell yes. But home improvement—no. We paid someone to do that stuff. My dad was an accountant, and we were comfortable. My dad knew as much about that shit as I did. He taught me everything he knew about sports yet that stuff, we hated.

Now, I'd be working side by side with him. He probably would be taking off his shirt. Fuck, what if he wore sweats? Oh, shit, the images broke through the clouds messing with my mind, and I was not thinking straight. I was out of bed in my boxers with the door opened, almost sprinting to where he was in the apartment.

When I turned the hallway corner, he was in a pair of jeans with his hands on the coffeepot and doughnuts on the table. He turned to me with a nod to acknowledge I was in the same room. But my eyes were hungry and not for the daily cup of java. When his eyes locked with mine, he put down the coffeepot, the chiseled cheekbones of his begging for something, anything from me.

I stormed over to him like I was pissed. Yeah, I was pissed at myself for letting it get this bad. So bad, we pushed our girl away. "Doc?" It was a question, and I didn't wait to answer him. Closing the space between us, I grabbed him by his shoulders, pulling our faces mere centimeters apart.

"Sorry, morning breath." I was finally about to take the plunge, and those were the words that formed on my lips.

A sweet smile, one where it met his eyes, was what I watched when he merely replied, "I don't give two shits about morning breath." His hands moved to my bare back. "Doc, you sure?"

My fingers moved to his cheeks, those fucking chiseled by the gods sort of cheekbones. I rested my forehead on his. "Yeah," I choked out, stroking the purple bruise on his face.

His emerald greens danced with excitement, yet he waited for me. But at the end of the day, this was still Levi. A wink from him was all it took, and my mouth crashed to his. Our tongues didn't dance. No, that was not the manly thing to do. We dueled for control. His hands were in my hair, and mine were messing with his short blonde curls. His moans made me push further. I couldn't help it when I physically slammed him against the closest wall, causing a picture to crash to the floor. Shit, we had other stuff to fix, so a broken picture was the least of my concerns at the moment.

He pulled away, and I let him. His face … how the fuck had I turned him down for so long? "Doc?"

"Yeah, I'm here. I finally pulled my head out of my ass." I leaned in, kissing his forehead when the sexiest chuckle left his kissable lips.

"Um, I know what I'd like to do with your ass."

I didn't know why that scared me, but it did. The same fire that Red elicited within me, I had with Levi. Before I could say anything, Levi cupped my cheeks. "No reason to rush this, Doc. We can take it slowly." Now, he rested his forehead on mine, and we stayed like this for a while.

I looked down at the broken glass and grinned. "Looks like we have more to replace," I began.

"Yeah, we'll add it to our list." He kissed me one last time. "Doc, we'll go at your pace. But for now, let's get ready so we can fix Scar's room." He released me, and the second he walked around the corner, I missed everything that had captivated me about him.

He'd closed the door behind him to the home office, and I'd collected my clothes, heading to the hallway bathroom. I'd get ready while Levi decompressed from my kiss. The steam from the shower filled the room. I was lost in my own thoughts of how our mouths fused perfectly together, and I needed some sort of release. Through the clear glass, while I stroked my dick, I looked up to see Levi watching me.

"Fuck, Doc, I'm sorry." He turned from me, walking toward the door.

"No, LT. You want a show, I'll give you one." What the fuck had gotten into me? I was horny, and I was daring. Yeah, the first one, I was a lot. But the second one, it normally wasn't me. I turned to the side to give him an easy view as I took the tip of my cock and stroked it just in that area. When I looked in Levi's general direction, he had stripped, his cock in his hands.

"This okay with you, Doc?"

I nodded, continuing to watch him as I worked the tip of my own. "Yeah, as long as you watch me the entire time." Sure, I was bossy, but this was so unlike me. A large smile covered Levi's face.

"Yeah, Doc, you watching me won't be a problem." His tone was low and controlled, and his eyes were on me, every part of me.

With my hands squeezing my balls, I moved my fingers up and down my shaft. Levi was not trying to be quiet. His moan, groans, and sometimes whistles had me so turned on, I didn't think I'd last much longer. And I didn't. My orgasm came on so quickly and so thunderous, I took my eyes from Levi. When I'd finally drained everything within me, I looked at him, his eyes hungry for my own. Fuck, I wanted him. But he nodded, winked one last time at me, and then gave me the privacy I required to right my thoughts. Shit, this would be an excruciatingly hard day.

chapter 40

levi

Holy fuck, we just jacked off together. I watched him explode. There was so much cum that if it had been blood, I would have thought someone died.

I left him to his demons. I'd be there for him, but he needed to work this out on his own. I hadn't planned to go to him, but when I walked by the door, I saw it was cracked. I wasn't sure if it was an open invitation, so I peeked in quickly, and I couldn't look away at him jacking off. I'd hoped our kiss had been the inspiration he needed to unload.

But there was so much more I wanted from him, and I couldn't spook him. There was too much riding on this, and fuck, we both needed our redhead seductress back in our lives. She was our everything. I missed her so much.

I'd walked to the kitchen to grab my cell I'd forgotten

about after the mind-blowing kiss. Picking it up to look at some instructional videos on drywall repair, I saw a text message from my sister.

Opening it up, my heart fell. At her name, which my sister had programmed in on her own, I knew I was in trouble.

Twinnie: *If you don't think there will be words about what you did to Scar, you're fucking wrong. My men are fucking pissed. YOU HAVE BEEN WARNED.*

What in the world? They knew we were going to be taking over the lake house for the next several days for our own sex-capades. But they were up there? How? Well, I guess logistics aside, I'd be pissed if anyone hurt Elliot like we'd hurt Scar. And since Scar was technically their little sister, we had it coming.

Me: *Is she okay?*

Twinnie: *We are drowning our sorrows in some rocky road, butter pecan, and moose tracks with a side of vanilla. We saw you this morning with doughnuts and thought you all had stayed at home. When the security firm did a drive-by and there were no cars, we assumed we'd have a nice romantic night at the lake house. So my guys are doubly pissed that Scar, of all people, walked in on our sexy times.*

Yeah, I could have lived never knowing about my sister's sexy times or what they called it.

Me: *But is she okay?*

My sister still hadn't answered my question.

Twinnie: *Fuck, Levi, I don't know. She's proud, having lived through a complete shit life. She's scared of losing you. But you two screwed up. Fuck, I'm too pissed off to even text you. Just know, I'd watch your back. Daimen and Arden don't take kindly to their kid sister being hurt.*

I knew that was all I'd get from my twin. I placed the phone down to look up into the dark eyes of the good doctor.

With a pair of jeans slung low on his hips, his face met mine.

"What's wrong?" His question was sincere.

"It was my sister. They didn't think we were at the lake house, so they went up there. Scar woke to them ... well, I don't need to know what she saw. Daimen and Arden saw her injuries, and if Ell doesn't kick my ass, I'm sure Arden and Daimen have dibs. Or maybe they'll take turns."

I poured him a cup of coffee while he sat on a barstool on the other side of the island. Placing the cream in front of him, I grabbed a stool near the wall and sat down in front of him.

"We fucked up bad, Doc. Really bad."

"I know." His face fell, but this wasn't all on him.

"You know, I meant it when I said this was supposed to be for Scar. I did; it was, well, my feelings for you multiplied each day we shared her. I wouldn't have shared Scar with anyone, but I couldn't deny you. It would be like telling my stomach I wasn't going to feed it for a month. Instinct would have kicked in, making me eat. It was what my love for you did. It took over."

Those words were out of my mouth before my mind processed what I had just said.

"Shit, Jordan ..."

He grabbed my hand. "Levi, I'm not shocked. I mean, I'm not sure how I feel about you. Telling you I love you, I don't think I can do it at this point, but fuck, these feelings are intense. I know it's deep 'cause they are like the ones I have for Red."

"So what do we do?" I asked, lost for once on how to fix this.

"Well, first, we fix Red's room. Then we wait for her like she asked. Until then, maybe we can hash this out between us."

His hand was still in mine. "Yeah, Doc, I like this plan — very much."

chapter 41

scarlet

One day was all I could handle with this threesome hovering over me like I was an invalid. This group was driving me crazy. At eight p.m., I'd finally had enough and retreated to my room.

I stared at my phone as if it was going to talk to me or read my mind. After a couple of minutes, I said screw it and placed a FaceTime call to Jordan. I needed to know if they were still together at my house, or if they'd caused more damage to my place and to my heart.

"Hey," I said the second both men came into view. They were still together, and it looked like they were eating on my couch. Pizza maybe.

"Scar." Levi's voice wasn't his normal confident tone. No, I'd scared him, and he was a little insecure of this call. I could see it in his face. "Fuck, Scar. Look at your bruise." It had turned purple, and though it hurt, it looked worse.

"Red, honey." I heard in Jordan's voice how fearful he, too, was. But what I hadn't missed was how close they were sitting. Sure, they both wanted to be in the screen so I could see them, but it was almost intimate how their bodies touched.

"I need to come home. I don't want to avoid this, not anymore. We need to face our future together." My words surprised me, especially after the ultimatum, but after a couple of days without them, I needed to embrace these two. I wasn't sure what our future held, but I'd fight for them, for both of them.

"We can come get you." It was Jordan. He was always my man of action.

"No, I'll be home in the morning. Just stay and wait for me." I didn't want to be away from them anymore.

"Yeah, okay, Scar. We'll see you tomorrow." Levi waved at me, and I ended the call. I never had a choice in foster care, but I had a choice now, and I'd do anything to make it happen.

chapter 42

jordan

Red was coming home. I wondered if she noticed how close we were. How our shoulders touched or the change in my stance. Sure, we'd spent the whole day together, though he did most of the hard lifting. And hell, something inside me shifted. The man, this man was hot, so very hot. The way his hard muscles rippled with all the hammering and heavy equipment he'd been in charge of. I acted like I was working, but I wasn't. I was watching him.

And it was freeing to finally admit what I had been fighting for the past several weeks. Levi's face was near me, at that moment, though his mouth was full of a Chicago deep dish pie from Vinny's. "Can you believe it? She wants to come back home."

He grabbed my face and brought it close to his. "Yeah,

we're being given a second chance. Our girl is coming back to us. I don't want to push you, but we gotta sort this out. I mean, we don't need to have it all figured out, but fuck, Jordan—she's coming home."

It might not have been a physical home that we shared with Red, but she was our home. He leaned over to take a swig of his beer. I did, too, in order to wash down the pie. We hadn't kissed, not since the morning, but we'd been close, an ease to us we hadn't shared in the past.

He turned his body from me for a moment, getting comfortable. Turning off the game that had been on, he stared at me. "So," he began.

"So," I replied, my eyes narrowing in on him. "I guess you want to know what this is?" I pointed at him and me.

"We don't need labels. Don't overthink this, Doc." I could feel the color drain from my face.

"Yeah, okay, let me get out of my mind." I stopped to gather my thoughts. "I'm scared, Levi. I won't deny it. I'm my own worst nightmare."

In the past, I'd pushed the idea of intimacy with Levi from my mind. I was accepting it when he leaned his head against mine in the most intimate of gestures.

"Just let me love you, Doc, and the rest will fall into place." I nodded my head, and it was all the permission he needed. He pushed me back to lie against the couch, straddling me. "This doesn't have to go any further but let me feel your body. Let me taste all of you."

I give him a little nod of my head, and when I thought his mouth would crash to mine, it took a detour, working toward my neck. He licked me, kissed me, and sucked on my shoulders while his hand roamed my inner thigh. It stayed put, not moving further. I wanted it farther north. I needed him to touch me and touch me there.

"It's okay, Levi. It's okay to explore."

He pulled his head from my neck. "Hell, baby, that's all the permission I need." His fingers were the first to reach my shaft after they worked them down the elastic of my boxers.

I took a deep breath just because his touch differed so much from Red. I could feel his calloused fingers, but they felt unbelievable against my cock. When he wrapped his hand around the length of me, I stopped breathing. Shit, this was beyond my wildest pleasures.

"Do you like that, baby?" Oh, where to begin. First, I loved him calling me baby. And sure as the night sky sparkled with stars, it felt fan-fucking-tastic.

"SHIT, don't stop. Make me come."

His hand stilled for a second as though he had something to say. "Wanna come on my hand or in my ass?" My eyebrows hitched at his dare. "Ah, shit, Jordan, forget I said that."

I sat up, pulling his hand from my cock. "No, are you serious? You'd give me that?" I asked.

His hands worked my cheeks, cupping them tight, bringing me into his gaze. "Shit, baby, I've wanted you to claim my ass from the second I saw you. Fuck, Jordan. I love you, and I need you. But if you aren't ready, I get it. We can slow this down."

I was sitting up when I pulled him from the couch into my arms. "If we do this, we do it right. Not on the couch. Let's be comfortable." I extended my hand to him and pulled him with me to the bedroom I'd been staying in.

He stopped me at the door. "You okay with this, baby?" His tenderness showed me he was a sweet lover.

"Yeah, I'm surprisingly more than okay with it. Make love to me, Levi. Break me in. Show me how you can love me."

In the doorway of my room at Red's place, I stilled, waiting for his reply.

chapter 43

levi

Was this for real? Early on, Scar had told me if there was a chance with him, just the two of us, to take it if it seemed right. She'd never be jealous of what we had. No, she wanted it for us.

"I'll love you so good. I'll teach you everything I know. I'll make it good for you, but now, I'll show you how to make it good for me—for the both of us."

His lips didn't crash on mine. No, they started at my forehead as he trailed kisses down my face, then to my neck and over my shoulder blades. He kissed both my nipples, working his tongue over them as he kneeled, grabbing my cock for the first time.

"Fuck, yeah, taste me. Have your way with me." My words seemed to give him permission.

As he licked my tip, I would try to burn this sensation into my memory. A hiss escaped his own mouth, and I continued to be happy by all of this. "Just a little, Doc."

"You got it," he said, pulling from me for a second. "Fuck, you taste good." I'd been with enough men in my life to know their taste was so vividly different than a woman's. I'd wondered if he, too, was noticing the stark difference.

After he deep throated me a couple of times, I needed him in me and now.

He stood, letting me taste myself on him. "I need you now," I demanded. I leaned in and kissed him. "Hold that thought, babe. I'll be right back." We needed something, and though Scar had it in her top drawer, I had been carrying this in my duffle bag that I shuffled from Scar's place to Jordan's condo.

He was waiting on the bed, his eyes instantly locking on the items in my hand. "Prepared?" he questioned.

"Yeah, more like hopeful." Jordan had taken Scar's ass before, so he knew what to do. Throwing him a condom, he smiled. I crawled in close to him, and started, "Babe, I want you so badly, but if you're not ready, I'll wait. Please tell me."

"I want you." It was all Jordan said when I rolled over to my stomach. "Levi, no, I want to see you, see your face when I enter you."

He was giving himself to me. Hell, my heart was so full of love for this man. I loved him; there was no doubt in my mind.

"Not sure I can be gentle," he warned.

It was one thing I loved about being with a man. With our bodies an even match, he could be rough with me and not worry about hurting me. I could get off on rough in a matter of seconds, too.

"Do what you like, Doc. Take me, I'm yours."

Jordan stilled, and I worried I'd overstepped when he asked, "Fuck, are we cheating on Red?"

Ah, he thought of Scar through this all, and it only

confirmed why I loved him. "No, Doc. We're fine. It was something we discussed. She told me if the time came, to have at it."

A smile spread on his face. "Really? Why am I not surprised? I think stopping right now would kill me."

I pulled him down to me and kissed him, but this time, I let him have the control. "Fuck, Levi, I never thought it could be this way. I'm sorry I fought you." The good doctor was going to psych himself out if he thought of the past.

"Doc, please fuck me. Take me and shut up—get out of your mind." I stopped briefly and added, "Please, baby, please take me now."

He pushed his tip into me, his way of stretching me out. "It's okay; don't be gentle." With that, he pushed into me so hard and so quick, but I welcomed the wonderful intrusion. "Fast, take me fast."

"Working on it, LT! You are so tight and feel so ..." He paused to lock eyes on me. "Shit, Levi, you feel fucking amazing."

"I love you inside me." My response was brief because it was all I was able to choke out.

Our connection was more than sex. Hell, I saw it and read it plain as day on his face. He was fucking me, yes, but he was making love to me at the same time.

After one more deep thrust, he yelled out my name as he came, and I let loose on his stomach. I didn't care that we were a sticky mess. I pulled him onto the bed and into the sheets and held on tight until his breathing changed. I was sleeping next to Jordan after we made love. Shit, the only thing missing was Scar, and she'd be between us tomorrow. Everything had changed but in the best fucking possible way.

chapter 44

scarlet

I couldn't wait. I was wide-awake at five a.m. If I left in the next hour, I'd be back by nine a.m. in time to talk to them over a plate of flapjacks. No, they weren't pancakes. No one better ever call my flapjacks fucking pancakes.

I was nervous; the voices in my head always got a bit cranky when I was both nervous and sleep deprived. Plus, I was positive Ell and her men wanted all five thousand square feet of this place to themselves.

I'd grabbed my suitcase and took one of the cars that the boys kept up here, just in case, and headed toward Chicago and to my guys. I wondered what they had done. Hell, they looked so cute last night, huddled together.

Logistics floated through my mind, and I wondered if someone had slept in my room or if they'd fixed the damage they caused. Had they kissed? My nipples hardened, and a warmth radiated between my legs at the thought. Was someone sleeping in the spare room? Did one of the guys take the uncomfortable as fuck futon in my office?

So many images filled my brain. And for once, I let the memories of my mom and dad dance around in my mind. It wasn't the life that had been stripped from me of them being my parents. No, it was the good memories. My dad showing me how to fish. He was determined to make me a sailor in one way or another. Or the times my mom taught me to cook. Her specialty was baking, but she began showing me around the kitchen at an early age.

My future, or my ideas of a future with my men, gave me hope. Before Daimen and Arden took me into their fold, I'd had lonely Christmases and birthdays. It should have been any kid's fantasy to wake with the knowledge and spirit that should have encompassed these two days. Sure, it would have been fun to have gifts to open, even if it was just a few like I had with my parents. Or smelling my birthday cake baking or helping my mom with the turkey or driving around looking at lights. It's all stuff the kids in school talked about after Christmas. And the stories they told about the birthday parties their parents threw for them physically hurt me. I wanted it all so much growing up. I didn't have it, but I'd have it with Levi and Jordan. One day, we'd have a family, and I'd be able to give our kids everything I never had. In that hope, my future would make up for my shitty childhood. With Jordan and Levi, I'd have the happily ever and never have to think about what I missed as a child.

In no time, all the beautiful memories of my parents and the future I had with my men entertained me through the drive, and I found myself navigating the streets of Chicago. I pulled into my parking garage before I knew it. I left my suitcases in the car and hurried to my apartment. I had no idea how I'd find them, but without a doubt, I know they'd be there waiting for me.

chapter 45

jordan

The room was pitch black, and I was in a haze, my eyes barely adjusting in the darkness. But when I felt a strong arm wrap around my waist, I bolted from the bed and opened the blinds just enough to give me an indication of where I was and what I had done.

It was a good thing Levi slept like the dead. I sat and looked at him as his chest rose and fell. I couldn't get out of my own mind. He was beautiful and tender, then rough, and then tender again. It was more than I had hoped for, and in my heart, I was already breaking for what I knew I needed to do. All my stuff was nice and neat next to the door. I grabbed it, closing it behind me after taking one last look at Levi. He had the gentlest of snores, and he looked so sexy with just a sheet draped over his body.

The idea of him naked with his cock that had come so hard made me want to wake him and let him have his way with me. I closed the door lightly, moving out to the living space.

I sat down on the table where just a couple of weeks ago, Levi had fucked Red so hard as she sucked my cock at the same time. I'd never felt a part of something like I did with them. So why was I doing this? When I freaked out, I left. It was what led me overseas to begin with. There was this girl who wanted more from me than I was willing to give at the time, so I up and left her. The saying, "When the going gets tough, the tough get going," was meant for me.

With a pen in my hand and a piece of paper on the table, I wrote:

Levi,

I'm not sure why I'm doing this. Part of me wants to wake you up and go at it again. And then this part, the one that is winning, feels like a chicken shit to let you wake alone. But I just need a second to catch my breath. I love you, and I've denied it for weeks. But I can't see how my constant fear of accepting that I'm bisexual at some level will ever be good for the three of us. Please take care of Red. I'll be out of town for the next couple of days, so come by and grab your stuff at the apartment then. I will never forget what you and I shared. I don't regret it, not ever, but Red needs more than I can give, and you're the guy for it.

Jordan

Looking at the time, I see it was five a.m., and the sun would be rising soon. I'd get back to the house just in time to grab a couple more changes of clothes and then I'd be out of the apartment and to our family cabin in Northern Illinois by the time Levi woke.

My brother would know where I was hiding, but for now, I needed to wrap my head around all of this. With the fear and hurt that had coursed through Red's eyes the day she left us to figure this out, I was selfish to let my inner desires win.

She needed us and only us for her. Could I get back to where we'd been? Until I could accept this, I needed time. I only hoped he would take care of Red while I did.

chapter 46

levi

I was typically a happy guy. But when I woke, my grin was like the fucking Joker from Batman. Shit, I'd fallen asleep with Jordan in my arms. Turning to the clock, I caught the time — 8:44. Grabbing for my phone, I smiled at Scar's text.

Redhead Seductress: *Got on the road early. Took one of the guys' cars. Will be back by nine.*

We had sixteen minutes to get coffee brewing and take a shower. Maybe, just maybe, we could save some time by catching a quick one together. This time, I'd suck him all the way dry.

Jordan was an early bird, so I wasn't surprised to wake up without him. He was probably at the gym or catching up on last night's game neither one of us cared to watch. For both Jordan and I, very few things were less important than our

Cubbies, but sex and Scar were the two things at the top of our list.

I'd hope that Scar would forgive us right away, then we could get to the business at hand of being together at the same time. I wasn't sure Jordan was ready for me to claim his ass, but if he was, he was going to experience one of the best days of sex ever. He'd be in Scar as I was in him. But fuck, if he wasn't, then I'd give him my ass again, and he could fuck me as I fucked our redhead seductress.

It was quiet in the room. The asshole was showing me up by getting to the gym first thing, apparently. As I rounded the corner, my eyes fell on the coffeemaker. The overachiever could have at least made me a pot of coffee before he left.

Something caught my attention on the table. Ah, my man had left me a note, telling me where he went. Maybe he was getting us coffee and breakfast in time for Scar's arrival.

Picking up the note, I read the first line and let the paper fall to the floor. He'd left. Nothing else mattered. My heart was racing a million miles a minute when the lock of the door twisted, and I waited for someone to appear. I needed it to be Jordan, telling me he'd realized his mistake. If he'd done this before Scar returned home, I could forgive him, but the second I had to tell Scar her number one fear of being abandoned had come to fruition, I wasn't sure I could ever forgive him even though I loved this fucker as much as I did Scar.

Reaching around the door was my gorgeous redhead seductress. She was a sight for sore eyes, but fuck, in her smile, she'd been working on the same false hope I had. "LT," she boomed, dropping her purse and throwing herself into my arms.

She kissed my cheek and pulled back. "Fuck, I missed you. By last night's phone call, I could tell things were better between you and Jordan." She looked around me and then back my way. "Where is the good doctor?" Her voice was low and breathy. She'd seen our closeness last night before I'd made love to him. Now I wanted to kill him.

I let her out of my embrace. Reaching down to grab the note, the one he'd woken up early to write while leaving me in bed to wake by myself, I gave it to her. What a chicken shit, I thought about Jordan, being the one to hurt our girl.

"Um, I don't understand. You two were together last night, and then he just up and left you?" The tears were already forming in her eyes as her cheeks flushed.

"Yeah, I told him I loved him, and he said the same to me." I'd had my hand on her hip, and she pulled out of my embrace so quick. "Scar ..."

"Fucking save it." She looked away from me as if she planned to retreat, but in a split second, she was back in my face. "You told me this was for me. When you suggested this, you promised us that you wouldn't push and look at what you did."

I closed my eyes because I couldn't bear to look at her. "Scar, he does love me. He's just scared."

"I'm not fucking blind. I saw it, but no, you had to go and push with your words and your actions. This is because you couldn't keep your promise." She pointed at her wrist, the one with the cast on it. "And you kept on and kept on. I thought it would happen naturally. But even I came to bat for you a couple of times because you were so cocky about it. Fuck ..." She looked down at the letter. "Don't think for one second Jordan gets off scot-free. I get it, Levi. He fucked you and ran. You should be mad. Shit, I'm angry for you." Her compassion gave me false hope for one second, but then her red-rimmed eyes looked up at me. "But in the long run, you broke your promise to me." She studied the letter a bit more, pointing to the last part. "And this right here ..." She choked up. "Take care of Red. This won't fucking happen. Don't you see that? It's the three of us, and if we can't have three, we have nothing." She crumpled up the paper, tossing it right in my face.

I stepped forward to offer her some sort of comfort or even solace, but she swung her arms around, making it impossible to do so. "Get the hell away from me." She leaned up against the wall, and though I wouldn't be gathering my things, I'd abide by her wish. Grabbing my wallet and my keys from her kitchen table, I made my way to the door. I turned around to say I was sorry, but I couldn't utter the words. I watched as Scar slid down the wall into a heap on the floor, and my whole body ached. This was my fault; she wasn't wrong.

chapter 47

scarlet

He closed the door behind him, and it was then I became that same little girl who'd just been told her parents died. It was just like yesterday, and I could even sense Miss Maizie trying to pick me up off the ground. I wasn't sure how much time passed until I was actually picked up off the floor this time. In his aroma, I knew it wasn't Jordan or Levi. Through the tears that had blurred my vision, I saw it was Andrew.

"Scar, honey, I got you, I got you, sweetheart." He murmured something else under his breath, some sort of slew of curse words. "Shit, honey, what the hell did they do to you, again?"

I was on his lap, on the couch, and I hadn't stopped crying. I fell asleep at one point, and when I woke, I was sprawled out on the sofa with a fucking bunch of people quietly chatting behind me like this was some sort of intervention.

As I sat up, Arden was at my side in a second. "Didn't I just leave you at the lake house?" It was the first thing that popped in my head and formed on my lips.

"Yep, but, Scar, when you need us, we'll be there for you, regardless." He enveloped me in his arms. As he released me, I turned to see Ell, Daimen, Andrew, and Brock at my table with a pot of coffee. Looking outside, it was dark already. How long had I slept?

Standing, I made my way to the table, a little lightheaded. Grabbing the couch to steady myself, my stomach began to growl. The traitor didn't know I was dealing with heartache. I couldn't feed her yet. Ell stood, grabbing Andrew and Brock.

"Hey, boys, let's run down to the Italian eatery nearby and get Scar some food." I didn't want her to go because she was the voice of reason with Arden and Daimen, and right then, by the look in their eyes, they were ready to murder a fireman and a doctor. With the rage coming from both of them, they'd probably be able to do it with their bare hands.

After I sat down, Arden rummaged through my fridge and brought me some carrots to snack on. "Here, you must be starving. We can't have you fainting on us, sis, or we'd really go kill some men." Those words came from Arden, who was normally the calmer of the two.

"Listen, guys," I began, crunching down on a carrot. "I understand you're pissed on my behalf, but I've got this. I've survived a breakup before, and I'll survive again."

Daimen, who'd remained quiet from his seat, pulled at my arm from across the table. Giving it a squeeze, he still had not lost his solemn look. "But here's the thing, Scar, you don't have to go through this on your own."

A thought popped in my head, and it made me giggle, welcoming the distraction to this fucked-up situation. "Could you two at least promise me that you won't go after Levi and Jordan like you did with Jefferey?"

This made both men smile, too. After my boyfriend strung me along for years and left me in bad shape after I found out he'd cheated on me, both of my surrogate brothers set out to get even with him. They'd ruined his credit, and the house he was about to close on didn't go through. Plus, with the type of job he'd applied to, a CFO of a major pharmaceutical company, the ruined credit was a red flag, and the company rescinded their offer. I'd, of course, only recently found out about all of this. I thought it was funny, and honestly, I was honored they loved me so much to destroy the guy who had ruined me for so many years. But as much as I hated both Levi and Jordan, I still very much loved them, too.

"Can't make any promises, Scar," Daimen replied. "But we will try," he relented. I was sure it worked in Levi's favor that both these men in front of me loved his twin sister fiercely.

"So let me have it," I began, still letting the carrots calm my angry stomach.

Daimen and Arden sat near one another, holding hands, while Daimen still had my hand interlaced with his. "Scar, we're just worried ... and pissed off at Jordan and Levi but more so worried about you," Arden started. "We saw what Jefferey did to you, and hell, we never liked that man, so it wasn't hard to protect you. But we honestly adore both Jordan and Levi and thought this was a good fit." He looked down at his reflection in my deep cherry oak table. Still not looking at me, he finally asked what everyone wanted to know. "So what happened? Last night, you thought they'd gotten close?"

I didn't know how much to disclose, but hell, I was tired of not being able to discuss it. I needed to dissect it to understand better. Finally, I replied, "They slept together. No, more than that, they made love to each other. Jordan finally admitted he loved Levi, so it was more than a fuck. But Jordan let himself get into his mind and ran. He left Levi a Dear John note, telling him to take care of me." The tears fell on my table, but I didn't wipe them away. "Now that I've had them both, I can't choose, nor do I want to."

Arden and Daimen gave each other a knowing look. "We get it, Red. We wondered if we'd make it through losing Elliot. Sure, we had a firm foundation already before Elliot had become a fixture in our life," Arden started, "but I questioned if we'd make it through losing Ell. Thank fuck we didn't have to."

Daimen stood, wrapping me in his strong brotherly arms. "We're here for you, Scar, always." He leaned around me, dropping a kiss on my cheek. Again, I cried in his arms, and because it was Daimen and Arden, it felt natural letting it all out with them in my presence.

***

Whatever Andrew and Ell bought for me, some sort of calzone, was not sitting well on my stomach. I woke the next morning, knowing I needed some kind of distraction to keep my mind off the two men who'd broken my heart. As I rolled out of bed, I rushed to the bathroom, tossing the shit from last night in the toilet. Fuck, on top of a broken heart, food poisoning was now messing with me. Shit, this was the last thing I needed. As I stood, after tossing my cookies or calzone, so to speak, I barely made it back to bed. I was dizzy, and all of a sudden, I was exhausted. Placing my head on the pillow, I didn't have time to worry about the future because sleep claimed me right away.

chapter 48

jordan

I'd stopped to get ingredients for mac and cheese. Oh, and beer, a fuck ton of beer. Maybe that would numb my pain. The second I got to the cabin, my phone didn't stop. I'd had several texts, but nothing from the two people I knew I was putting through hell.

The ugly brother: *You are a chicken shit, you know that? I held YOUR girl as she cried herself to sleep. Since her parents died, being abandoned is her worst nightmare.*

Yeah, I was a chicken shit. There was no better word to describe me.

Arden Blakely: *You and I need to have a talk, but I'm not sure you're ready for what I have to say to you yet. But running away only hurts those you love, and fuck, stop denying yourself the love you deserve, too. Right now, the only thing I feel you deserve – is a* *beatdown for hurting my sister. She was our girl first, don't fucking forget it, so yeah, you have me and Daimen to contend with.*

Arden's was undoubtedly the longest, but it didn't stop. I'd known Elliot for years, and her text affected me, too.

Elliot: *I don't think I've ever been more disappointed in you than I am now. Somewhere, deep down inside of me, I'm trying to understand because I was there, too, when Arden and Daimen both pursued me, but you walked out, left a Dear John letter, and left Scar like every other man has. How could you?*

But when the last text came in from Daimen, I couldn't take anymore.

Daimen Torano: *You ran. You left. She's destroyed.*

It was the last message that did me in the most. Red was destroyed, at my hands. I wasn't sure I'd ever forgive myself.

———

Fishing was the one thing in this world that brought me peace and comfort. I'd been in my own world when footsteps alerted me that I was no longer alone. I'd expected to look over at my brother.

Nope, when a man in boots and jeans sat next to me, it wasn't my brother. It was another man I loved in a very different and very genuine way.

He said nothing as his legs dangled over the dock like mine. He had a Chicago Bears ball cap on and a lightweight jacket. October was cold up north, especially on the lake. My pole was extended, and we sat in silence a good ten minutes.

His touch was quick and effective, his hand reaching my knee. I tried to ignore it. Tried was the key word.

His hand remained on my knee, but we didn't say a word. After about an hour without one bite on the line, I packed it up. I hadn't expected to catch anything with it being so cold, but fishing always calmed me. Levi even held his hand out and pulled me up. Of course, as he did, I was right in his face, his eyes beckoning me to break the silence. I couldn't look at him, not for a second, but he drew me into his embrace and his warmth.

"I need you to know how much I truly miss you." I nodded my head in his direction.

When I thought he'd follow me into the cabin, he walked to his truck, started it up, and backed out of the little makeshift driveway my dad had installed for this cabin years ago. I turned and watched as he shifted his little pickup truck out of reverse to drive and sped away.

Did he really come all this way just to tell me he missed me? Yeah, he did, but more so, he left so as not to pressure me. It was then I realized I missed his touch, too. Shit, I missed Red and his touch so fucking much.

Waking the next day, I grabbed my duffle bag and headed to my car, leaving the place where I came to get clarification. I found it, but I wasn't sure what I'd do with it. Not yet.

chapter 49

levi

It took a lot to get Andrew to give me Jordan's whereabouts. "I'm just as pissed at him as you are, but he needs time, so give it to him," he'd insisted. Yet I had to make sure he was okay. Even if I saw him for a moment, the two-hour drive was worth it.

After I parked my beat-up truck in the garage kitty-corner from my building, I'd tried to unlock my door, only for it to be unlocked already. Opening the door slightly, I'm met face-to-face with one of the scariest motherfuckers I know when he was angry. And because he'd been waiting at my place for only God knew how long, I braced myself for the worst.

"How's Scar?" I asked, grabbing two sodas from my refrigerator. I'd asked my sister this same question many times, and her only reply was you don't deserve to know.

But with Daimen Torano, I was positive I'd get the same response.

I handed a soda to him, and he took a long swig. Putting it down on the end table, he turned squarely at me. "How do you want me to answer this question, Levi? She's a fucking mess. What did you expect?"

I took a deep breath. Of course, he was pissed at me. "I know. I'm not sure what to say, Daimen. This got out of hand, so quick."

His fingers raked through his thick black hair. "Yeah, because you pushed. You couldn't leave well enough alone. Even when Andrew wanted you to decompress, leaving Jordan to be, you went half-cocked to confront him."

He was wrong on this. If I had gone up there half-cocked, I would have followed Jordan into the cabin. I would have pushed him up against the wall, laying claim to his ass as I made him admit I owned his heart, too. But no, I walked to my truck after my question was answered. He was okay, and that was what I'd set out to do.

"I honestly needed to make sure he was all right. We didn't even speak. We sat in silence." He shook his head.

"Well, you can't keep doing what you've done. You have made no progress with him. And I will tell you what, if you hurt Scar again, brother or no brother to Elliot, you and I will have problems."

He stood, taking one last sip of his soda. "I understand wanting him so bad it aches, but right now, Scar has gotten herself so sick she can barely peel herself out of her bed, so back off. I know it's a fucking cliché, but if you love them, set them free. If they come back, they loved you, and if they don't, they were never yours." In his parting words, I understood how much truth was packed into them. So. Much. Fucking. Truth.

When I arrived for my shift the next day, Garner was waiting for me in the common area. "When you have a second, I pulled together all your old cases, and I want to go over each one." He pointed at his iPad. It does beat going through tons of boxes.

"Wait for me in my office, and I'll be there soon." My men had been on edge since hearing through the grapevine about the note found near the fire and how I was the target. It had not been the right time to share with Scar or Jordan about the threat to my life. I didn't keep it from them on purpose, but between Scar kicking me out and Jordan not saying a word to me up at his cabin, I hadn't had a chance to tell them.

Ell had barely spoken to me. However, she'd at least responded to my last text telling me Scar had been sick. They believed it was an emotional breakdown. I wanted to go to her, but Elliot said between Daimen, Arden, and herself, they had forbidden it.

After the turnover, I met Garner in my office with two cups of bad firehouse coffee. Sitting down, I went through record after record of my previous cases, stilling at a file from the call that still haunted me.

I was a rookie in my first year, and I'd officially started seeing Cami and Dane, together. I'd left from their apartment for my shift. I was so green, so inexperienced, and when we got to the house, a young woman was trapped. The father and brother attempted to run back into the house. I tackled the brother because it was suicide to attempt the rescue. The whole time, the brother screamed for his father and sister, and all we could do was watch the flames engulf his home. I got it; if it were Ell, I would have done anything to protect her, yet my goal at that moment was to protect the almost grown man so he'd have a future. I never saw him again. He only yelled at me, but his face was so full of smoke, I was glad his features were never ingrained in my mind. As I looked back at the file, a memory assaulted me. His exact words were, "One day, brother, Karma will get you." It was the voice that hit me like a punch to the gut. In the here and now, the tone rang in my head like a face I had just recognized.

Taking the iPad from Garner, I went back, looking further into the files. "The Cassie Deckland case, I think we have something." He pulled his phone from his pocket and called someone, asking for the case from the evidence locker. Arson had never been ruled out, and the Aurora police had it.

"I don't care," he almost growled into the phone. "Get it rushed over to me and get more digital records."

I grabbed for my mobile phone but remembered placing it down during turnover in the large conference room. I searched through the case file, trying to get a glimpse of the young man, and at the very end of everything that had been downloaded to digital records years ago, my heart stopped. I knew this kid. In the file, it said his name was Kevin Deckland, but I knew him as Kevin Driscol, the other lieutenant who took over for me after my shift. I stood, my hands shaking as I pushed myself from my seat. "Fucking son of a bitch, I got it. I figured it out."

My first thoughts were for those I loved. Understanding the fucking nutcase Kevin was, I feared for those I called my own.

chapter 50

scarlet

Daimen and Arden insisted I see a doctor. After a couple of days, I wondered if it was more than just stress. Their trusted doctor, Dr. Serrin, was on call at the hospital, and he worked me in. After the appointment and my mind and a fuck ton of other things, I was not paying attention on my way through the tight corridor and ran smack dab into someone. Looking up, out of the thousands of people who came and went from Mercy daily, I saw Jordan.

"Red," he started, grabbing for my hand, but I quickly yanked it away. "Hell, Red, I'm so sorry."

"Yeah, yeah." I turned, trying to give myself space. I couldn't look Jordan in the eyes.

"Red, wait!" he yelled after me, attempting to sidestep me. "Did you get it, too?"

I stopped. I was dizzy, queasy, oddly enough hungry, and fucking pissed off. With my hair color, it was a lethal combination. "What?"

"Levi texted me." He stood in my space. "He needs to see us. Something about the case. He fears we're in danger."

I rummaged through my phone, pulling up the messages.

My Hot Fireman: *I know you need time, and I get it. But you and Jordan are in danger. Meet me at a place I know you'll be safe.*

Jordan showed me his text, which was basically the same message. "I just found another physician to cover for me. I'll drive." He pulled at my hand, but I still yanked it away. In danger or not, I could still be fucking pissed at these men. And I was just that.

Levi was not the only one blowing up my phone. Elliot was, too.

Elliot: *What did the doctor say?*

Me: *I will tell you when I'm back. Levi needs to see Jordan and me.*

I powered off my phone because I couldn't handle her twenty questions. In the car, we said nothing at first, then I had to know. "Where did you go after you left that chicken shit letter for Levi to find?" I didn't try to hide my disgust with my tone.

"My family cabin." He was quick and to the point.

Looking out at the streets of Chicago, I only continued, "You didn't stay long."

I was attempting to bait him, make him mad with my tone and my harsh words. Something that would get him to explain this all to me. "Yeah, leaving didn't solve the problem."

"You mean, leaving Levi to wake up without you after you shared a night of passion or leaving the city, yet another person I loved abandoning me!" I was yelling, and I wouldn't be dialing it down.

He raked his hand through his hair, and replied, "Both, I guess." He didn't say more, not when we arrived at the address. "I guess this is it," he continued, getting out of the car. It was an old warehouse. It was something that looked like it could be refurbished, similar to the building he lived in now. I didn't think it was odd. After all, a safe place was inconspicuous, and that certainly was what this old building was.

chapter 51

levi

I found my phone in the conference room where I had stopped earlier to talk to Matt Shirley. Garner was already in with my chief as I looked at all my texts, still reeling from the revelation that Kevin Driscol was the man behind the fires.

Before I had a chance to call Scar, Jordan, or my sister, the phone rang in my hand. Picking it up, I began, "Ell, I was about to call you."

"Forget that for one second. Do you know where Scar is?" she demanded.

"Um, no. Why, what do you mean? She's not at home? Or at work?" My hands were shaking.

"She went to the doctor. Daimen made her—she's been so sick. She met up with Jordan and told me you'd texted her and wanted her to meet you someplace." I didn't say a word, but my voice had to indicate my concern when I'd spoken earlier. "Shit, Levi, what's going on?"

"I didn't text her, Ell. It wasn't me." With my phone on speaker, I scrolled through my texts but didn't see anything in the history. It had to have been wiped. But wait, Driscol wasn't on this morning. Who texted her and Jordan?

"What the fuck do you mean? It says right here, 'going to meet Levi, he needed to speak with Jordan and me.'"

Through the glass partitions of our firehouse, my chief and Garner had me in their sights. Waving them my way, I began to explain to my sister, "Listen, Ell, it was not me. A lot has come out concerning the arson case. Don't go anywhere without Daimen and Arden. Do you understand me?"

"What?" Of course, my sister was going to argue with me. It was a part of who she was. "What the hell is going on?" I looked down at an incoming call, and it was then it all got real.

"I gotta go. I'm going to have Garner call his brother now. Promise me, you'll stay put. Don't go anywhere unless you have your guys with you." She was silent. "Fuck, Ell, I gotta run. I can't go if I can't trust you to stay put."

I knew my sister's pout. "Fine, but call me the second you know anything." I told her I loved her then answered the incoming call quickly.

"Hello?" I didn't recognize the number.

"One day, brother, Karma will get you, and today is that day."

My phone was on speaker, and Garner and my chief were listening in. I took a piece of paper, writing for Garner. Scarlet Reeves and Jordan Peters are missing. Call your brother soon and make sure he understands to keep Ell close.

Nodding at my request, we all listened in carefully when my response didn't come.

"You're quiet, brother. Of course, I didn't have time this morning to text your sister, but I did find a way to get a text off to your boyfriend and girlfriend. You really are a kinky son of a bitch, aren't you, Arnold?"

Garner mouthed at me to be calm, but I was anything but.

"What the fuck did you do to my guy and girl, Driscol?"

Laughter floated through the phone. "Ah, funny you ask. You gotta love it when a plan comes together. Don't worry, you are about to see them very, very soon." The line died, leaving me staring at my phone.

chapter 52

jordan

"Red, wait." She was so eager to get out of my presence, she opened the side door that was oddly marked with the entrance sign when I followed in behind her. The second I let go of the door, it slammed shut. "Scarlet." I pulled out her full name because she'd been ignoring me.

"What, Jordan?" She shouted my name, stiff and forced.

"Um, this doesn't seem right, not one bit."

She got in my face, ignoring her surroundings. "Why is that?" she began. "You mean because it's just you and me, and you may have to actually talk to me and be honest with me about your feelings for Levi?" She shoved me, and though there was a semblance of truth in her words, I decided to ignore it for now.

"Sure, you're right, Red, but look around. Something's

not right. We would've heard from Levi since we've gotten here, and this place has all the feels of a bad horror movie." She turned her hand now, taking in the bottom floor of the warehouse. The windows were full of dust, and there was one lonely light on. In front of us were two brown metal fold-up chairs with a note on it reading, "Get comfortable, you'll be here a while."

With one look at it, Scar hightailed it to the door. "Yeah, you're right, Doc. This place is scary as fuck. Let's get the hell out of here. We can talk later." It was a good sign she was calling me Doc again.

I followed her, moving toward the door, but when she pulled, it was so forceful, with her one good hand, she fell back into me. "Shit, it won't open."

"What do you mean it won't open?" I asked. She had her cell phone in her hand as I grabbed for mine in my pocket. I watched as she powered it on.

"Shit, Jordan, I have no signal."

Turning my phone over, I realized how much danger we were in when my phone wasn't working either.

chapter 53

levi

Garner's phone rang as I got an incoming text. But it was not a message. It was a picture. No, I realized it was a video.

Jordan was pulling at a door in what looked like a dim lit warehouse while I watched Scar move her cell phone around over her head. In my mind, she was trying to get a signal. The feed was quiet at first. I snapped my fingers at Garner when I heard the tail end of his conversation.

"Gotta go. Trust me when I say, don't let Elliot out of your sight." He ended the call. At least Ell was safe. I showed him the feed of Scar and Jordan, and we looked on in awe, unsure what the hell was going on.

Soon, a voice flooded my phone, but I realized it was meant for Scar and Jordan, too, when their heads whipped around to listen to the voice. It was Driscol.

"I'll tell you now, you two, you don't want to try to escape. The warehouse is rigged with explosives, and if you try, not that I've made it easy for you two to get out, but if you somehow figure out a way, the building will blow to kingdom come."

I heard Scar attempt to reason with the lunatic. "Why are you doing this to us?" Her voice was so shaky, and a little bit of me died right then.

"Aw, glad you asked. You see, your man was responsible for the death of my father and sister. He took two people I loved from me, so I'm returning the favor." My body broke out in sweat, dripping, as I could barely steady myself when I sat. "And because he took my sister away from the love of her life, we both decided the son of a bitch you both loved without question should be taken from you."

Another person? It had to have been the one who texted Scar and Jordan from my phone after the meeting. But the only two people in the debrief were my chief standing next to me, and my dear friend Shirley. My brain worked backward about a name that all of a sudden stood out at me. Matt Shirley's daughter was Cassie, who he'd told me was named after his girlfriend, the love of his life, he lost when he was in college.

After one look at Garner and my chief, I continued to watch Jordan through live feed take our frightened girl in his arms. My hand came down on the cheap plywood that we called a table, splitting it in two. "Fuck!" I screamed so loud, everyone in the open common area stopped to look in at me through the glass windows. When I tossed a chair across the room, neither man tried to stop me from taking out my fear and frustration on the furniture. "I know who the second person is, Garner. I fucking know who I'm about to go kill." And if I got my hands on Driscol or Matt Shirley, I'd tear them both to pieces.

chapter 54

jordan

The voice over the intercom was freaky as hell. The allegations of Levi killing anyone had me almost laughing but not in that ha-ha sort of way. Scarlet had propelled herself into my arms upon the revelation that we'd been lured here as some sick revenge plot against our fireman. Yeah, I said ours. I guess in life or death terror, everything was put into perspective.

The voice continued to haunt us. "Do you two have anything to say to your man? I mean, he can hear you. But I didn't want to give him the satisfaction of you three being able to communicate."

"Fuck you!" Red screamed toward the mystery guest.

"Ah, Arnold, I know you hear me. You have a feisty little thing. Hot, too. I hate to have to kill her, but now you know the whole sordid story. The second I was called this morning, knowing that the detective had all your late files, I understood you'd figure it out. After all, you're a coward, but you're not dumb."

He was baiting Levi, and our LT wasn't even here to defend himself. "Probably figured out my partner, too. He was happy that you'd suffer like he had since he lost the love of his life."

None of what the son of a bitch was spewing made much sense to me, but I had led Red to the chairs as the color drained from her face. I'd been told she was sick, very sick. Looking at her, I whispered in her ear, "Red, you okay? I know you've been sick."

Knowing Red like I did, it was a light bulb moment as though she'd forgotten she'd been ill for several days. "Red, honey, you look even worse than you did a minute ago."

She whispered in my ear, only something I could hear. I pulled back as she nodded her head at me, confirming what I'd just heard was indeed correct. I brought her close to my body. Her head resting on my shoulder while tears streamed down her face. "We'll get out of here, Red. I swear, if it's the last thing I do." It was the most truthful promise I'd made in my life.

chapter 55

levi

"Bomb threat." The speakers blared throughout the fire department. At least, we had the address where Scar and Jordan were. It took ten seconds to explain to my chief who Driscol's accomplice was, then I hopped on my rig, taking me to the warehouse where both the people I loved were being held.

The mere minutes it took to arrive at the warehouse were maddening. In my mind, I didn't know how to live in this world without both Jordan and Scar a part of it. The police had already barricaded most of the street when my crew arrived.

When both the fire and police commissioner arrived with the entire chain of command, I got the full extent of this situation. Garner had taken control of the crime scene. I was merely a spectator witnessing the breakdown of two men. One of them was Matt Shirley, a man I'd come to deeply respect.

I had been avoiding calls from my sister, especially with the news stations getting a glimpse of the story. When a phone call came in from someone I'd once called my friend, I answered, in the hopes I'd been wrong.

"Shirley, please tell me you aren't a part of this."

The person who answered on the other end was not the same man I'd once known. No, this man's voice was cold and distant. "Do you know how hard it was to be friends with you when all I wanted to do was turn your life upside down? Now I'm here to tear it apart, and I take great pleasure in this." A chuckle filled the static on his end.

"You planned this for what, the past twelve years? Got close to me to just take me down?"

"So you're not too stupid after all. You understand what we did? We had to avenge Cassie's death."

My mind, it wasn't forming coherent thoughts. "What about your daughter, the one you named after your Cassie? I've held her; I was at her baptism. I've been in your house with your wife. This will kill them."

There was a silence on the other end, and I'd hoped mentioning his daughter and wife would mean something. "My heart has only ever belonged to my Cassie. My life doesn't work without her. Same with Kevin. And because I can't love — though I've tried, you can't either." He ended the call.

What could you do when someone hated you so much? One look at Garner and I knew he was coordinating efforts with the bomb squad. My phone rang one last time as I was watching the live feed of Jordan holding Scar.

"Hello," I answered quickly.

"Arnold, here's the deal." It was Driscol on the phone. "We have the bomb hardwired, but we have it on a timer, too. I will give your lovers one chance — one you never gave to my sister or father. The door will disengage in thirty seconds. They have a short amount of time to run from the building. I won't tell them how long 'cause what's the fun in that?" His maniacal voice could be heard over my cell. "And in this way they stand a little chance. Though prepare yourself to watch them die. Now, this all will bring pleasure to Matt and me."

I didn't have anything to throw, not one thing, and I needed a release. With the live feed still on, I heard Driscol's orders. "Okay, you two kinky partners of Arnold's, the lock will disengage in thirty seconds. You have mere seconds to escape the building. You may want to lose your heels, Ms. Reeves." The hair on the back of my skin stood on end. "I'll not hesitate to push my control button as I see fit and good luck."

I watched as Jordan and Scar lined up at the door, and he placed her in front. He whispered something into her ear, and she kissed him. We waited for the door to disengage. In a split second, I heard the psychotic voice of Kevin tell them, "Go!" The door opened and Scar took off first, Jordan right behind her. What happened next was like watching a film in slow motion.

chapter 56

jordan

The second the door unlocked, I almost pushed Red out of it. With what I knew, she was in front of me, and I was on her heels.

I saw Levi. His was the first set of eyes that I locked on when Red and I frantically took off running. The control freak in me counted to myself for some sort of understanding. In my odd mind, I calculated we needed a good ten seconds to get out of blast range, but we'd still probably take on some force. It was the main reason Red was in front of me.

I got to nine and braced myself, pleading with Red to hurry up. She had long legs, and it could have been our saving grace. I reached ten, which was actually in my mind quite generous for the psychopath who locked us up in the building.

The second my mind reached ten, a loud, piercing sound

exploded behind me, and I tackled Red, pushing us a couple more feet from the blast site. As the explosion sent shards of glass through my white doctor's jacket and into my back, my mind was only on one thing—Red and the baby that was both Levi's and mine.

chapter 57

scarlet

I woke the second I heard the familiar beeps of the hospital where I'd been just a couple of hours earlier. "Ms. Reeves?" I had no idea who was talking to me, but everything began to piece together with every second my eyes remained open. My head felt as though someone had split it open with a jack hammer, and then I remembered—oh, fuck, everything. The building, Jordan shielding me, and the baby. I sat up, screaming, "The baby, the baby. Jordan and the baby. Save Jordan and our baby."

At my side was Levi, his eyes on me and his hand in mine. "Scar, honey, you're in shock."

My words kept coming. I couldn't stop the screaming, the yelling, and the fear I'd lose two more things in my life.

"Levi, Jordan?"

He turned from me with that question. "Levi!" My hands shook, and my yells and screams continued to fill the air around us.

"He was rushed into surgery. He took the majority of the blast, and his back was burned badly."

His words didn't make sense. They did, but they didn't. Jordan couldn't be taken from me, and in my thrashing, his simple touch on my arm calmed me.

"And the baby?" I asked.

"Scar, you're in shock, honey. There was no baby. Just you and Jordan."

Dr. Serrin rushed into the triage room, Levi holding on tight to me liked he'd never let go. "Ms. Reeves, we're setting up an ultrasound right now. I just found out. Let's make sure your little one was protected by you and the brave Dr. Peters."

His words had taken a second to register for Levi. The nurses and Dr. Serrin were quick with their intentions, setting up the ultrasound right away. He had the cold gel on my stomach, searching for the little being growing in me I'd just seen earlier today. And shit, somehow, I already loved him or her so fucking much, already.

"Scar, shit, are you??"

I couldn't answer him. As soon as I thought I could form something, anything, Dr. Serrin began, "Ah, there it is, your little baby."

Levi held my hand, watching the screen. All we needed now was the other person who completed us.

I'd been moved to a private room to monitor the pregnancy and the blow to my head. Andrew had thrown himself at me before he went down to the OR waiting room for news on his brother.

Levi wouldn't leave my side, though I needed him down with Andrew and his family. Ell popped in from the waiting room to my room every half an hour as Daimen and Arden wouldn't leave me, not yet.

We hadn't shared my pregnancy with anyone. And when we'd finally gotten a moment to ourselves, Levi asked, "Will we find out who the bio daddy is?"

I shrugged, my mind on Jordan and what he did for our baby. "Does it matter? I mean, you both are the father in my eyes."

He leaned down, peppering kisses on my cheek. "No, you're right. It doesn't matter, not one bit. My DNA or the doc's DNA, I will love our little baby with all I have."

Settling in next to me, he held me. It was the only thing we could do until someone arrived with an update on our man.

chapter 58

jordan

I blinked my eyes, but they barely opened. On my hands, I could feel small squeezes. And shit, something hurt like stab wounds and burn marks down my body. But all I cared about were the voices beckoning me out of my sleep.

"Doc." The voice and tone had been one I'd run from just days ago, but I wouldn't be doing that today.

"Jordan, honey." This time, it was the sweet vibrato of a woman, my woman.

I struggled to keep my eyes open, but I had to, to witness the beauty that claimed them both.

I tried to speak, to say something, but Red spoke for me, "Don't speak, honey. Just let us hold your hand."

I nodded, but that even caused pain. I had to know, and they had to know what was on my mind. "The baby?" Those two words were all I could piece together.

"He or she is doing just fine." I turned to Levi, who was holding my other hand. Him here, with me, was everything, especially after how I'd treated him.

"Dads!" Levi rubbed my face gently, a tear forming in the corner of his eye. "Doc, we're going to be dads." He leaned down and kissed me, and in return, I squeezed his hand. They stayed with me until I couldn't keep my eyes open a second longer.

———————

Three weeks was how long I'd been cooped up in this hospital. Fuck, I couldn't wait to get home. We hadn't talked a lot about us, and the same fear crept up in the past three weeks that had made me run to begin with. Scar had planned to move a couple of things over to my apartment to help me out as I continued to heal from home.

On my last full day, I was surprised when the door opened, and it wasn't Levi or Red, but Arden. He'd been here to see me many times, but today, it seemed different, almost like he had an agenda. By the look on his face and as he sat in one of the chairs, scooting it close to me, I realized I was right.

"Ready to go home tomorrow?" he asked, and it wasn't like Arden to shoot the shit with me. By then, I'd gotten mobility in the arms that had been hit the worst with the shards of glass. My back still hurt like a motherfucker, but hell, I was alive, and the little baby that was a part of me, regardless of paternity, was growing in Red.

"Yeah, I'm so tired of physical therapy. You know what they say, doctors make the worst patients."

He was sitting directly next to me and I attempted to push myself up in bed, moving to see Arden better. "So this is not a social call." I was an older brother. I got it.

"Yeah, I've had to wait, honestly, because you weren't ready for what I had to say beforehand, but now, I think you may have some perspective."

Perspective. It was a good way of saying I'd pulled my head out of my ass, yet somehow, I still kept Levi at arm's length.

Arden steepled his fingers together, waiting for me. I nodded in agreement, and he continued, "But knowing you, like I'm starting to, you still have reservations."

I shrugged my shoulders as my answer. "Well, I understand, believe me," he replied. "But I have to say I wasn't quite so fucking stubborn as you. I mean, I see it, we all do, in your eyes. And the world be damned, I choose my own happiness over anyone's opinions."

Nodding, I started, "It's not other people I care about. Sure, it's unconventional, but for me, it's one gender or the other. It's about my own preconceived ideas."

He closed his eyes, thinking on my words. He stood, pushing back the chair. "So what you need to ask yourself is will your preconceived ideas keep you warm at night when your heart aches for the two people you love more than anything in this world?" He was at the door when he stopped and looked back at me. He seemed to have one last thing to add. "Only you, Jordan Peters, can answer this question. But if you can't accept the love you have for a man, they will only wait so long, and then you won't have a choice at all."

He shut the door quietly behind him and left me with his parting words. The idea was more than I could fathom, and in the quietness, I had many tough decisions to make. But really they weren't hard at all. Grabbing my phone, I figured I had twenty-four hours. Could I pull it off? With help, I possibly could.

chapter 59

Levi

I saw him every day, and it took everything in me not to grab his arm as I had when he woke up. I'd hoped he'd understand how fragile life was and welcome me back in his arms, but he was just as confused as before.

Though the one thing that linked us was knowing we were going to be fathers. But if we were not together, would Scar find out the bio daddy and exclude the other one? Scar still insisted that it was all of us or none of us. And when she made plans to move in with Jordan and stay in his guest room, I wasn't invited. I was crushed but after almost losing them both, I'd take the stubborn as fuck doctor as long as he was breathing his next breath.

I was placed on desk duty until the fire department's shrink cleared me. And the fuckers who almost killed the loves of my life were caught fleeing Illinois at the Kentucky border. It was a good thing they were almost a state away, or I might have killed them myself. In the investigation and their confessions, they admitted the truth to why they let Scar and Jordan go. They'd tried to blow the building the second my eyes found theirs. They wanted me to witness their deaths. It was dumb luck, I guess one could say. There was a short in the detonator—it was what saved them. I chose to think of it as fate.

Finishing up some arson reports they'd had me investigating until I could get back to my firetruck, I looked down at my phone at a picture of Scar, Jordan, and myself we'd taken at the Navy Pier one day. We'd had so much sex and wanted to get out and mingle with the world. Of course, all it did was make us want each other more. On the big wheel, we'd both fingered Scar, causing her to orgasm as we rode it. It was the best. Of course, she insisted on a selfie for her Instagram account, and I'd saved it as my screen saver. I'd spent hours looking at this picture. I couldn't get enough of it, of them.

With one glance at my clock, Jordan was being released right then, and I wasn't there. Actually, he didn't ask me to come, and Scar suggested this morning to give him some space. I'd moved in with her to be close after her injuries caused a severe concussion. I'd used any excuse to be near Scar. And I didn't want to miss out on any of the pregnancy. I was going to be a dad. The thought scared me and sent chills up my spine. What if we had a girl who looked like her mama? We'd be fucking screwed.

My text alert brought me out of my daydreams. Looking at the message, I smiled. Jordan and I talked every day. Hell, I saw him all the time, but it was all surface level shit and nothing super deep.

The Good Doctor: *Meet us at Red's apartment.*

It was all I got, but fuck, I'd take whatever he gave because I wanted him more—both of them more than anything in this world. Grabbing my coat, I turned to the receptionist. "Something came up, and I'm not sure I'll be back."

I didn't know what to expect, but he never really had to truly ask. Good or bad, I'd always be there for Jordan. And Scar and now — our baby.

chapter 60

scarlet

The man was fucking stubborn. I'd come by the hospital to get him, and the staff said he'd checked himself out. I was hurt because he'd fucking run again from me, from us. When we'd made plans for his recovery, I didn't want to push. I suggested I move into his place until he was fully able to be on his own.

Levi didn't press Jordan for an invitation to join us. He came in every day and spent time with our good doctor. He was careful not to touch him unless Jordan initiated it, and he hadn't. Levi was disappointed, but after almost losing us to those psychopaths, he was content that we were still alive. He'd been staying with me, claiming he wanted to experience every bit of my pregnancy—even the horrible morning sickness which had hit with a vengeance. He was staying in the guest room. I still was clear. It would be all of us or none of us. Both men were cautious and I stuck to my guns.

Hormones overtook my body, and I started to cry at being abandoned by Jordan again. Then one of his nurses handed me a note. I opened it slowly, unsure what to expect but confident he'd left me again. Now, it was just not me. I had a passenger, and I felt more outraged for him or her than myself.

Red,
You probably think I ran again, but I didn't. Please meet me at your apartment. I promise, I'll explain everything then. But for now, take care of our baby and get your sweet and beautiful ass home. I love you.
Yours always,
Jordan

I stuck the note in my purse and made my way to a cab outside Mercy, bracing myself for what could be waiting for me at home.

The elevator was closing when I heard, "Hold it please." It was a voice I knew all too well. He was out of breath in his uniform, though he was on desk duty. "Scar, hey beautiful." He leaned in and kissed me on the cheek. "You're heading to your place, too?"

"Yeah, Jordan left me a letter. And you?"

A smile spread over his face, and I tried not to let any of this mean anything. "LT, let's not get ahead of ourselves." He nodded in agreement but reached for my hand, pulling me to him.

"I've missed you, Scar." Yeah, I understood what he was saying. Though we'd seen each other for the past three weeks every day, I missed his intimate touch so much.

"Yeah, me, too." I leaned my head against his forehead until the doors to the thirty-seventh floor opened, and I kept my hand intertwined with his. Using my key, I opened the door but had to do a double take. This was not my apartment, not the one I had left this morning.

Jordan was sitting at a new dining room table that was shoved up next to my other dining room table. Boxes were everywhere, and my once small television the guys complained about without fail was replaced by a television the size of what Levi had in his house. Upon further inspection, it was Levi's television and the table Jordan sat at was his from his apartment. Jordan's recliner was in my corner along with bookcases that had once housed Levi's video games in his own place.

There was so much stuff, and in front of my window sat Levi's couch and Jordan's coffee table.

"What in the world??" I asked, taking it all in.

"Yeah, I couldn't decide, so I thought we'd decide together and the rest we could donate to the women's shelter I volunteer at."

But he hadn't answered the most obvious question. I didn't think I had to ask it, but apparently, I needed to. "Okay, but what is all this doing here?"

I looked up at Levi, who was smiling. He hadn't said a word either. It was like he understood when all I saw was so much fucking clutter.

"If we are going to all move in together, I thought the logical choice was your apartment. It's the biggest. But I wanted it to be ours, a little bit of all of us. I don't have much, but I wanted to contribute something."

My mind was not catching up with the reality when Levi tipped my chin to his. "I think he's trying to show us what he wants, beautiful."

Jordan stood, and by the grimace on his face, he was in pain. He grabbed both of our hands. "Yeah, that's exactly what I'm trying to tell you. I want you both. I want to be committed to both of you because I love you, Scarlet Reeves and Levi Arnold, more than the stars, the moon, and the sun combined." He took Levi's face in his hands and pulled him close to his own body. "I'm sorry I've kept you far from me. It was not that I didn't love you. I didn't think I could give you what you needed."

"I need you, you stubborn fucker, any way I can get you," he replied.

"Yeah, I get all of this, now." I'm star struck, seeing these two together in this way, and if I wasn't already pregnant, my ovaries on their own would have figured a way to conceive at their sexy as sin display of affection. Jordan turned to me. "And hell, Red, I'm so sorry, so very sorry I've done this to you, making you go without either of us because you refused to choose. And I'm so fucking glad you didn't because I want you both if you both will still have me."

I was to the side of both men, watching them. I circled my arms around their waists. "I've never wanted anything more than I want you both, right fucking now." But I would have to do gentle, and I didn't want gentle. I wanted to see them fuck one another, and I wanted them both to take me at the same time. These thoughts floated through my mind as I was about to demand they take me to bed. If we could make it to my room. Shit, there was so much crap around my house, but I didn't care one bit. I only needed them.

Jordan stopped both of our advances right then. "Don't worry, there will be time for us to make love—all together. But first, I have one more surprise for you."

He weaved us in and out of the maze of boxes and furniture, bringing us to the closed door of my home office. He stood facing us when he began, "Last night, I thought long and hard about the love both of you have brought into my life. As I said, I love you more than the stars, the moon, and the sun combined. So I was thinking those three things represented us, our love, and who we are to one another."

I loved this side of him, how he became deep at times

and wooed us as he was doing right now. I saw it with the mild shaking of his hands or how he touched his chin because he was nervous. I loved this Jordan. I loved every part of him, and I couldn't believe both him and Levi next to me were mine and would be for life. And our love for one another was growing inside me.

"Red, you are the star in our life. You continue to sparkle. They are, in essence, a nuclear fusion, and you are exactly this. You bring us together; you're the beginning of us." He paused, looking at Levi. "And you're the sun. You give off both light and heat, making us both warm in your presence." He stopped for a second, and it was then I saw beads of sweat forming on the crown of his head. This was him being vulnerable, and I didn't see it often, but I loved him even more for this. Just when I didn't think I could love him more, I did.

"And that leaves us with the moon." A small smile appeared on his face. "The moon's gravitational pull causes our ocean's tidal waves. Sometimes, they are high and sometimes low, depending on a bunch of scientific lingo that's not important. The important part is sometimes it has caused major riffs, and sometimes, it has been calm. But the ocean would not be what it is without the moon. And without you two, I wouldn't be the moon; I'd be some black hole searching for you to make me complete." He paused, giving us both a weak smile. "I hope you guys can accept me for who I am, knowing I'm trying to work out stuff within me. I'll make mistakes, and I will cause tidal waves in our lives, but if you guys are next to me as my sun and star, I know I can make it through anything."

Holy shit, who knew this man in front of me was so romantic. I wanted to throw myself at him, but I couldn't. I gently walked toward him, bringing him as close to me as I could. "Jordan, as long as you're here, I will be next to you every step of the way."

Levi's strong arms were around us. "I fucking love you, your stubbornness and all. I won't ever let either of you out of my reach again." Levi began to pull us toward my room between the boxes, but Jordan wouldn't budge. "I have one more thing for you both." We stopped, waiting for whatever grand gesture was next. My mind had still not caught up to him moving our stuff here or the whole stars, sun, and moon analogy. Surely, he couldn't top any of this.

He turned the knob to the door where my home office was. "I hope you don't mind, but I called in every favor I could think of. If you don't like it, we can change it before the baby comes, but I thought she or he should have a little bit of us in his or her room." Turning on the light, I'm greeted with a mural painted on the wall. And just not the wall but the ceiling, too.

The ceiling had sparkling stars. Over the baby's crib were a moon and the ocean tides. On the other side of the room, on the opposite wall, was the sun painted to a dazzling brilliance. And on further inspection, the crib was the one I'd showed Elliot I'd wanted a couple of days ago. A deep cherry sleigh crib. In the corner was the rocking chair that matched the crib.

I couldn't speak. "If this isn't what you want for our baby, we can redo the nursery, but I wanted you to see how the three of us loving each other is the best thing for him or her, and certainly for all of us."

I turned to him, Levi's arms were around my shoulders, when I replied, "You touch this room, and I'll gut you." They both laughed at me, my mind on the beauty he'd created in just eight hours.

"I think that is her way of telling you she loves it, Doc." But before I could take in anymore of this room, Levi scooped me up in his arms. "Are you coming, Doc?"

"Yeah, I'm right behind you." And he was. Looking over Levi's shoulder, I saw the heat in Jordan's eyes could not be contained. I had braced myself for the worst-case scenario, and now, I was bracing myself for one hell of a ride, mainly all three of us riding one another in one way or another for the next several hours.

chapter 61

jordan

This was going to be tender, so very tender. First, I was in pain, yet I'd taken some pain pills just so I could make love to these two. Secondly, we'd be gentle with Red for the next eight or so months. After she healed, of course, all bets were off.

Levi climbed over Red, straddling her. Somehow, I blinked my eyes, and they were undressed. I had to catch up. Thankfully, I was in track pants and a large sweatshirt my brother had given me of Brock's. The man was huge, and I needed clothes that wouldn't be tight on me. At the moment, I was glad I could shimmy everything off very easily.

I stood to the side, watching them kiss. How I loved it before, but now that I was willing to admit my love for both a man and a woman, it was more sensual. "Doc, what are you waiting for, a formal invitation?" It was something we joked about a lot, but that was Levi. I'd always thought it was weird the names that Arden and Daimen called one another like asshole and fucker, but now I got it. This man I loved, loved being an ass at times.

"Yeah, ass wipe, that's exactly what I'm waiting for."

"Then get your fine-looking ass up here. I'll be gentle with you, I promise." I climbed onto Scar's bed, lying next to her naked body. It wasn't long before Levi's strong hands wrapped around my hard cock, stroking me lightly.

"Straddle him like you are with me," Scarlet demanded, and Levi moved gently from over Scar's naked body to mine. She sat up, her legs crossed, watching us. "Hell, you two are sexy as sin." Her words only increased Levi's motions, and I wasn't far from coming. I didn't stop him. I needed a release, and I wanted Scar to witness me letting go of my own preconceived ideas. Arden was right. Those would not have kept me warm on a cold lonely night.

But his stroking stopped for a moment as he readjusted his position around me until the wetness of his tongue touched the tip of my dick. I couldn't suppress the moans that overtook me, and as I held Scar's hand, I came in Levi's mouth.

"Orgasms, that is what I want, too." She kissed me on my lips, then moved out of the way when Levi's lips crashed on mine.

"Scar, you're next, I promise," he said, pulling away from our sensual kiss. "Did you taste yourself on me? You taste almost as good as Scar."

I'd never been more at peace in my life with the two of them next to me and me coming in Levi's mouth. "Yeah, she's pretty tasty." As Levi moved from over me, I sat up slowly, pushing Scar down. "I'm about to find out." My mouth snaked over her beautiful little red curls she kept trimmed for us. "Hold on tight, Red, we're about to have our way with you," I warned.

"I'm buckled up. Bring it on." My tongue found her clit. I looked up for the briefest of moments in time to see her engulf all of Levi's beautiful cock in her mouth. It wasn't long before she came, and I heard Levi's pre-orgasm groans. Coming down from our high, I'd looked at Levi, silently questioning what was next.

"I have to have you both at the same time." He didn't even wait for us to fully recover because I'd gotten hard again, and looking at my man—he was just as hard. "Doc, you think you can stand?" Ah, and this was why I made sure to take my pain pills.

"Yeah, I'm good." I walked over to the end table where we kept our lube and condoms. He took no time entering Red as I coated my hand with lube. As I worked one finger inside his ass, he moaned and groaned.

"I can feel you, Doc," Red croaked out.

"You're about to feel a whole hell more of him, beautiful," Levi replied. "And hey, Doc, we'll work at your speed, but one day, I want to claim that virgin ass of yours."

My reply surprised me when I said, "Yeah, can't wait."

Entering him, I could feel Scar, too. Hell, this was amazing. And one day, very soon, I'd let both Red and Levi sandwich me like this. Holding him tight and watching Scar over his shoulder, I'd never felt more alive as I did at this moment. My star and my sun were everything to me.

chapter 62

levi

eight months later

It was hard to see Scar in so much pain. She'd been screaming since her water broke. With one look at my doc's face, I understood this was more than simple childbirth. I'd not questioned him, not in front of Scar. With a quick cab ride to the hospital, Jordan bypassed normal check-in and took her straight to an operating room where Dr. Serrin met us right away.

It was then that Scar knew something was not right. "Jordan, what's wrong?" A slew of doctors appeared out of nowhere, and Dr. Serrin looked at Jordan. "You can assist, but this is my patient, you got it?" Oh, even Scar's OB understood the way our man worked.

No words were exchanged, just a little nod of the head. Jordan kneeled at her head as I leaned over to listen. Between her doctor and our man, they silently understood what the next step was, but I didn't have a clue.

"Listen, Red, everything is fine. The baby is breech, which means Dr. Serrin has to perform a C-section. They're prepping you for surgery. We can get the baby out in minutes, and it's what is best for him or her."

We didn't find out the gender of the baby. It was Scar's call, but both Jordan and I wanted to know. And it was surreal that, within minutes, we'd meet our child. I was given scrubs to put on over my clothes while Jordan left us to go wash up. When he returned, he gave both of us a kiss on the cheeks. "Stay next to her, babe. She'll be fine."

I loved when he called me babe. He had no problem showing me affection, his fears had subsided, but I could tell he still struggled in public at times. But it would come; I had no doubt we'd get there eventually. And we'd already come a long way.

Scar's eyes watered. "Levi, I'm so scared."

Oh, she was preaching to the choir. "Yeah, but I'm here, and Doc won't let anything happen to you or our baby."

"The heart rate is dropping; we need to get the baby out of her now." Dr. Serrin's orders were met with quick action. "Now, Scarlet, we will have your baby out in thirty seconds. Don't worry, you will be a mom soon."

Thirty seconds came and went, and we heard nothing. Jordan's eyes followed the doctor's hands, but I couldn't see over the drape at Scar's midsection. He looked at me for a brief second, then said something to the doctor. He quickly placed a silent baby in Jordan's hands as he flew to a team of nurses at what looked like a warming table.

"Why is it quiet, Levi? What's going on?" Scarlet demanded, crying next to me.

"Doc?" I called to get something, anything from him. He hadn't moved, not one twitch of his head toward mine.

"Jordan," I said louder with Scarlet in tears next to me.

Another couple of seconds passed. And then it came, a scream so loud it was music to my ears. "You hear that, Scar? That's our baby." I still didn't know if it was a boy or a girl, but it didn't matter.

Jordan walked over to us with this baby swaddled in a blanket and Dr. Serrin on his heels. "Red, meet your baby girl." She had reached out to hold her, and Jordan shook his head. "She seems okay, but it's procedure to take her to the NICU. I wanted you to meet her first." He looked at me, and in his smile, I knew he was telling her the truth. "I swear, it's just to check her over one last time."

Scarlet's cries turned almost hysterical. I certainly would not be telling the mother of my child to calm down, not when she wasn't able to hold her baby. Somehow, in her sobs, she asked, "Jordan, will you stay with her?"

"I won't let her out of my sight." He leaned down, giving her a kiss and me a little view of our girl. "Stay with her, baby?" he asked of me.

"Yeah, there's no way I'm leaving her."

He kissed me. "It's exactly how I feel about our daughter right now." With Jordan watching over one of our girls and me watching over our other one, I knew we'd be okay.

Thirty minutes after moving to our own private room, Scar was going out of her ever-loving mind as a mother without her child.

"Where the hell are they?" She kept asking every thirty seconds. I'd gotten a text from Jordan saying it would be any time, but that had been ten minutes ago and was far too long for Scar. For me, too, I couldn't wait to hold our daughter. The texts kept on coming from Ell, Andrew, Kayla, and Dane. All three of us, Jordan included, had become close to Cami, Dane, and their kids. They'd even healed enough that they were exploring triads again. Looking at my girl and waiting for the rest of my family to arrive, I hoped they were close to finding their missing piece because I certainly had found mine.

The second the doors swung open, Jordan appeared with our daughter in his arms. "Ready to officially meet our little girl?" he asked.

"Yes, bring her to me now." Oh, Scar would be the fiercest of moms. A true mama bear.

"Okay, Red, I got her, just for you." Jordan placed the small little human in her arms. She was a natural, holding her tight to her body. It was the most beautiful thing I'd ever seen. With both Jordan and I sitting on the same side of her, we took in every little noise our baby made. Pulling back the little beanie cap that sat on her head, I saw a full head of red hair. I couldn't have asked for anything more perfect.

"Um, guys, we never picked out a name," Scar mentioned. Hell, names led us to out and out fights, and we'd stopped all negotiations, promising to be more civilized when the baby was born.

I was the first to offer up, "I was thinking about using your parents' names, Scar. What do you think?"

Jordan was nodding his head, agreeing with me. "I love this idea, Scar. Katherine Michelle?" However, when I looked at our little angel, she didn't look like a Katherine. But I thought it was a great way to honor her parents.

"Um, I love the idea of making my parents part of this day, but I was thinking something a bit less traditional than Katherine and Michael." Well, this was Scar we were talking about, after all, so the idea didn't surprise us.

She looked at our little girl one last time, placing a kiss on her sweet head. "I was thinking about my parents' passions. My dad loved to sail, and my mom was a baker, at heart. Taught me at a young age how to cook and bake, which came in handy in foster care." She paused, and I was wondering where she was going with this. "I've had this idea for a while, but since we couldn't calmly pick a name, I thought I'd suggest in honor of my parents, Baker for a boy or Sailor for a girl."

She didn't wait for an answer, not yet, when she continued, "And after both her daddies, I want to use your middle name that you share — Aaron but spelled with an E — E-r-i-n."

With one exchange between Jordan and myself, I understood we had a name for our baby. I reached out, and somehow, Scarlet let me hold our girl. "Welcome to our world, Sailor Erin Arnold-Peters." And it was then that everything we had fought hard for made it all worth it.

epilogue

scarlet
nine months later

Sailor was the easiest baby. And being a mother came naturally to me. I looked at her sleeping in her crib, and tears were about ready to fall down my face; after I'd spent an hour applying makeup, too.

In his touch, I understood it was Jordan. "Red, we'll be upstairs. Greta is the best nanny. She has come highly recommended by Cami and Dane. Sailor will be fine."

I never returned to work, though I did work some from home. Sailor was my focus, and she would remain it always. "I know, but I've never left her by herself before." Not even with her Auntie Ell or Uncle Andrew. She'd always been with either me, or one of her dads, or all of us.

"We've talked about this," he began, stepping back, still quiet not to wake the baby as he looked me up and down, a new mission popping in his mind. I knew this man too well, and I recognized when he was about ready to eat me alive. "We will come get her after the ceremony. It will be less than an hour. During the reception, we'll bring her upstairs with us."

He was right. It wasn't every day our best friends got married. But they were more than our best friends; they were our family. Elliot was pregnant with triplets, due in a couple of months, and she was as big as a house. But her men were putting a ring on her finger today. I'd wanted to bring Sailor with us, but the second she woke from her nap, she'd be crawling around. These past nine months had gone by too quick.

Levi popped his head in. "Greta is here. Let's go."

Jordan almost dragged me out of Sailor's stars, moon, and sun room. I left Greta with a dozen different lists as both the men barely got me out of our home we shared together.

In the bridal suite Ell had taken over for the day, she was talking about many things. I tried to stay focused, but my mind was on my baby downstairs, and one surprise I was sure to give my men after the reception. Trying so hard to stay focused on Ell and her big day, I looked over, and she was about to cry.

"Ell, what's wrong?" I asked.

"I don't know. Damn hormones, I guess. I mean, I'm marrying the loves of my life. How can I not cry for joy?" Then she asked the one question plaguing her. "But did they show up?" Of course, she was asking about her fucking family who refused to be a part of her life or Levi's. They had not even met Sailor. They claimed, how could we know for sure she's your baby and not that other guy you all live in sin with.

"I'm sorry, Ell. Besides your brother and Andrew's family, there's no one else." Why was I the bearer of bad news?

"I told myself I wouldn't be upset," she claimed. I tried to offer some sort of comfort, but I knew between the proverbial middle finger they'd given her and her pregnant with triplets, of course she was more than upset.

"I know, and you're right. Everyone is happy. You found your happily ever after, and Andrew found his, too. It's how it should be. I love my new family, you, and Andrew, and my guys, and these creatures growing in my belly." We all somehow found happiness; there was so much truth in Elliot's statement.

"If you're good in here, I'm heading to go check on your men. How does that sound?" Looking at the blonde curls that matched her brother, I counted myself lucky to call Elliot one of my best friends.

I could feel her eyes on me as I made my way to the door. "Can you send Levi back? I wanted to speak to him before the service." Levi couldn't be happier for his sister. He knew she'd always be loved.

"Sure, I'll have someone find him. I haven't seen him in a while." I wondered if the sly son of a bitch had snuck down to our place to check on Sailor.

I immediately ran into Jordan. He brought me in close, caressing my cheek. I couldn't help but kiss him. "Could you do me a big favor, Doc? Can you go get Levi for me? I'm not sure where he is—gonna check on the grooms." He smiled at me with an all-knowing look. Levi—the fucker did go check on our daughter. And he gave me a hard time.

After the ceremony, I couldn't make my way to the elevator fast enough. I wasn't waiting for Levi, the traitor, or Jordan, his accomplice. In the foyer of Ell, Arden, and Daimen's penthouse, two large set of arms encased me. "Where are you going, Red?"

I stood tall and proud, not ashamed of the anxiety I felt

being away from my baby. "To get Sailor, as we agreed upon."

Both of these men chuckled at me. "Okay, we get it, but can you give us just five minutes of your time?" I was skeptical but curious.

"Okay, five minutes, then if you try to stop me, I'll gut you both."

Levi had me by the arm, his looped in mine. "Why is she always threatening to gut us?" he teased.

"You get in the way of me and my baby, and I won't think twice." I laughed at my threat. They led me into Elliot's library where Belle from Beauty and the Beast had nothing compared to what the boys did to house her books. They ripped out three walls, combined four rooms, and gave her a library any president would have been proud of. As a matter of fact, it could have been a presidential library. The room housed every architectural model she'd ever built along with the designs she created. She even had a Dewey decimal system on display, like the old-school libraries in elementary school.

"Okay, guys, what's so important that it can't wait?"

They looked at one another and back at me. "Well, after today, we know we won't ever get you away from Sailor, nor can we take leaving her with a babysitter either," Jordan admitted. I knew it; they were just as attached as I was.

"And with that being said," Levi began as they both lowered to one knee, "we love you so much. You're our life. And we'd like to know if you'd do the honor of ..."

Jordan finished the question, when he asked, "Marry us?"

We'd always talked about making it official. After all, Sailor had their last names hyphenated.

But now it was surreal, especially after my visit to the restroom today before the ceremony. I didn't hesitate to answer. "Yes, the answer is yes."

It was then they pulled out a large ruby ring that was at least two carats. "We thought it would match your hair and that of our daughter."

Ah, that was all I needed as a segue. "What about other children? What if this ring doesn't match our next child's hair color?"

"Then we'll buy you a ring for every kid we have," Jordan answered, standing up to bring me in his arms. I couldn't keep the tears contained, but I had more to say.

Levi stood, kissing me, both of them holding me tight. "Then you better get me one, just in case he or she doesn't have red hair. I expect our next child to have black hair like yours." I kissed Jordan and then looked at Levi. "Or blonde like yours."

"Scar, we'll cross that bridge when we get there, I promise." Levi's arms were already undressing me while Jordan's hands were plunging into my cleavage. I guess we were going to take some time for ourselves in the library to really break it in, but before we could, I had my own surprise for them.

"We're getting ready to cross that bridge, guys." Both of their advancements stopped.

Levi leaned back. "What? Are you telling us …?"

"A baby, we're going to have another baby. Sailor will have a sister or brother."

It was then that my gown pooled to the floor, and Jordan walked over to the door and locked it. "Well, this is cause for celebration, and boy, do we have a celebration for you."

And, I melted into my men's arms, where I fit perfectly.

bonus epilogue

eight years later

Who would have thought that a trip to the dentist would be less enjoyable than being poked in the eye by an ice pick? I don't have the latter to compare it to, but being at the dentist with three kids by myself made me want to take part in any type of torture session rather than taking them to their next appointment in six months.

This was where it came in handy having two more partners who could be there with me normally. But it was Levi's first month as the new fire commissioner for Chicago, and Jordan had just been promoted to the chief of staff at Mercy. My men were busy, but I'd already sent reminders to their secretaries to clear their schedule for the next appointment.

Maizie was still all puffy faced from the tears she'd shed

during the routine exam. Baker was chill, like Levi was in most situations, trying to calm his sister. Of course, Sailor thought the world would end at the idea of braces.

"When are daddies going to be home?" Maizie's deep chocolate eyes and olive complexion left nothing to the imagination of who her biological father was. But it never mattered in the eyes of both men. Hell, they took being a daddy fiercely and loved all three of our children equally.

I scooped our five-year-old up in my arms, kissing her as she wiggled and giggled. Soda Pop, our golden retriever, came at her cries, thinking he'd rescue her by licking me to death. Sailor, who was as serious about life as Jordan was, pulled out her next Margaret Haddix book, taking over Levi's recliner, her red curls pulled up in a ponytail. Baker, of course, at the age of seven, grabbed the controller from the gaming console to play his favorite game.

Looking around our house, I still had to pinch myself at the life I'd built with two men together. Elliot had designed our sleek and modern home full of windows and light. The living room was behind a set of angular walls to separate it from the foyer. When Ell and her men bought enough land right outside the city for a small village of their own, she went to town designing the house of our dreams. It differed greatly from the house she'd built with Daimen and Arden who were essentially our neighbors, with them about a thousand feet down the property we now all owned.

After I had Sailor, I never returned to work full-time, though I still helped with Daimen and Arden's schedules from home. I owned five percent of the company, and the annual dividends from my checks were enough to ensure we lived a very comfortable life.

Jordan was still as committed to his job as he was when I'd met him. Working as chief of staff was hard and the hours were long, but he'd never been happier in his job. Levi became one of the youngest fire commissioners in the history of Chicago. I had to admit I loved the idea of him not running into burning buildings. He was a good and fair commissioner, and his love for his job never changed.

The second we heard the garage open, Soda Pop and Maizie were at the door waiting for their daddies. Most days, Levi and Jordan tried to drive into the city because they could spend quality time together.

The second they were over the threshold of the door, my two men's hands were interlaced with one another. I never tired of this sight. Soda Pop and Maizie were jumping up and down, ready to greet them.

Levi saw the tear-stained face of his girl and pulled her to him tight. "My baby hates the dentist, don't you, sweetheart?"

"Daddy, I won't be going back," she claimed, and as I shook my head, Levi only held her tighter. Maizie was a bit on the dramatic side, and her dads' continual doting only made it worse.

Jordan leaned in to give his girl a kiss when Baker yelled, "Daddio, got us all set up!" Jordan stopped briefly, dropping a peck on my forehead. "Don't worry about dinner. We got it covered." After the day I had, I needed a break.

He sat down on the floor next to his son. "You want me to go easy on you, or just kick your butt right away?" Oh, he talked the most trash to his son, though Baker won nine out of ten times.

"Keep telling yourself that, old man," our son chimed in, and his quick wit had come from Levi. Boy, our son was a mirror image of our hot fireman.

Levi leaned over to kiss me with Maizie still in his hands. Walking over to the chair, he kneeled next to Sailor, still engrossed in her book. He whispered something about braces in her ear making her laugh. Yep, the second these men were here, they completed our family. An hour later, Andrew appeared at our doorstep, and both my men had backpacks for all three kids.

Our kids were jumping up and down because Uncle

Andrew's house was absolutely chaotic but in their own words, "Crazy fun." A house ran by all men, for all boys, I had to admit, it was more than I could take at times. But the kids loved it. And through this all, I was getting my men to myself tonight, so it was the best of both worlds. Gone were the days I had become anxious with the kids being out of my sight for the night.

Turning to both Levi and Jordan, I saw that the dinner they'd talked about was not food, but they'd be feasting on me. "Come on, Red, let us take good care of you tonight," Jordan began.

"Can I have many orgasms?" I asked.

They had me in their arms before I knew it when Levi answered next, "What do you think?" We were in our room, and with the life we'd built, I'd never felt more complete.

The End

a note
from the author

I'd initially wanted Scarlet and Jordan to call Levi CAP— as in their real life Captain America. Researching the rank of the Chicago Fire Department and knowing the storyline of the story, I needed to switch it around. A captain would not work.

If you have read any of my previous books, you may see I have a thing for nicknames. With Cap being nixed so to speak, LT was born. I could see both Scar and Jordan calling Levi the two letter initials. It worked for the spunky redhead and the broody doctor.

As always, I love writing this sexy threesome story. I hope to bring you more soon! There are so many that need their story.

I hope you enjoyed this sexy threesome!

~Leigh

it takes a village!

First and foremost, to the women who take the very rough draft of my words in the rawest form and treat it with the utmost care and respect. Nancy George—you've become my friend and I treasure you! Kymberly—you and your eagle eyes—I can't thank you enough for your help. Megan Damrow—you're such a godsend in my writing. I thank my lucky stars for you. Megan Harris—AKA Vomit Sister! You are wonderful and I count myself lucky to have met you. Mary Moore—I've enjoyed getting to know you better and being able to call you friend. Melody Hillier—I enjoy working with you so very much. Kelly Green—you were such a great addition to my beta team! I can't tell you how much I appreciate the time and effort you took to help make this book a success.

Auden, you are my writing bestie and I couldn't do this without your support! I absolutely adore you. And thank you so much for letting me include Prelude and Interlude in this book. It was a great addition to Scarlet, Jordan, and Levi's story.

Jenny Sims—Your editing services are always top notch. I love working with you.

Julie Deaton—I'm in awe of your professionalism. You're the last set of eyes on my books. I consider it a true honor to be able to work with you each and every time,

Najla Qamber—You continue to blow me away with each and every cover you design for me. This one is truly amazing as every single one has been. Thanks so much.

Angel Nyx—Thanks for being another set of eyes for me.

Annette—Thanks for running Leigh's Lovable Arc Team. I honestly can't say enough good things about you!

Kelly—You've come in and truly been a huge help with my social media and the arc team. Thanks so very much!

Megan D.— Thanks for helping me run Succulent and

Sassy Reads! You are a true gem.

Thanks to my dear friend, Elizabeth. I tell her every story so many times, she knows my characters as well as I do. I love you!

Dawn—My best friend after twenty-five plus years! I love how much I shock you by my subject matter and how my ideas make you laugh. I adore you, DW!

I can't say enough to my Facebook group page; Succulent and Sassy Reads! You all are so awesome and I am humbled you follow me and encourage me to continue writing.

Thanks so much to my incredible arc team and to everyone who read an advance copy and posted a review. You ladies are so valuable to me!

I want to thank my readers because without you, this would not be possible!

Of course, none of this would be a possibility without the Hubs and our little ones who call me mom. I love you more than I can express.

about the author

Leigh Lennon is a mother, veteran and wife of a cancer survivor. Originally with a degree in education, she started writing as an outlet that has led to a deep passion. She lugs her computer with her as she crafts her next story. Her imaginary friends become real on her pages as she creates a world for them. She loves pretty nails, spikey hair and large earrings. Leigh can be found drinking coffee or wine, depending on the time of the day.

Please stalk Leigh Lennon on social media:

Facebook group page - Succulent and Sassy Reads:
https://www.facebook.com/groups/1257849247670788/

Facebook author page:
https://www.facebook.com/leigh.reagan.7

Twitter: @4leighlennon

Instagram: https://www.instagram.com/leigh_lennon/

Website: Authorleighlennon.com

Good Reads: goo.gl/dWw8pQ goo.gl/dWw8pQ

Amazon:
https://www.amazon.com/default/e/B074WMY4XV

Have you met Daimen, Arden and their girl — Elliot from Foundations?

Excerpt from Foundations

elliot

The second the masculine voice referred to me as a man, I motioned to the secretary not to correct him. The call ended, and she looked at me when I explained. "Don't worry, I get more business this way. It's the main reason I don't have a picture on my website." I paused to catch my breath, and it was a shame in this day and age having a man's name worked to my advantage. "I love seeing the shock on their faces when they realize I have boobs. Most of the time, they think Andrew is the boss, and I'm his assistant."

"Ell," Andrew's deep tone warned, "you get too much pleasure out of shocking men."

I could almost imagine my eyes sparkling with mischief at my best friend's caution. "I like shocking them. It's too much fun," I teased back.

"Alright, Ms. Arnold and Mr. Peters, let me show you in." Scarlet knocked on the door, then opened it at one of the men's request. "Mr. Blakely, Mr. Torano, let me know if I can get you anything," she said, leaving quickly, but their eyes were averted down, still not on Andrew or me.

Witnessing the beauty of the two male specimens standing in front of me, I instantly felt light on my feet. Normally, I would be attracted to these men, but it was a known fact they were partners in more than just the professional sense. As indicated by all the newspapers, they were in a very committed relationship.

As I predicted, both men walked toward Andrew, when the blonde man extended his hand toward him. "Mr. Arnold, it's nice to meet you."

Andrew's head turned, looking in my direction, and he flashed a smirk at me. I have them where I want them. I internally laughed at that thought. Snaking my way in front of Andrew, I extended my own hand. "Actually, I'm Elliot Arnold." I paused, wanting to have some fun with these two. "I would think with two people like yourselves who live out of the mold of what is traditional for most, you wouldn't be shocked that a woman could have a reputation such as I do in this industry."

Arden's gaze fell on his partner, then moved back at me, and if his baby blues could write an apology, I think he would have done that. Before I fell victim to his eyes, something hit me in the gut. A memory assaulted me, and I looked away for the briefest moment.

"I'm sorry, Ms. Arnold, it's not meant as disrespect. We just assumed with the name Elliot, it sounded more masculine," Arden claimed, his apology pulling me back to the here and now.

Concentrating on the business at hand and not wallowing in my past, I silently scoffed at them. I was used to this sort of reaction. Though this was not our first meeting, Arden Blakely had the warmest mannerisms of anyone I'd known. That part of him had bewitched me the first time—that and the ocean blue of his eyes.

He was articulate along with handsome and sexy; again, something I'd never forgotten. "Well, now that I know you'd work with me whether I was a man or woman, let's get down to business," I said curtly, and though I caught wind of Arden's little smirk, Daimen Torano or whom I'd named Mr. Grumpy, didn't change the scowl that had graced his face since I arrived. "Alright, in corresponding with Mr. Blakely ..."

"Arden, please, Ms. Arnold," he insisted, and for a second, if I had to guess, his eyes danced with understanding when he examined my body. He hadn't given me any indication he recognized me yet.

I reminded myself that he was a taken man; though, in my expert opinion, he liked what he saw. Just as he had the first time too. This was all about business right now. Even though my womanly regions had certainly experienced a cold zone recently, they still remembered his touch. I finally croaked out, "Alright, Arden, as I was saying, while I was corresponding with you, I saw the design sketches from your last architect. Obviously, you're bringing me on mid-project, so I assume you weren't happy with who you hired before."

"That would be an understatement," Daimen, AKA Mr. Grumpy, replied, brooding, apparently still stroking his ego at such a regrettable decision when I simply nodded. I got a feeling this storm cloud of a man might never like being wrong—ever.

Want more? Be sure to check out Daimen, Arden and Ell at https://amzn.to/2skCrGM

fahrenheit

Made in the USA
Columbia, SC
29 December 2019